GREAT BRITISH HORROR I

GREEN AND PLEASANT LAND

Great British Horror I
Green and Pleasant Land

Edited by
Steve J Shaw

BLACK
SHUCK
BOOKS

First published in Great Britain in 2016 by

Black Shuck Books
Kent, UK

HERMANESS © Victoria Leslie, 2016
MEAT FOR THE FIELD © Rich Hawkins, 2016
STRANGE AS ANGELS © Laura Mauro, 2016
THE CASTELLMARCH MAN © Ray Cluley, 2016
OSTRICH © David Moody, 2016
BLUE-EYES © Barbie Wilde, 2016
A GLIMPSE OF RED © James Everington, 2016
MR DENNING SINGS © Simon Kurt Unsworth, 2016
HE WAITS ON THE UPLAND © Adam Millard, 2016
MISERICORD © Alexandra Benedict, 2016
QUIET PLACES © Jasper Bark, 2016

Cover design and interior layout © WHITEspace, 2016

The moral rights of the authors have been asserted in accordance with the Copyright, Designs and Patents Act, 1988.
All rights reserved. No part of this publication may be reproduced or transmitted in any form or by any means, electronic or mechanical, including photocopy, recording, or any information storage and retrieval system, without permission in writing from the publisher.
This book is a work of fiction. Names, characters, businesses, organisations, places and events are either the product of the author's imagination or are used fictitiously. Any resemblance to actual persons, living or dead, events or locales is entirely coincidental.

978-1-913038-03-8

Dedicated to the memory of Robin Hardy

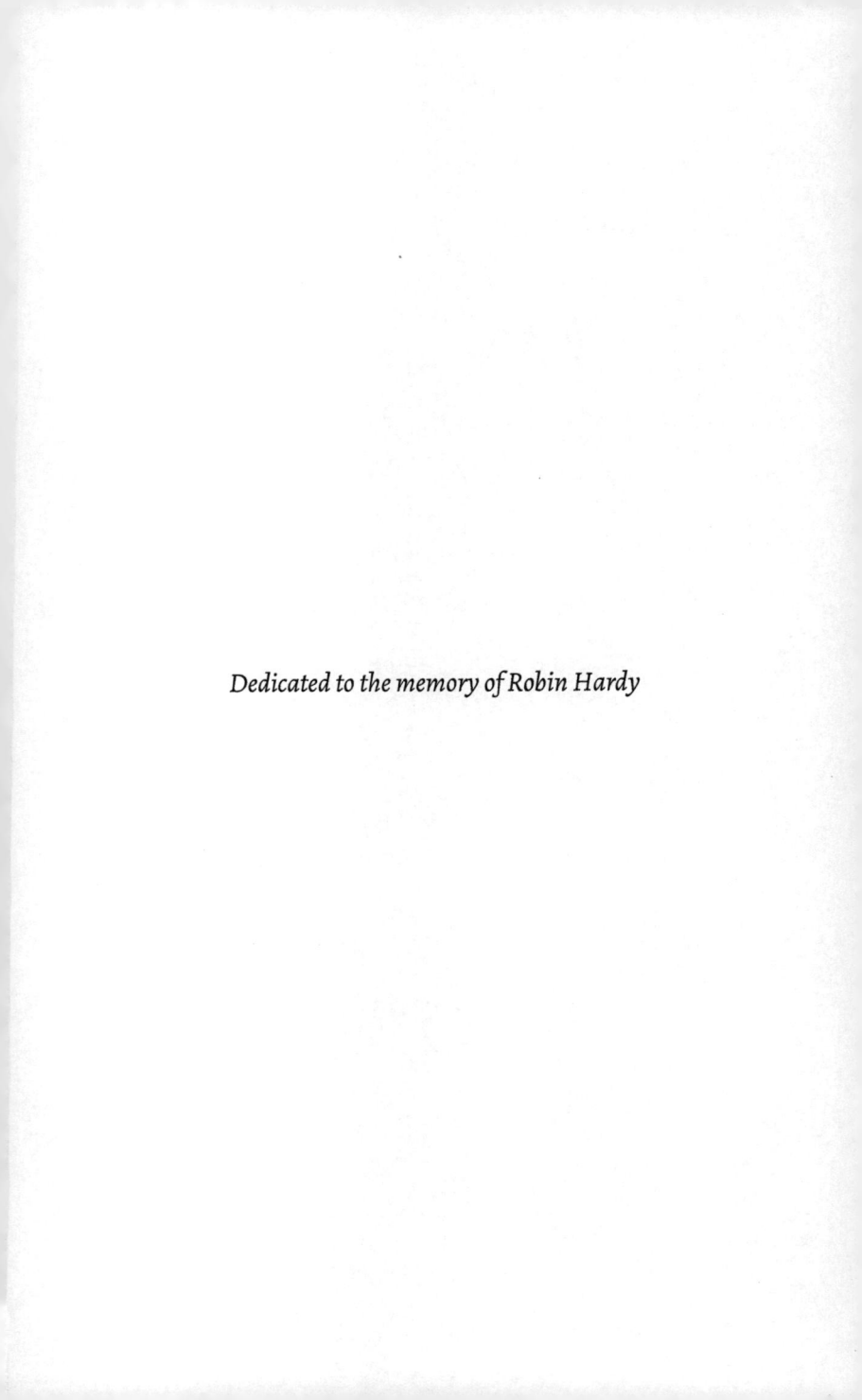

Hermaness	9
V.H. Leslie	
Meat for the Field	37
Rich Hawkins	
Strange as Angels	57
Laura Mauro	
The Castellmarch Man	87
Ray Cluley	
Ostrich	127
David Moody	
Blue-Eyes	151
Barbie Wilde	
A Glimpse of Red	163
James Everington	
Mr Denning Sings	191
Simon Kurt Unsworth	
He Waits on the Upland	205
Adam Millard	
Misericord	225
A.K. Benedict	
Quiet Places	239
Jasper Bark	

Hermaness
V.H. Leslie

It was a hard ascent to get to the edge.

They were used to being on the edge. They'd been skirting it for the last few months, forced toward it by the arguments, the brooding silences, as much by the things they didn't say as by the things they did. They knew how to hurt one another now; life at the edge had taught them a whole host of new survival skills. They could push hard or dig in their heels, hardly caring which one of them would eventually fall. Plus, the air was thinner closer to the edge, the pressure unremitting so that tempers would flair up over trifling matters, causing chaos and disarray, broken crockery, broken egos. It was too much of an effort to make their way back down to the way things were, or to haul themselves up and over and see what existed beyond. You needed strength to do that and the climb up had taken everything they had.

It was almost too much of an effort to go on the trip but it had been booked nearly a year before when they hadn't imagined such troubles ahead. They had both shared the same vision then, to make their way to the edge of it all, to Hermaness, the most northerly point in Britain, the last accessible landmass before the North Atlantic Ocean held sway. In the summer months the northern tip of the island of Unst in the Shetland archipelago became home to thousands of seabirds and Hermaness Nature Reserve welcomed visitors from all over the world keen to glimpse puffins and red-throated divers, the great ocean stacks swarming with life. But it also appealed to hikers intent on reaching the farthermost limits, keen to stand at this final, hallowed edge with its exclusive panorama. Besides the birds, there was the slender hope of seeing killer whales or orcas, a fitting if elusive reward for such an arduous journey. For Nell, it was the prospect of seeing the puffin colonies that made Hermaness so appealing, whereas Brian was keen to add it to his list of accomplished feats.

But as their relationship began to fragment, their enthusiasm for the trip waned. Neither wanted to back down, to admit they were too exhausted emotionally to spend a week in the other's company or to lose out on their deposits. A strange stalemate existed, both overcompensating for their lack of interest. Nell made her way studiously through guidebooks, bird-watching guides and the greats of Scottish literature to get a better feel for the place. Brian, not to be outdone, absorbed himself with the road maps and ferry itineraries, pouring his efforts into making the trip there and back as efficient as possible. Secretly they both envisioned going it alone, of the other turning back at the train station or the airport, dragging their luggage behind them amid curses and recriminations. And both had imagined having the two-man tent all to themselves, the canvas interior a dark and quiet sanctuary.

But they had both boarded the small plane, which

came down neatly on the narrow tarmac strip sandwiched between the sea on either side. They had picked up the hire car and visited a few tourist spots before pitching their tent beside a bay, working perfunctorily with little interaction, realising too late that the tent was far too small now there was so much discontent between them. But they had crawled inside anyway and into their separate sleeping bags, keen for an early night despite the unnatural brightness; the extended twilight the Northern islands experienced in midsummer casting a strange luminosity over the land. Because they both knew how much depended on Hermaness.

Perhaps it was providence that the trip was already booked, Nell thought as she settled against the hard ground, a well-timed panacea to fix everything that was wrong in their relationship. After all, they'd been together a long time – nine years – and it was normal, she supposed, to grow apart. She tried to think of Hermaness as an opportunity to bring them closer; that in this remote wilderness they might be able to rediscover the person they fell in love with.

But the two-man tent, far from facilitating the kind of intimacy you'd expect from being in such close proximity, only brought home how much they'd come to value the distance. With daybreak, Nell rolled up the tent-opening as quietly as possible and snuck out into the cold morning, pretending not to notice that Brian was also awake. She watched the sunlight on the bay, the grass dewy, and thought what a perfect moment this was to share with someone you love, though that paled against the desire to keep it all to herself. Guiltily she thought of Brian lying on his back in the dim tent, watching the gnats darting against the canvas, trapped in the netting parapet at the top amid the beads of condensation.

With still no stir from the tent she made her way down to the bay, stepping over a succession of grey slabs that jutted out from the shore like a row of enormous teeth. She watched a couple of sheep amble down onto the shingle, grazing on grasses that sprouted sporadically from between the rocks. She remembered reading that their meat was particularly sought after, tasting of the seaweed they consumed. Carefully she made her way back between the rocky peaks and troughs, the formations like frozen imitations of the waves crashing against the shore. She glanced up and saw that the tent had disappeared, and for a moment she thought that Brian had actually gone, that this really was the end, left on the foreshore with the wandering sheep. She played out the scenario in her head, wondering if she could make it back on her own; thinking of the practical things, touching her pockets to check she had her mobile phone, her credit card, before even considering the injury to her heart.

But as she crossed the field, she saw the blue canvas deflated on the ground, looking pitiful. And there was Brian beside the shower block, brushing his teeth.

He'd nodded courteously as if greeting an acquaintance.

"How about some breakfast," she called but he merely looked at his watch.

She tried not to show her annoyance, knowing that Brian was punishing her for her morning of solitude. She'd forfeited breakfast for her walk on the beach.

They packed up the rental car and began to drive. The road to Hermaness is not particularly long but can only be reached by crossing through a series of islands. The inter-island ferry operators had clearly timed the journey to perfection so that you could catch each adjoining ferry in succession, if you didn't dally. Despite the raw beauty of the landscape, the impetus to make each ferry – most of which ran only every hour – curbed the desire to stop and marvel at sights along the way.

Not that there was much to see, as Nell realised as they drove through Yell, a foreboding and austere island that lived up to its name. The islands were hardly distinguishable from each other; low-lying land surrounded by the sea, a few homesteads perched here and there but possessing neither beauty nor charm. Rather, they were strangely like the landscape, firm and rugged, built from stone or concrete in lieu of wood, as the islands were barren of trees. In days gone by, Shetlanders had traded with the Scandinavians for timber for their shipping vessels. At one point in the journey, they passed a series of newly built Norwegian-style houses.

"Look," Nell pointed, as if spotting a marvel of nature, "what a relief to see an attractive house."

Brian winced, as if personally offended by Nell's statement.

"Don't you think most of the houses here are ugly?" she pressed.

"No."

"They look like bunkers. Look, that one has a corrugated roof."

"They don't need to be pretty, they just need to stand the weather."

"Shouldn't houses do both?"

"I'm not an architect Nell."

He had a tendency to make things personal. Nell looked out of the window and thought instead of their house back in the south and the compromises they'd made in making it a home. The sacrifices they'd made for each other: a lamp here, a pile of books there, an objectionable item given by an ex, whilst other parts of themselves were consigned to boxes in the attic because they didn't fit into this new identity they were forging for themselves as a couple. Instead they'd opted for furniture and fittings neither of them liked all that much, selected because they were an acceptable midway point between their preferences.

Nell decided to drop the subject when she spotted another pebble-dashed façade. "It's just surprising. The houses here are so... severe, despite being in such a beautiful part of the world."

But perhaps that wasn't entirely true. Though the landscape was indeed spectacular, breathtaking with its vast moors and dramatic coastline, it wasn't exactly beautiful. It was severe, foreboding almost. Even with the sun glinting off the sea, making their way closer to Hermaness, the landscape appeared darker, hostile.

Following the signposts to Hermaness Nature Reserve, Brian eventually pulled into a car park at the foot of hill, parking beside a large, modern camper. It irked Nell that he'd parked so close to another vehicle when the car park was so empty. But he seemed to be appraising the camper, either that or the blonde woman stepping down from the back door. A rather overweight man was stood in front of her, leaning over a tripod. Though this was their second day in Shetland, Nell had already come to value the space and solitude the landscape offered. Being so close to this couple made her feel strangely claustrophobic.

Brian closed the door and smiled at the couple. They greeted him cheerily. The blonde woman strode toward him and took his hand.

"Morning," she said in a thick American accent, "I'm Lorraine and this is Don." Don didn't look up from his camera but lifted his hand.

"Sorry about him, he's a bird-watching *fanatic!*" she said with emphasis. "He's pretty excited about the climb."

"We are too," Brian said, sounding more enthusiastic than he had all morning. "I'm Brian and..."

"Nell," Nell said from her side of the car. The American woman looked very stylish in her hiking gear. Nell found she'd instantly forgotten her name, distracted by her lilac outfit and neat blonde bob. Nell wished she'd taken more care dressing or perhaps put on some make-up.

"You've come pretty far?" Brian asked.

"South Carolina. It's been Don's dream to come to Hermane*ssss*." She elongated the suffix making it sound much more alluring on her lips.

Nell gathered her backpack from the boot and made her way to Don. He didn't say anything but adjusted the tripod, inviting her to look through the lens. Each grain in the tarmac was crystal clear, enlarged to gigantic proportions. Nell shifted the camera that was hung around her neck towards her back, hoping Don wouldn't notice such an inferior piece of kit.

"I don't know a thing about birds," she heard the American woman say.

"Me neither," Brian agreed and Nell was stung thinking of all the things she'd taught him over the years.

She found herself talking to Don about puffins and fulmars, the great skuas, which Shetlanders called 'bonxies', in an attempt to drown out the inane exchange between Brian and the American woman. But she was interrupted intermittently by the American woman's shrill laughter, which wasn't all that dissimilar from the cries of the herring gulls flying overhead. Nell wondered how Brian could be so amiable in the company of strangers, yet so morose and sullen with her. When she ran out of things to say to Don she looked to Brian, hoping they'd engaged in enough pleasantries to be on their way.

"Maybe we could head up together?" the American woman suggested.

She saw Brian nodding.

"Actually, we're going to check out the Tourist Info Centre," Nell said, relieved to spot it across the car park, "I'm keen to read up on everything before we begin and I don't want to slow you down."

Don began to pack up the tripod. "We should get a move on anyway."

Brian said goodbye as he fell in step with Nell, glancing back at the American woman and the camper in the same covetous way Nell had looked at Don's camera.

"See you at the top," the American woman called, her laughter following them across the car park.

They made their way across the moors, through patches of heather and crowberry, areas of blanket bog they'd read about at the Tourist Information Centre for being a particularly favourable habitat for golden plover and snipe. They were nearing the edge but it was hardly perceptible in the heavy fog, known by the locals as sea haar. In the Shetlands, the weather was especially inclement and the fog could roll in off the sea with alarming speed, caused by the hot air currents passing over the water. It would be easy to lose your way, to stumble off the cliffs or vanish into the mist. But Nell and Brian kept doggedly to the path, which ran quite a distance from the cliff-face. Visitors were advised to stick to the route to avoid disturbing breeding birds, warned of the chance that great skuas often dive-bombed hikers who came too close to their nests. Occasionally you could see them hovering in the distance, or swooping suddenly through patches of fog. You had to keep one eye on the ground, one on the sky, vigilant always of the edge, just out of sight.

"You didn't tell me the bloody birds attacked," Brian said, waving his stick in the air as the Visitor Information leaflet had advised.

"They rarely make contact," Nell replied, trying to

sound certain. It was a calculated risk, she'd reasoned, the price to see bird colonies of such size, if only the mist would clear a little. She could hear birdcalls all around, a shrill cacophony indicating they were nearing the gannet colonies just offshore, eerily out of sight. She knew that Hermaness could be a dangerous place if you were not adequately prepared but what she hadn't accounted for was such a strong feeling of threat. From the moment they began their journey across the moors, she'd felt the hostility of the place, an uneasy, knotted feeling in her core.

It didn't help that Brian was walking so far ahead of her, keen to catch up with the Americans no doubt, treating the trip like another exploit to be ticked off a list rather than an opportunity to spend time with her. She could see the sea haar closing in around him, wisps coiling up his body, conscious that he was vanishing before her eyes. She wondered if it was that simple. That eventually, when the fog cleared, he would have disappeared from her life for good and she would be left alone at the top of the cliff to make her way back down and begin over.

She found him perched on a low wall containing a grassy hillock.

"Bloody fog," he muttered at her approach, as if she were responsible for the weather.

Nell looked at the stone wall, curved as if it were part of a circular structure, and she wondered if it was the remains of an Iron Age Broch like the ones they'd seen at Jarlshof when they first arrived. Those ancient homesteads had been excavated to reveal hollow-walled structures arranged around a central hearth, like a roundhouse. Or perhaps this was an ancient burial mound.

"Maybe we should sit over there?" Nell suggested but Brian ignored her, digging in his backpack for a sandwich.

He didn't seem to listen to anything she said lately. She'd tried to persuade him to change out of his waterproof trousers into his regular hiking gear before they began their ascent. The Tourist Information Centre recommended such measures in case you fell, the waterproof fabric increasing the likelihood of sliding further. But Brian had merely laughed, citing the certainty of rain and fog and how wet through she'd be at the end of it all.

Nell knelt down on the grass, the fabric at her knees dampening. Despite the wet ground, she was reluctant to sit on the wall itself, hoping it wasn't inauspicious to be here at all.

She'd read somewhere about the custom of walking widdershins around ancient burial sites and barrows. According to superstition, the act of walking counter clockwise, against the motion of the sun, could transport you to fairyland. It put her in mind of a curious story she'd read on the ferry by Robert Louis Stevenson. A king had built his daughter a castle on the beach between two seas but she never gave any thought to the future until she saw an old crone dancing widdershins across the shore. The crone hailed the coming of the morrow before disappearing into the stalks of seaweed and specks of sand.

It all felt very allegorical. It seemed to imply that the possession of knowledge, the awareness of our mortality, went against the natural order of things, and that this knowledge had to be summoned via magic. The crone, having predicted the future, was transformed into nothing more than the detritus upon the shore. But Nell couldn't help but wonder if the old crone's motives were more selfish. Perhaps what she desired was what the King's daughter already possessed – youth – walking backwards to turn back time.

Nell had been so lost in her thoughts that she hadn't noticed that the fog was lifting. She looked up towards the grassy mound but there was no sign of Brian.

She stood tentatively, trying to peer between the patches of fog.

"Brian?"

She was rooted to the stone wall, unsure which direction to take, knowing Brian had the only map.

"Brian?" She called again, aware suddenly of the sound of birds all around her, as if they were summoning the fog away. She began to walk, overcome by the feeling that life was starting up again after this strange misty hiatus, realising how deathly silent it had been beside the grassy knoll.

And there was Brian in the distance, pointing down the slope.

"Look!" he called, and despite the uncertainty he caused in her mind, the fog that seemed to linger there though it was dispersing all around her, she ran toward him and toward the edge.

"There they are," he called. Nell followed the direction

he was pointing toward, unsure whether he meant the puffins or the Americans. For lower down the cliff face stood two figures hunched over a tripod, one dressed in bright lilac.

"We thought you'd never make it," the American woman smiled as they approached.

The fog had cleared to reveal a breath-taking vista. The sea glinted beneath the sun, the sky crowded with flocks of gannets and fulmars. Nell trained her binoculars on one such assembly and felt her heart quicken.

"We thought you must've lost your way," she heard the American woman say.

Nell spotted a flash of black and orange further down the cliff-face, scanning the rock until a lone puffin hopped into view.

"We stopped for some lunch," Brian said, as if the fog had been inconsequential.

Don hadn't looked up from his camera, immersed in the view, his body bent protectively around the tripod. Nell searched the cliff-face, hoping to see more puffin burrows in the rock crevices.

Brian and the American woman seemed to hardly notice the birds, engrossed in conversation.

"It's such a curious name," the American woman said, "Hermanesss. It must be named after Herman someone-or-other."

"Herman Munster," Brian offered jovially and the American woman burst into high-pitched laughter.

"It's named after a giant," said Nell.

The laughter stopped and she could feel them both looking at her, annoyed perhaps that she'd interrupted their repartee.

"Herman and his brother Saxa lived here on Unst. They were the last of their kind and they'd probably be here still if it wasn't for a mermaid."

"Mermaid?" Nell could tell she had the American woman's attention. She'd already read Brian the story from the guidebook on the flight over, though she could tell he wasn't really listening. But he was captivated now that the American woman thought the story worth listening to.

"What happened?"

"They were rivals for her love, throwing huge boulders at each other across the cliffs, forming the stacks you see now. She promised to be with whichever one could swim to the North Pole with her."

Nell looked back out to sea, imagining how small and insubstantial the world would have seemed to those giants. How they were prepared to give up their lofty outlook, to follow a woman off the edge of it all.

"Well, who won?"

"No one knows. They could both be at the bottom of the ocean. Or one of them made it and is now living in even colder climes with his prize."

"So we don't know who got the girl?" The American women seemed put out.

"It doesn't matter. All that matters is that the giants left."

Brian, hovering close to the American woman, shrugged in apology at such an inconclusive ending.

Don, either sensing his wife's bemusement or stirred by the story, placed his arm around her proprietarily.

"Take a look," he offered, leading her toward the tripod. And, as the American woman peered through the lens, Nell wondered if she was aware of the two men appraising her, studying the way she inclined her head, elongating her neck, her manner of tucking her blonde hair behind her ears. And she thought of the power of women to beguile. She'd forgotten that power. She'd had it once, she must've, to have ensnared Brian. But he was looking elsewhere now. Her magic had run out.

"Why don't you take a look?" the American woman said to Nell, challenging her to take the pedestal. Though Nell had no desire to compete with this woman, she was eager to see the puffins more clearly.

No wonder Don guarded the view so vigilantly. The lens had been trained on one particular burrow, nestled into the nook of the cliffs. She watched the puffins converge at the entrance, waddling in their comical manner, as clear as if they were only a few metres away. At the centre, a pair were engaged in billing, rubbing their beaks together affectionately, and further back she glimpsed at least three chicks huddled in a nest of feathers and grass.

She looked up to beckon Brian to come and see but he was further along the ridge now, looking toward the horizon with the American woman.

The puffins would come back each year to this same nest for the purpose of breeding, travelling far out to sea in the winter months. The family secure and safe, tucked into the cliff-face. Nell's own home in the south felt suddenly very far away. Standing at this summit, encircled by the sea, the home she shared with Brian seemed almost illusory. Maybe it was. All those years building a space to house the better parts of themselves, with room for the children they'd envisioned, seemed little more than a vague dream. The future she had thought was so certain and concrete had turned vaporous, slipping further and further into the distance.

The American woman's laughter pierced the air and inadvertently Nell tipped the lens forward. She watched the view as it tilted downward, feeling herself plummeting through the air, though the camera remained fixed firmly in the tripod. And suddenly she could see waves crashing against the rocks, a slither of shingle between peaks of grey stone. And there, walking slowly in circles, was a lone figure on the beach.

Nell gripped the camera. It had to be a trick of perspective or she'd pressed something she shouldn't have. Her hands fumbled with the settings and dials, though she was incapable of taking her eyes away from the view.

"Careful," Don said, pushing his way in front of her, righting the camera and stooping to inspect the damage.

It had all happened so quickly, a matter of moments, the camera tipping, the strange vision on the shore, growing more hazy in her mind now that she could see the world around her with her own eyes. But before she'd been forced aside, she'd glimpsed the long white hair of the figure, blown about like cobwebs in the wind.

"Everything ok?" The American woman and Brian had reappeared, drawn by the commotion.

"I thought I saw something. Down there, on the shore."

She could feel them all looking at her now, could feel Brian's embarrassment.

Don sighed heavily, as if pacifying a child. She watched him move the lens in the direction of the foreshore.

"Just sand and seaweed."

"Are you sure?" She wanted to check herself but knew that Don wouldn't let her touch the camera again. She couldn't be trusted. She hesitated in lifting her own binoculars, feeling the pressure of the group watching her.

"Of course he's sure," Brian said.

And to prevent any further debate Don began to dismantle the tripod.

"Won't you walk down with us?" the American woman offered, though she looked only at Brian. "Maybe we can get a drink?"

"I thought you wanted to get to the edge?" Nell said, a little more curtly than she'd intended, but a challenge nonetheless. "Now that the fog has cleared we might be able to see the lighthouse."

The American woman looked to Don, breathless with the effort of carrying the camera and tripod a few paces; there was no way he'd be able to hike much further.

"Well, we're staying at the pub in Baltasound if you change your mind," she said and Nell and Brian watched the Americans make their way down from Hermaness.

❖

They made their way along the edge, following the coastal path through swathes of thrift and angelica. They were heading toward the most northerly point, where, if the weather remained clear, they'd be able to see the lighthouse on the adjacent island of Muckle Flugga. The lighthouse had been built by Robert Louis Stevenson's father, which seemed appropriate considering the far-reaching ambition of his son.

Brian walked ahead, beating his hiking stick through the low vegetation, though the path was reasonably clear.

"I can't believe you broke their camera."

"I didn't break it. It just slipped."

"He wasn't happy," Brian continued, "we'll have to get them a few pints."

It was pointless defending herself when Brian had so clearly made up his mind that she was at fault, especially as it served as a convenient excuse to see the Americans again.

"I'm sure they'll survive."

Brian turned and looked at her as if he couldn't understand her at all. When he began walking again it was with renewed conviction, impatient to complete the trip and catch up with the Americans.

Nell slowed her pace on purpose, happy to put further distance between them. She thought instead of the figure on the beach, though the memory was becoming more vague. But she had seen someone down there, she was sure, a women – it had to be – with long white hair, turning slow circles on the shoreline.

Up ahead, she saw Brian hesitate at a crossroads. He unfolded the map. As Nell approached she saw a laminated sign attached to a fence post, a diagram of the coastal path.

"This side of the path has eroded," Brian explained, pointing, "it says we're to take the other route. But the map says different; that we should carry on to get to the end."

"The notice looks pretty recent," Nell said. "Perhaps it would be better to take the diversion."

Brian cast his eye over the sign then back at the map.

"There's no guarantee we'll even get to the edge."

"It's what *they* recommend," Nell said, careful not to include her own opinion. She didn't want to be blamed for anything else.

Brian looked for a moment at his preferred route, snaking further toward the cliffs, before reluctantly folding up the map and heading along the diversion, which receded further from the edge.

It was a long upward trek, through muddied grassland, interspersed occasionally with equally muddy wooden boards to negotiate the most slippery and worn sections of the path. Oddly, without the presence of the sea, the land felt devoid of identity. The muddied terrain was so indistinguishable, even with the boards and route markers appearing at regular intervals to punctuate the sense of homogeneity, it gave the journey a strangely repetitive feel. The feeling was enhanced when they rounded the curve of a hill and saw the grassy knoll bordered by the low stone wall.

"How can we be back here?" Brian said. The tone was accusatory.

"We followed the signs," Nell shrugged.

"I knew we should have taken the other path."

When Nell didn't answer, Brian slumped against the stone wall.

"Why does this have to be so fucking difficult?" he shouted, waving the map.

"Shall I take a look?" Nell offered, but he clung to it even tighter.

She wanted to tell him that she was disappointed too. That she'd been disappointed ever since they'd arrived at Hermaness, that she could trace the disappointment all the way back across the North Sea to their life back in the south. It had become the staple of their relationship. But Brian had the monopoly on anger for now. Silence seemed like the best option.

It was a long time before Brian spoke again, staring vacantly at the map.

"This isn't working."

"Maybe if we head back toward the puffins," Nell suggested.

"Not that. Us."

Nell sat down against the hillock, hardly caring about invoking the ghosts of the past or creatures from fairyland. She was conscious again of how silent it was here; the birds were far away, circling the boulders Herman and Saxa had thrown out to sea.

"This relationship," Brian continued, "it's not right. I've tried to make it work but I'm so tired."

"I'm tired too," Nell said but her voice sounded small and far away, "I'm still trying."

Brian stood, as if her contribution was insignificant.

"I can't see a future, Nell. I'm sorry." But that wasn't

true; he could see a future, just not with her. Brian had reached the edge that bit faster and could see a way down. And whilst he was ready to leap over in a new chapter of his life, she was still clinging on.

"Let's talk about it later," he said, opening up the map. "Let's just concentrate on getting to the edge and back down."

Nell squeezed the grass beneath her fingertips. He hadn't even considered that she might not want to continue the journey. That he might have hurt her too much that she'd be forced to make her way back down on her own. Maybe he knew it wasn't in her nature to storm off dramatically, that she was too keen to mend and persevere. Or maybe he had counted on her eagerness to see the bird colonies to leave him up here on his own.

She was loath to miss out on the birds for the sake of her ego but it pained her that he had chosen this moment to end it all. It was ill timed. He had marred Hermaness. He hadn't given the trip a chance; he hadn't allowed the magic to return.

Nell lay back against the grass, realising how tired she really was. There was no need to rush, no fear of encroaching darkness with the eerie prolonged twilight. She could just curl up and fall asleep. She would refuse to leave the cliff and nestle into the grassy bank, letting her body sink into the ancient soil, replete with the remnants of forgotten times, of primeval peoples, and allow herself to disappear into its history.

What would Brian do if she vanished here, right now? He would head back down to the car and drive to Baltasound, drown his sorrows with the Americans, missing Nell the appropriate amount in company to gain their sympathies, before making his way back south to begin again with someone new.

Nell thought of the American woman, her youthful figure tucked into her neat lilac outfit. If it wasn't her, it would be someone else, all exciting and new, with stories unfamiliar and strange. That was what it had been like at the beginning of their relationship, when Brian couldn't get enough of the novelty of her. He'd listened to all her stories then, hanging onto every word.

These things move in cycles.

She was hardly aware that she'd stood up, buoyed along with the rising fog that coiled its way from the ground in vaporous stems. Maybe if she walked widdershins around the mound, the door to an invisible world would open, a place where she could seek refuge from the interminable repetition of life. Or better still, she could reset the clock, return to the time she'd been the happiest.

She felt a strange recklessness, despite the cautiousness she adopted in everyday life that extended to superstitious beliefs. She had nothing left to lose.

She walked around the bank nine times, one for each year of their relationship.

Brian hardly noticed what she was doing. She was already invisible to him. It was as she completed the final lap that Brian looked up from the map, as if to conclude the spell.

"Nell, would you stop pacing. You're blocking the path."

She couldn't help but smile. There was hardly an

abundance of visitors at Hermaness at the best of times. It wasn't as if a group of hikers were about to round the bend at this late hour, to find her inconveniently in the way. They were undoubtedly alone up here, with the exception of the birds that she could hear calling in the distance.

They stood at the crossroads again. Nell re-read the laminate sign, saw the diagram of the eroded coastal path crossed through with neat diagonal lines.

"We can't go that way," she said.

"But this is the way," Brian replied, pointing with his stick for emphasis.

"Maybe we missed another path on the route we took?"

Brian shook his head. "It will just take us back the way we came. If we want to get to the edge we have to cut some corners."

Nell heard a group of gannets swoop close by, screeching in warning.

"But it says the path is worn away."

"It'll be fine," Brian said, turning to face the prohibited trail.

At least for the first part of the journey, Brian was right. The path ran a considerable distance from the edge and was less muddy than the inland route. And from this vantage, the view of the great sea stacks was unsurpassable. Nell had never seen such numbers of gannets before. The sound was raucous, incessant, the air filled with the overpowering smell of guano. She alternated between her binoculars and camera, keen to see and record everything she possibly could.

"We should carry on," she heard Brian say, his voice competing with the sound of the gulls.

For a moment she had forgotten Brian was there, perhaps already coming to terms with life on her own.

"Why don't we get to the edge first," he continued, looking towards her camera, "then come back?"

"What does it matter what order we do it in?"

"In case of the fog." True enough the fog still lingered but it was low-lying, no higher than their knees and had been that way for some time, like a good dog brought to heel.

Nell took some more photos then followed Brian further along the path, casting backward glances at the sea stacks. The route had begun to slip further toward the cliff edge, the rocky underbelly visible between the mounds of grasses and sea pinks. How easy it would be to lose your footing and to fall over the edge, to plunge through the air before your body crashed upon the rocks. Nell doubted whether the rescue crews would even be able to recover a body in a place like this. Hermaness was too hostile, the rocks too jagged and the incline too steep to allow for an easy retrieval. Far more likely that the sea would salvage what it could, dragging the strewn remains down to ocean floor, where perhaps, the colossal skeletons of Herman and Saxa rest beneath the waves like sunken galleons.

Nell leant toward the edge despite herself, feeling the air rush past, along with a wave of vertigo. But she looked on, thinking of the old woman down there somewhere, dancing endlessly round and round. Had she been cast down too? Left on the shore to dissolve into the sand and spume. She thought of her own body dashed upon the rocks, shredded like stalks of seaweed.

"Careful," Brian called, but it was an involuntary caution, prompted by his own slow progress along the cliff. He had not looked back at Nell, he did not see how close she was to the edge. He was concentrating on his own footing, casting guarded glances up into the air.

The great skuas were more abundant here than elsewhere, soaring alarmingly low, forcing them to stop intermittently to wave their hiking sticks in the air. They were overly protective parents or maybe they'd remembered the wrong those nineteenth-century ornithologists had done them, hunting them to near extinction for the collectable quality of their eggs. Still wary of man and eager to exact revenge on all who strayed too far into their domain. Nell thought again of the laminated notice, the coastal route crossed through with sharp diagonal lines and considered that it wasn't just the state of the path that presented danger.

As if to drive the point home, the fog that had previously accompanied them harmlessly enough through the journey began to rise. Nell looked down but could hardly see the ground, let alone the ocean at the bottom of the cliffs. She looked backwards and the view was much clearer. The great sea columns stood obstinately despite the steady erosion of the waves, seemingly held upright by the millions of gannets, thrashing their wings higher and higher. But it was a transitory perch and would eventually sink into the sea with everything else.

"Come on!" she heard Brian call, noting the impatience in his voice. She could just about see him in the distance, striving forward, looking ahead. She cast one last glance back at the sea stacks teeming with life – great towers of shit and noise – before plunging into the fog.

Brian had put some distance between them. The path Nell walked now was a solitary one. Hermaness was indeed a lonely place. She pondered the name *Herman* but the word *Hermit* sprang to mind. The place should be renamed *Hermitess*, she thought, thinking of the lonely woman on the shore. Thinking of herself, wandering aimlessly in the fog.

"Brian?" she called, aware now of the silence rising with the sea haar.

She slowed her pace, taking cautious steps forward. She couldn't see the lighthouse she knew stood on the adjacent headland. She could barely see in front of her but she could see the woman on the shore, turning round and around in her head. And she thought of Brian's words, of all the hurtful things he'd said over the years, whether he'd meant them all or not, coming to the fore of her mind with ready clarity. His habit of going headlong into arguments, while she tried to sidestep them. And she was sidestepping still, making her way steadily across this path of eggshells between the two of them, only to be cast aside. How could he do that to her after all these years, after such a hard climb together? How come he'd reached the end first, whilst she was still stumbling to catch up?

"Nell," she heard Brian call, across the blank expanse of the fog. "We should go back, it's too dangerous."

She scanned the misty cliff-face, could make out an indefinite silhouette in the distance, turning slowly on the spot.

"Nell, where are you? Call to me and I'll follow your voice."

But as Nell opened her mouth she heard the American woman's laughter perforate the silence. A gloating, triumphant laugh echoing through the twilight, before realising it was just a flock of gannets flying close by. But it was enough to break the unnatural lull and Nell watched the figure in the distance turn toward the sound, stumbling almost at once as a great skua swooped suddenly out of the fog in a bid to chase the gannets away.

Nell ran into the fog and despite the obscurity, she was conscious that she was nearing the precipice. Simultaneously, she heard the thump of an impact, the unmistakeable sound of nylon against wet grass, screeching as it gained momentum down the slope.

"Brian!" she called, as she reached the edge. But there was only silence. She peered between the swathes of fog, lifting her binoculars to scan the rock-face, almost relieved when the lenses clouded over, scared of what she might see. But she looked on, until the fog slowly ebbed away and she could see right down to the bottom. To the narrow shingle beach between the crenulated rocks, a spot similar to where she'd seen the mysterious figure turning circles. But there was nothing there now. Just sand and seaweed.

When she eventually moved away from the edge, she could see the lighthouse in the distance, about which the gannets flew widdershins.

Meat for the Field
Rich Hawkins

Gregor woke from dreams of dark soil and cold earth. In his lonely bed he pushed the sheets away from his chest and sat up, wiping sweat from his face. His hands trembled. He let out a breath and looked towards the window, where the first light of dawn breached the thin curtains.

Another day. One day closer.

He rose from the bed and dressed quickly, shrugging on his shirt and jumper, thick trousers and old boots. He walked to the kitchen and tightened his father's old watch around his wrist as he waited for the kettle to boil. After that, he went to the window above the sink, pulled back the curtains and stared out at the cold dawn slowly defining the fields and the horizon beyond.

❖

He stepped outside with his mug of coffee and lit a cigarette. Inhaling a lungful of smoke, he held it in for longer than was healthy and then breathed it out into the cold air. The sky was brightening from a washed out shade of white to marine blue. He drank and smoked as the sun rose. The empty barns behind him were silent, and despite not being inhabited by livestock for years now they still retained the faint odour of dung and sheep urine. He'd grown used to the smell during his childhood, helping his father on the farm and running errands.

He should have burned them down by now – they held no sentimental value – but whenever he decided to act, he inevitably forgot about it again, because all that mattered now was the crop.

He finished the cigarette and crushed it under one boot.

Dark soil and cold earth. Blood in the dirt of the field.

❖

With a burlap sack in hand, Gregor walked down the narrow lane and out to the wheat field. He stood and looked out over the crops. His heart fluttered. There was no scarecrow, but the birds stayed away. They always stayed away.

He looked for movement amongst the crop. The wind swept shadows across the wheat, to chase each other in the tall stems and stalks, and Gregor listened for a long while as the sun began to climb its arc in the sky. But there was just the silence in the field and the others around him. And then he stepped into the field and walked along one of the furrows until he reached the small clearing at the centre of the crop.

He stood before the small pile of dead animals and put one hand to his nose. A few flies droned, alighting from the corpses of rabbits, crows, pheasants and stoats. There were mice too, and moles, stiffened and rank, bled out onto the ground of the clearing. Gregor walked to the pile and crouched down, his eyes watering, looking at the crumpled, broken bodies mutilated by the hands of true believers. Tiny hearts and livers and kidneys scattered amongst the wheat stubble.

Gregor was inured to the sight of such slaughter; the offerings, the tributes, the gifts to the land. The wind whispered through the wheat. He closed his eyes for a second.

The dark soil. The cold earth. Blood in the dirt.

He took the gloves from the burlap sack and put them on then began filling the sack with the stiffened corpses.

❖

Gregor took the dead animals around the back of his house and burned them in a pile. He sucked on a cigarette while he watched the black smoke rise and writhe into the sky. The smell of burning flesh stung his nostrils and filled his lungs. When the animals were reduced to charred bones and ashes, he climbed into his car and drove to the village to fetch supplies.

The houses, all in bland rows, were of dark brick or whitewashed walls, with small gardens and stagnant ponds. Occasionally there was a face at a window, peering out as the car passed. He glimpsed furtive eyes and pallid skin, and knew he wasn't imagining the leering grin of crooked mouths.

Farther on, people appeared and stood in gardens or loitered on pavements. There was distant laughter and some cheering. The villagers were looking forward to the festival.

He passed the church, which hadn't been used for

worship since the days of the Black Death. Ancient gravestones and Christian markers slowly degrading into nameless forms. The reverend was a liar, and not a follower of the Nazarene, but appearances had to be upheld and illusions kept.

Deeper into the village, he saw people on the streets, walking their dogs or pushing prams in which plump babies wailed. A man with shockingly white hair that reached to his shoulders nodded at Gregor and smiled. Gregor returned the smile, although when he glimpsed his own expression in the rear-view mirror, it looked pained and false, and by the time he had formed something more convincing the white-haired man had turned away, and Gregor had no one to smile at.

More people waved to him. Some of them spoke, but their voices were muffled and slow, as though they were lightly sedated. A woman sitting on a low wall laughed and held her hands together, rocking back and forth, raising her face to the sky.

Gregor stopped the car outside the shop. He turned off the engine and climbed out. He crushed his cigarette upon the road and grimaced down the street. There was silence, and when he looked back at the people, they were watching him, and he knew that they were grateful because he tended the crop and kept watch over it.

The door opened and gave a dull chime as he stepped inside, grabbing a wire basket from the leaning pile near the entrance. The recycled air was humid and stifling, and even before he stepped into the first aisle sweat beaded on his forehead and above his upper lip. He scratched his face and looked around. The linoleum floor was covered in old stains. Something smelled overripe and sickly sweet, and the reek of it grew stronger as he walked deeper into the shop. He moved between shelves laden with tinned fruit, dog food, bags of salt, bags of sugar, and flour. Tins of soup, spaghetti, ravioli, and baked beans. Faded labels flaking from old tins. He stepped over a damp patch. Everything was overpriced.

At the back of the shop, Gregor stood before the refrigerated section and examined the plastic bottles of milk, checking them for ruptures and spillages. One bottle of semi-skimmed had leaked, and some of its contents had dripped onto the shelf below and hardened into a yellowy crust.

He picked a bottle of whole milk and cleaned the dirt from it with the sleeve of his jacket, then placed it in the basket.

The sickly sweet and overripe smell was coming from the fruit section. The produce on offer made his mouth water, but only with faint nausea. Bunches of overripe bananas splitting in their trays, next to dusty apples and peaches, spoiled oranges and satsumas. The green grapes were bruised and glistening.

Gregor moved on. When he reached the counter, he laid down his basket and looked over the racks of chocolate bars and other sweet treats. Immediately a woman emerged from the doorway straight ahead, stepping from behind the beaded curtain as if she'd been waiting for him to arrive at the counter. She was old and slightly hunched. She looked at Gregor and wiped her pursed lips, smearing a silvery dampness on the back of her hand, like a snail's leavings. Thickly-applied mascara, blusher and lipstick made her face appear clownish and artificial, like she was something made of wood and sawdust trying to imitate a human being. One side of her mouth drooped.

"Hello, Gregor," she said, her voice cheerful and soaked in the local accent.

"Hello, Edith," he replied, trying not to look at her face for too long. Flashbulb memories of teenage afternoons spent lying in the meadows and using each other's bodies returned to Gregor and curdled the juices in his gut.

"We usually don't see you in the village this close to the festival. Nothing's wrong, I hope..."

"I just needed some groceries, is all, Edith."

She snorted. "I don't think I've ever been so excited about the festival. Must be those cod liver oil capsules I've been taking."

Gregor grunted. "Maybe."

"Everyone else I've spoken to can't wait either. The whole village is buzzing. In the pub last night, it was all they could talk about. Even my old mam's been in a giddy about it all."

"Is she still bed-ridden?"

"Yes, but we'll get her into a wheelchair so she can be at the festival. She's attended the festival each year since she was a toddler back in the twenties – if she can't go, she'll get angry with me, and I don't want her shitting the bed again."

"Yeah, that makes sense."

Edith ran the items – a tin of kidney beans, a packet of biscuits and a box of soup sachets – through the till and put them all in a bag. She hummed to herself as she worked.

Eager to leave, Gregor watched her. She smelled of lavender and dust.

"Anything else?" Edith asked, revealing browned teeth with a smile that creased her face and made hardened patches of make-up crumbled into powder. She didn't seem to notice.

He asked for a few packets of his favourite cigarettes from the racks behind her, and watched as Edith put them in with the other items in the bag. When that was done, he handed over the money and told her to keep the few pence change. He said goodbye, turned and stepped away, but then stopped and looked back at her.

"Is something the matter?" Edith said.

Gregor breathed out, glanced at the floor. "I heard that we've got a young girl for the offering. For the festival."

Edith nodded, smiled. "Yes, a runaway. Colin Flaycross found her stealing apples from his orchard. She's a bit skinny, but she'll do. Better than what we usually have."

"Is anyone going to notice her disappearance? She got any family?"

"A mother, up north, so she says, but I don't think anyone will trace her to us."

Gregor nodded. "Okay. See you at the festival."

The old woman giggled as Gregor walked away. "It'll be a great night."

She was still laughing when Gregor emerged outside, into the bright sun of the afternoon.

❖

He drove back to his house, past the fields where scattered pensioners from the old people's home prayed on their knees upon the sun-dappled grass. He increased the volume on his radio to drown out the chanting that rose from florid meadows and wild thickets.

❖

He sat in his armchair in front of the television and chain-smoked while watching an old black-and-white film. When the film finished, he rose from the armchair and went out to watch the wheat field for a while.

Nothing stirred except for the wind rippling across the crops in shapeless patterns. The air wavered with the summer heat. He exhaled, wiped sweat from his face then lit another cigarette. The sun blazed hot and white.

He listened for voices from the crop, but there was only silence, so he returned inside to shelter in the shade.

Then he fell asleep and dreamed of dark soil, the cold earth, and blood in the dirt.

❖

Gregor woke to the sound of scuffling footsteps inside the house. He sat up and looked around while pawing for the brass fire poker nearby, but he couldn't find it.

A low voice spoke from just outside the living room doorway, but Gregor couldn't discern the words. A shadow drifted across the hallway floor. Gregor rose from the armchair and bunched his hands into fists.

A short figure with the face of a raggedy hare appeared from beyond the doorway. Floral dress, white stockings, and buckled shoes. Coarse hair and crumpled ears atop the small head. Dark, vacant eyes and a furred cleft for a mouth. Gregor halted, stifling a scared noise in his throat.

The figure waved at him and said his name. Then it peeled away its face, but there was no blood or dripping flesh.

"Hello, Mister Higgins," the little girl said. She smiled.

Gregor sighed with relief.

"Are you okay, Mister Higgins? Did you have a bad dream?"

"I'm fine, thank you, Amelia."

The girl blushed. "I needed to use the toilet, and your front door was unlocked..."

A woman's voice came from the front of the house. "Amelia Kittridge, what are you doing in here?" The school teacher, Miss Bloom, appeared and stood beside the girl, glaring down at her. Then she looked at Gregor, who shifted awkwardly on his feet.

"Hello, Gregor," Miss Bloom said.

Gregor cleared his throat. His face flushed with heat.

Miss Bloom smiled. "I'm sorry about this. I told the children not to enter your house without asking."

"It's fine," he said. "No harm done."

"Thank you for being so understanding." She was in her twenties and yet to be married, despite being the most beautiful woman in the village. Gregor had fantasised about her many times during the lonely night-hours in his bed. He imagined that she only saw a withered old man when she looked at him.

"I better get back to the children," Miss Bloom said. She glanced at the girl. "Let's go, Amelia."

Gregor raised a hand to them as they left.

❖

He went outside and walked down the lane and found the children of the village gathered at the edge of the wheat field. Miss Bloom stood before them and led them in a prayer to the old gods of the dirt and the trees and the fields. And he watched them and found himself whispering the same prayer, but he could not finish it, and in the end he turned away and walked back up the lane with sharp aches toiling in his gut.

Miss Bloom's voice echoed after him.

"Only one more night until the festival!"

❖

After Miss Bloom and her children left, Gregor went out to the wheat field and sat down in the clearing. The ground smelled of dung and animal blood.

His hands worked at his face, pressing at the aching cheekbones and the tender parts of his skull. He sagged and let out a tired breath, then looked up at the sky as the light began to fade. The wheat field was silent around him. He lay down and ran his hand through the dirt, which became stuck under his fingernails and dusted the calluses on his palm. With one ear to the ground he listened to the earth and the things that toiled below: the insects and the burrowers, the mammals and blind foragers with hides of glistening white and pale pink.

And something else. Something greater. Something beyond the comprehension of the rational mind.

Gregor closed his eyes.

❖

He dreamed of a place where tall stalks of wheat stretched across the land in all directions to each horizon. He stood amongst the wheat and turned in a slow circle, his hands brushing through the crop that reached to his waist and bristled in the foul-smelling breeze.

The sky was a deep shade of red. A yellow moon glowed, bloated and diseased, an awful satellite scarred with trenches and craters. Gregor had to look away.

Around him, the grey ghosts rose from the wheat and turned their heads to stare at him. They were the ones sacrificed over the many years. Hundreds of them like scarecrows in the crop, men, women and children, glassy eyed and motionless and sullen with the memories of the death brought to them by the people of the village. Lost souls. And then, as if of one mind, they raised their right arms, pointed at Gregor and opened their mouths, and from the dank holes in their faces came a low wordless whispering of entwined voices.

Gregor shook his head. He tried to look away, but wherever he turned, they were staring at him, accusing him, reminding him of the past and all the lives given as offerings.

He put his head in his hands, spluttering apologies to the ghosts. But the ghosts weren't for listening to his pleas and they closed in on him.

Gregor cried.

The grey ghosts halted and went silent, and when Gregor took his hands from his face and looked at them, they were staring at the ground. He got the impression that they were waiting for something.

The ground beneath his feet began to tremble, and the leaves and stalks of wheat stirred and shook.

The dirt cracked, fractures splitting beneath the crop. A fetid smell, of mould and mildew, old rags and squalid bones, rose from the ground.

It happened fast, and there was no time for him to scream.

The ground collapsed and he fell into cascading plumes and billows of dirt, soil and dust, until he was grabbed and embraced by something made of squirming pink flesh and sopping wetness. He was squeezed so hard that the air spilled from his chest and out of his mouth. And he closed his eyes again, because he had already seen the cavernous maw waiting for him below and didn't want to witness his descent past its dripping lips and hooked teeth.

❖

He woke when someone's foot prodded his stomach. An old voice told him to get up and arrange himself. He looked into the reddened face of Colin Flaycross. The man was standing over him, small eyes set close together in a displeased glare, piggish and pale green.

Colin helped him to his feet. Gregor rubbed his head, glancing around at the wheat field, expecting to see the apparitions from his dream lurking amidst the crops. He did his best not to stare at the ground around his feet and watch for tell-tale cracks and growing fractures.

"What are you doing out here?" said Colin.

"I was just having a sit down," Gregor replied, wiping at his mouth and chin, his heart still racing from the dream-memory of being pulled into the ground. He looked past Colin, at the other men gathered at the edge of the field. They had brought a cow, a pig, and a sheep, held by lengths of rope attached to loops around the animals' necks. The men appeared uneasy and nervous, but excited. The growing season had that effect on the villagers.

The animals had already pissed and shat on the ground. Gregor wondered if they sensed the fate that waited for them. He eyed the long knives in the men's hands.

"Are you sure you're okay?" Colin said. He put one hand on Gregor's shoulder and squeezed lightly. Gregor shifted on his feet and hid the shiver in his spine. It felt like his limbs were full of water. He looked away because he was sure his eyes displayed all the guilt, shame and fear inside him.

"I'm fine," he muttered to the ground. "Just feeling a bit under the weather lately."

Colin frowned. "I hope you'll be okay for the festival tomorrow night."

"I'll be fine."

"Glad to hear it. You're a good man, Gregor, and you've done us proud."

Gregor looked across the fields and said nothing.

❖

He returned to the house, and when the terrified lowing and bleating began and the men started slaughtering the animals, he put his hands over his ears and sat on the floor and slumped against the wall. He didn't move for a long time, and all he could think about was hot blood gushing upon the dirt of the field.

❖

The dark arrived early, before Gregor even realised that the daylight had bled away. He rose from the kitchen floor and stood in the lightless kitchen, breathing slowly, his shoulders slumping as he stared out at the lane that led down to the wheat field.

After drinking from the kitchen tap and splashing his face with water, he went outside, past the back of the house and out to the garage, with a plan slowly forming in his head.

❖

Gregor walked down the lane with a jerry can in one hand and a torch in the other. The beam of light from the torch moved across the ground, swaying with his movement. Despite the chill air of the late hour, his face was beaded by droplets of sweat and pin-pricks of heat bristled under his skin. The night was completely silent, starlit and silver-tinted by the moon. Gregor imagined the nocturnal animals moving soundlessly through the fields and woods.

When he arrived at the wheat field, he stood at the place where the crops met the yellowing grass and the lane, and breathed in the air that was tainted with the slaughter of livestock. He could still smell the blood. He felt a little sick and dizzy, and thought that maybe he was losing his mind.

His limbs trembled. Something stirred in the silence, and he looked out over the field. He walked into the field, swarmed by the crop, then halted in the hidden clearing where the ground was red and festooned with the scattered bones of executed farm animals.

The wheat rippled, but there was no breeze.

Gregor laid the torch on the ground and unscrewed the cap on the jerry can. The petrol fumes stung his nostrils and made his mouth water. The box of matches in his pocket held no weight, like the bones of little birds.

"Forgive me," he whispered.

Before he could start pouring the petrol around the clearing his vision flared with white-hot light. The explosion of pain inside his head was crippling, and he collapsed to his knees and dropped the jerry can. Knives jabbing at the inner walls of his skull. Talons slashing behind his eyes. Grinding metal in his ears. The sheer agony of creation. And he cried out, cried for mercy then screamed as flashbulb images in his mind showed him the bloodied faces of the victims sacrificed over the many, many years of toil and harvest.

He grabbed the jerry can and staggered from the clearing. He left the torch behind. Through the rows of crops he stumbled blindly, tripping and flailing and crying in the darkness, expecting at any moment the grip of fleshy pinkish limbs around his ankles.

But the field let him go, and as he fled down the lane and away from the crops, the pain subsided and lessened to something like the low pulsing of rotten teeth and cavities inside his skull.

❖

Gregor spent most of the next day in bed, dosing himself with aspirin to soothe the aftershocks of pain from the night before. He gulped whiskey to numb the images still lingering in his mind; the faces of those who'd been sacrificed on his family's land. He wished his heart was hardened and cold, as it had been in previous years, but his conscience was a needle that pierced deeply.

When the day began to dim and the night of the festival was almost upon him, he rose from the bed and dressed in his best clothes, then finished the bottle of whiskey in several gulps that burned his throat raw. He looked at himself in the mirror and spat hysterical laughter, because he was a fool and there would be more death during the night ahead.

❖

The villagers arrived, more than two hundred people blended with torchlight and flickering candle-flame, as the sun sunk below the horizon. They moved in an untidy procession, chanting and singing, offering prayers as they made their way past Gregor's house and towards the wheat field. They were people he'd shared many days and nights with, sharing laughter and companionship, even love. But now he could only look upon them as bright-eyed devils craving sacrifice.

He stepped outside to join them.

❖

Colin Flaycross and the other elder men dragged the girl

into the clearing while the rest of the villagers gathered around the edges of the wheat field and murmured in expectation and shrill excitement. The children held corn dollies and figures made of dried sticks. Edith the shopkeeper sang an old song in a low, mournful cadence. Gregor knew the words to the song, and found himself muttering them despite the anxiety frothing in his throat. He tried not to make eye contact with anyone, as he made his way through the eager ranks. Miss Bloom called to him, and he looked up to find her holding the hands of her children. He looked away and kept moving.

One man, whose name he did not remember, shook him by the hand and spluttered compliments and stinking gusts of breath into his face. Gregor simply nodded and muttered his thanks, feeling sick inside and close to tears. The voices of the gathered villagers, all clamouring in the anticipation of sacrifice, were like a chorus of agitated beasts. It was all Gregor could hear as he crossed the field and stood with the other men around the girl.

Colin nodded at him. Gregor returned the gesture then looked away. He wiped his mouth and regarded the girl. Her hands were bound with rope and she was dressed with the traditional garments of frayed cloth. She was beautiful, he thought. Her feet were bare and sore. She glanced at Gregor, her eyes imploring him, her face tight and trembling. She was crying. Gregor turned away and tried to ignore her sobs and pleas.

Colin raised one hand to silence the villagers around the field, and their chattering stopped immediately. They all watched, riveted, motionless. Hundreds of eyes gleamed in the light of torches and candles.

Two of the men, rugged field workers who liked to brawl, dragged the crying girl to her knees and straightened her upper body as Colin stepped towards her with the ceremonial knife. The long blade, its edge sharpened to no wider than an atom, caught the light and gleamed. The knife had been passed down through the generations. Even the elders weren't sure of its age.

The girl begged, but the men held her fast. She struggled, jerking her head in every direction, trying to rise from the ground, until one of the men drew back his hand and slapped her around the ear, the dull clack like a stone hitting the ground.

She stopped struggling. Her head drooped on her shoulders. Her eyes fluttered.

She was barely conscious when Colin lowered the knife and drew the blade across her throat. She gurgled, choking on her own blood, unable to breathe, and as her eyes rolled back into her head she fell forward and slumped on the ground. There was only the trembling of her body and the last convulsions of dying nerves until she bled out and died.

Gregor watched, grinding his teeth, the blood draining from his face.

Colin stood back and raised the knife.

The villagers cheered and whooped. The men in the clearing shook hands and patted each other on the backs.

The celebrations began. There was dancing and singing, with much laughter and joy.

Gregor stayed for a while, and even joined in with some of the old songs in some meaningless tribute to the past. And when he was too tired and sick of it all, he walked back to his house and sat in the darkness of the living room and drank whiskey into the night.

❖

As the first light formed past the eastern horizon, Gregor walked out of his house and climbed into his car. He drove down the dirt lane and past the wheat field, glancing at the grey figures that watched him from the site of their deaths. The radio hissed static. He continued into the village as the sky began to brighten and birdsong drifted from the gardens of empty houses. Apart from the birds' dawn chorus the village was silent and the streets were deserted and lifeless.

Gregor stopped the car outside the village hall. Before he climbed out, he stared at the windows along the side of the building and saw the dancing candlelight within. Then he took the jerry can from the car boot and hefted it up the stone steps to the front of the building. He peered through a window, and it gave him no pleasure to see the entire population of the village asleep on the floor or in chairs. It was a tradition for them to return here after the festival and the sacrifice to pray and give thanks before passing out from exhaustion. When he noticed the sleeping children, and the babies cradled in their mothers' arms, he felt such a deep swell of loathing and regret that he almost walked away. But he had to see this through, all the way to the end. There was no compromise. After this, there would be no more horror in the fields and no more victims.

Gregor tied a rope around the handles on the double doors at the front entrance, and then did a circuit of the outside of the building to ensure that the windows were closed and sealed.

Once that was done, he unscrewed the cap on the jerry can and pulled the cigarette lighter from his pocket. His hands were steady and he did not hurry.

❖

It didn't take long for the flames to take hold of the village hall, and he stood there watching from the other side of the street as the fire grew and roared and the screams rang out. He smoked a cigarette and thought about old traditions and ceremonies.

The fire consumed the building and soon the screaming and crying stopped. Even from across the street, the heat reddened his skin and leeched the moisture from his mouth and throat. A column of smoke climbed towards the sky.

He stared into the flames. "I'm sorry."

And when it was all over, Gregor went home. The sun rose and turned the sky pale blue.

The grey ghosts were waiting for him in the wheat field. He went to join them.

Strange as Angels
Laura Mauro

Frankie drives with the window down and a cigarette between her lips, the taste of autumn night and nicotine crisp in the back of her throat. The radio is tuned to one of those weird nonsense-chatter stations that only seems to exist out here in the sticks. The cold air is going some way towards sobering her up. She drives one-handed, cruising at a steady speed down pitch-black country lanes. Thick trees line the road on either side, a ragged cleft of dark sky running between them like an old scar. No stars out tonight.

Jimmy is slumped in the passenger seat, face pressed hard against the window. Condensation blooms from his open mouth. It's his car, he ought to be driving, but he's so appallingly wasted he can't even put one foot in front of the other, let alone man a vehicle. She had anticipated this outcome; she's downed just enough vodka and lime to quell her nerves, and a little more for luck.

Jimmy had driven on the way up; it had been an exercise in florid catastrophising, and Jimmy had laughed at the way she shrank into her seat every time a car came in the opposite direction. "I'm not drunk enough for this," she'd muttered. The woods had seemed sinister then, dark and foreboding, the kind of place monsters might lurk.

But drunkenness has a way of lending a certain fuzzy-edged perspective to things, and it seems now to Frankie that the trees are protecting them somehow. That it's the world beyond them which is sinister.

She flicks ash out of the window.

"Are there wolves in Sussex?" Jimmy asks.

Frankie looks across. Jimmy's pale eyes are grave and bleary, his body contorted into an improbable knot of skinny limbs and seatbelt. She's used to this: sometimes, when the alignment of strange chemicals in his bloodstream is just right, his dreams bleed out into his perception of the world, and he can't quite find the divide between reality and hallucination.

"Wolves?" A thick plume of cigarette smoke catches on the breeze, spilling out into the night. She watches it dissipate in the rear-view mirror. "There aren't any wolves anywhere in England, I don't think. Only in zoos."

"Oh good." Jimmy smiles. His teeth are crooked, the ivory keys of an old piano. He leans forward, slow and deliberate, reaching a single finger to the radio panel. He misses the 'change station' button by inches. "Why are we listening to the shipping forecast?"

She likes him better like this. It's a perverse thing to think, that the accumulative funk of booze and coke and weed improves him as a person, but it does. He's quieter, more amenable, less inclined to pick at the frayed edges of whatever screwed-up kind of friendship this is. Less inclined to push for more. "I've not been listening. I've been driving. One of us has to be a responsible adult."

"I get to pick the music," he slurs. "That's the rules. That's the rules of shotgun."

She flicks the cigarette butt out into the road. It glows briefly in the dark, a scarlet firefly guttering on the tarmac. Jimmy cycles through seven different types of static, briefly discovers – and loses – a station pumping out crackly bossa nova.

There's a sudden spark of motion from the woods. Something pale and quick emerges from the trees, careening wildly through the air towards them. Frankie hits the brakes but they're moving too fast and the road is slick with yesterday's rain; tyres yelp as they skid out, car arcing gracefully across the tarmac. She's dimly aware of Jimmy beside her, still cycling through those fucking radio stations even as the car turns a full three-sixty, a whipcrack of motion; something bounces off the windscreen with a hard, wet thump, and she thinks *jesus shit, I killed someone.*

They come to an abrupt halt ten metres from where she'd hit the brakes. Her seatbelt is the only thing standing between her and violent defenestration. For a long moment she is perfectly still, fingers like talons wrapped tight around the steering wheel, heart pistoning in the base of her throat, staring at the shape imprinted on the windscreen: the pale, smeared outline of an improbably tiny human being.

Her hands fumble frantically, fighting to open the door, to unlatch the seatbelt. The sweet-sour stench of bourbon-laced vomit rises in a thick wave, and she realises Jimmy has puked all over himself. She stumbles over her own feet as she scrambles out; she lands on outstretched palms, dark mulch seeping between the gaps in her fingers.

The car sits diagonally, front half listing slightly into the ditch at the side of the road. Frankie stumble-crawls back into the road, blue-black braids hanging in her eyes, grazing her bare knees on the wet tarmac. Somehow, Jimmy is already there, crouched in the glare of the headlights. His skin is so white it's almost blue, stretched thin and tight over the long contours of his face.

He points. There's a pale shape at his feet.

"Frankie, come here," he says as she approaches. His smile is lopsided and beatific. "Look what I found."

It's a delicate little mannequin, tiny limbs curled and foetal, skin bloodless and ricepaper thin. A pair of membranous wings sprout from the nubs of its scapulae, folded up tightly like the petals of a sleeping flower. She slips her fingers beneath it, gentle, afraid it might crumble in her hands.

Tiny black eyes flicker open, regarding her without fear.

"Look Frankie," Jimmy whispers, reverent. "It's an angel."

❖

In the morning her body feels like the aftermath of a street riot, a burnt-out shell smouldering in the cold light of day. Her head is horribly heavy, her spine a too-taut rope, and her hands and knees are crusted with a filth she does not remember accumulating.

Frankie gingerly disentangles herself from Jimmy's arms, her mouth a moue of disgust; the proximity of his skin to hers is almost physically repulsive, the masculine scent of him intrusive. She did not give him permission to enter her bed. They've had this conversation before – he, oscillating wildly between childlike hurt and indignant sulking, she grinding teeth at his inability to accept the sanctity of her personal space. And still, some mornings she finds him, emboldened by chemicals and by her own dead-body stupor, coiled snakelike and overwarm around her like a too-friendly dog that can't understand 'no'.

He has never tried to touch her intimately. Not yet.

She shambles to the bathroom, peeling off last night's clothing as she goes. Her black skin shimmers with glitter-paint; in the dim light she is a galaxy, a broad sweep of faraway stars glimmering in the darkest reaches of space. She smells resolutely terrestrial, though: old sweat, cigarette smoke, damp earth and mouldering leaves. She does not smell of Jimmy, and for that at least she is grateful.

Frankie perches on the edge of the bath, soaks a flannel in hot water and scrubs her face until her skin shines, passing it cursorily beneath her arms. She shrugs on a clean t-shirt and shorts. Specks of glitter cling stubbornly to her forearms, her clavicle; she'll have a proper shower later, when her brain has stopped throbbing.

Jimmy is awake by the time she gets to the kitchen. He's appropriated one of her oversized band t-shirts. His thin shoulders barely stretch the fabric. He turns, alerted by the soft press of her bare feet on the tiles.

"Holy shit, Frankie. " His wide, bloodshot eyes stare out over a mug of coffee which, at a glance, must be at least eighty percent milk. His breath smells sour, even at this distance. "I thought I was dreaming."

A glass aquarium sits on the kitchen counter. She's had it for years, though she is certifiably incapable of keeping any kind of pet alive for more than two weeks. At the bottom, half-buried in a litter of torn paper towels and newspaper, is a creature the colour of dead skin.

"The angel." She looks up at Jimmy. "We brought it back with us. Don't you remember?"

"No," he says pressing his fingers to his forehead. "The *angel?* What the fuck's a... oh, Jesus, what did you let me take last night?"

Frankie taps a finger on the glass. The angel doesn't even stir. It looks dead. It probably *is* dead; she can still feel the impact, recall the perfect imprint of its tiny body on the windscreen. "There's a syringe," she says, waving vaguely at Jimmy. "In the medicine box. Fetch it here." While he's searching, she takes the kettle, pours lukewarm water into a glass. She stirs in four teaspoons of sugar. This is what they do with hummingbirds, she tells herself. She can't remember where she might have learned such a thing – watching the Discovery Channel blitzed at three am, probably – and she isn't sure such knowledge can even be applied to such an unusual beast, but she has to try something.

Gently, she lifts the creature from the fishtank. It is unresponsive, a little clammy, as though it is only a puppet fashioned out of pinkish clay. She feels Jimmy's presence close behind her, a peripheral warmth.

"It's just a doll, Frankie," he says. "We must have been off our faces and seen this in the road, and..."

"*You* were off your face. I saw it open its eyes. It flew out of the woods, Jimmy." She pries gently at its mouth with her little finger, poising the syringe just above. Its head is a smooth, hairless quail's-egg sloping down to hard little eyes; the rest of its face is a plateau, flat and featureless except for the thin gynaecological slit of its mouth. "I don't know what it is," she says, "but it's alive." It's insubstantial in the crook of her arm, matchstick limbs floppy. She holds it like a baby, feeding individual droplets of sugar-water into its open, toothless mouth.

It blinks. Light pink membranes slipping up and over like a lizard's. Its wings are folded against its back, crumpled like loose, elderly skin.

"Shit," Jimmy murmurs. "What the bloody hell is it, Frankie?"

In the bright light of morning it seems smaller, more fragile, a pale flesh-puppet. Its eyes meet hers, bright and curious. There's a pang somewhere in the vicinity of her heart, startling in its intensity.

"It's beautiful," she says.

❖

On the third day the angel refuses to drink the sugar-water, choosing instead to bury itself in the litter at the bottom of the aquarium. It wriggles and burrows until it disappears, forming a hillock beneath the shredded newspaper and kitchen towel. Occasionally, passing by, Frankie catches the gleam of sharp eyes peering out, observing her from the safety of its nest. Once, she holds its gaze for an entire minute; somehow she feels as if it can see into her eyes, into the back of her skull and *up*, penetrating the thick, tangled bolus of her spinal cord, the soft matter of her brain.

At first, Frankie thinks this must be some new and exciting stage in the creature's development; perhaps it's forming a chrysalis under there, seeking darkness and warmth until it's ready to emerge, bigger and more beautiful. But two days pass and the angel remains stubbornly entombed, withdrawing further until even its eyes are lost from view. She's afraid to reach in and touch it, afraid that she might disturb some kind of vital process, but as strange a creature as it is, it surely must need some kind of sustenance.

"It might be dead," Jimmy says, peering into the tank. There's a scattering of chopped fruit in one corner, a heel of bread torn into small chunks. She's tried saucers of milk, crumbled biscuits, sugar cubes. Raw beef mince sitting in a dish for six hours, the smell growing increasingly unbearable in the still warmth of the flat. She's so desperate to see it eat that she has barely slept.

"It's not dead," Frankie replies. Her voice is tinged with an unpleasant hysteria. She nudges Jimmy aside, presses both palms to the side of the tank. She would *know* if it were dead, she thinks; she would feel it deep inside of her, a hollow ache like something torn out of her and thrown aside. The certainty of this baseless conviction scares her, a distant kind of fear like the far-off possibility of terminal disease, or lonely destitution. She wills the angel to move but the nest remains stubbornly undisturbed.

A single lamb's kidney is pooled in a dish beside the tank, a glistening mass the colour of old blood. Tentatively, Frankie plucks a knife from the wooden block. The blade hovers, reflecting the blue-red sheen.

She cannot bring herself to destroy the taut architecture of the renal capsule; she imagines the kidney deflating, a burst water balloon leaking blood.

Jimmy sprawls out across the sofa, jeans riding up, revealing threadbare blue socks. "The internet says it's a hoax," he says, waving his phone at her. "Some kind of animatronic puppet. CGI's a popular theory too."

"You put it on the internet?"

He shrugs. "Well, yeah. I thought maybe someone had seen one before. Might've been able to tell us what it is."

A tremor of useless anger runs through her, petering out at the tips of her clenched fingers. She still can't cut into the kidney. "I don't want anyone else knowing about this," she says. "If someone catches on that the angel is real..."

"I wish you wouldn't keep calling it that," Jimmy mutters.

"You called it that first."

"I was *off my tits*, Frankie, it doesn't count."

She waves the pristine knife at him. "Seriously. Don't put it on the internet. Delete whatever you've already posted. I mean it. This is between me and you, all right?"

"Oh," he says, eyebrows raised. "So there's a 'me and you' now?"

Hot blood creeps up Frankie's neck, burning at her cheeks. She does not know if it is anger or shame that causes the breath to catch momentarily in her chest; this same old debate, one-sided as always, trotted out like a dying horse every time he feels vulnerable. *You won't let me touch you. You won't let me love you.* Except that isn't quite it. There is an element of longing in him – a yearning for the kind of affection she'll never show. But there's also a proprietary undercurrent, a greedy possessiveness that makes her flesh crawl: *you won't touch me. You won't love me. You won't give me what I want.* She does not want to be owned by him, touched by him, and she has never feigned otherwise but guilt sours her stomach all the same.

"I was referring to our friendship," she says, forcing neutrality despite the tightness of her jaw. "Because I like to think that maybe the last two years haven't just been about you slowly wearing me down until I give in and sleep with you."

His lower lip protrudes in a perfect three-year-old's strop. "I don't know how you can even say that," he says, pulling his arms protectively across his chest.

"Because every time I think we're done with this conversation you go and resurrect it. And I have to ask myself if it's because you think you're going to get a different answer if you just keep being patient." She slices into the kidney, slow and deliberate. The texture is surprisingly firm; the knife glides through with ease. For a split second she imagines it is Jimmy's face. Just a split second. "I don't want that kind of relationship with you, Jimmy. I need you to understand that, because if you don't..." In goes the knife. Thin slices of kidney accumulate, silk-glossy. She gains confidence as she cuts.

"I understand," he says, a little too sharply. He's looking down at his feet, worrying at a hole in his sock with his toenail. Mouth still cartoonishly sulky, like her scolding is entirely unprovoked. Like she's in the wrong. "Doesn't mean I have to *like* it though, does it?"

Knife slides in, negotiating delicate renal architecture. Paring matter into paper-thin slivers. She can't argue. She has nobody else, and loneliness terrifies her. If she shatters this delicate pretence – the illusion that they are comfortable like this, that Jimmy's obsession doesn't matter – he will leave, and the days will pass in silence, one blending into another, because nobody else has ever been able to tolerate Frankie for longer than a month. Her fingers close tight around the knife handle as she peels off a slice so thin the light shines through, illuminating veins like the branches of dead trees. She wants to tell him to go, if he's so unhappy. But he's nitroglycerine, and if she pushes hard enough he'll explode, destroy everything, burn it all to ashes, and there'll be nothing left but her own voice chiding her endlessly from inside her skull.

The knife slips in her hand, skewing to the left. She registers no pain at all as it cuts into the meat of her thumb. A bead of blood wells up, garnet-dark; it quivers for a moment before collapsing inward, spilling down her palm. She inhales sharply at the sight of it, a wide pink cleft against dark skin.

"Are you all right?" Jimmy asks.

She looks up at him, blank and calm. "It's just a nick," she says, although the pain has started now, and she can tell by the slow, deep pulse of it that she's cut far deeper than she's willing to acknowledge. She searches the counter for the kitchen roll, a towel, anything to staunch the wound. And there, pressed gecko-like at the side of the tank, is the angel. The cloven nubs of its hands are splayed against the glass, slit-mouth gaping, tongue probing the air the way a snake scents it prey. Slowly, she lifts her injured hand. Blood trickles down her wrist, forking off into smaller tributaries. Her eyes never leave the angel as she moves towards it.

"Frankie?"

Thin, ragged slivers of kidney line the dish like rafflesia petals. A trail of droplets stain the counter, a prolonged red ellipsis. The angel scrabbles at the glass as though in desperation, upright on thin limbs which seem ill-designed for movement. She lowers her hand into the tank, expecting it to pounce at her, but it doesn't. A cry emerges from its open mouth, shrill and childlike, the pitiful sound of its hunger. Clumsy fingers grasp the knuckle of her thumb, gently guiding it into the waiting cavern of its open mouth. The pain is brief and intense, but it warms her, flowing to her core like there's something volcanic inside of her. Its tongue is like warm suede.

"Yes," she says, watching the angel suckle with something like pride. "I'm fine."

❖

She buys little white mice from the pet shop. They tumble over one another like breaking waves, an undulation of tiny bodies, baby-pink ears. The shop owner eyes her with suspicion, which abates only a little when she explains it's for her snake. This is a small town. Small enough that a black girl with a snake might be considered a talking point, though she can't be sure.

The mice have inquisitive eyes; they are unafraid as Frankie slips her hand in among them, scooping up a warm, squirming bundle. Feet pitter against her hand, tiny claws prickling at her palm. The angel emerges from its burrow, all hands and knees, fixated on Frankie's cupped palms as though it can smell what's inside.

With comical care, she deposits the mouse in among the shredded paper. The angel straightens, limbs poised. A cat ready for the kill. She turns her back, hurrying away before the brittle crunch of small bones and the obscene contrast of blood on white fur conspire to turn her already sour stomach.

"It's like the Chupacabra," Jimmy says later, retrieving a cluster of desiccated corpses from the bottom of the tank. Tissue paper clings to their diminished bodies, fluttering as Jimmy lifts them out. Frankie peers at one from the corner of her eye, cradled in the cup of Jimmy's palm. It barely resembles a mouse anymore: a chrysalis of skin and bone, an empty ribcage gaping like an open mouth. There is no blood.

"The heart's gone," Jimmy says, prying with a fingernail. "Guess we've figured out what it eats."

"How would something like this survive out there?" Frankie asks. "It doesn't look equipped to kill anything. It's got no teeth or claws."

Jimmy shrugs. "Could be a baby," he says. "Maybe it's still dependent on its parents to bring it food. Hey Frankie, maybe you could chew up some mouse hearts? Isn't that what hawks do?"

"It's not a hawk," she says, faintly nauseated; she can imagine the gristle against her teeth, the wet pop of a heart bursting between her molars. "Anyway, it's managing fine by itself. It's eaten four mice since yesterday. It keeps begging. I can't tell if it's hungry or just greedy."

He frowns, sceptical. "I doubt it's begging, Frankie. It's not a puppy."

You don't know, she thinks, filling a ceramic hamster dish with water. The angel is presumably resting – she has not seen it since she slipped the first mouse into its tank, but the pile of corpses – car-crash messy, limbs stacked beneath limbs – reassures her that it must be all right. And it's true that she can't bring herself to watch it feed, or reach in and touch the bodies it leaves behind, but at three in the morning she'll crawl silently out of bed, eyes adjusting slowly to the bleary monochrome of early dawn, and she'll sit for a while at the kitchen counter, watching it sleep. Sometimes it's awake, and it will pause as she approaches, perhaps judging her in that instant as friend or foe – small body tight as a wound spring, ready to leap for cover – until it recognises her, somehow, by her gait or her build or her scent. And then it relaxes, because it knows she is its benefactor, a surrogate mother whose determination makes up for her lack of knowledge.

It doesn't trust Jimmy yet. Jimmy doesn't talk to it, or sit beside it, marvelling at the intricate architecture of its wings, the way the light illuminates branched veins, rendering skin the colour of a sunset sky. The alien beauty of it is discomfiting, like the bioluminescent lightshow of deep-sea creatures gliding through black ocean trenches. To Jimmy the angel is a curiosity, something to study and to observe, but from a distance.

He is too preoccupied with her refusal to love him that he cannot see just how precious, how special this strange, beautiful monster is.

The angel grows. It goes from a fragile little mannequin to a hunched preybird, limbs slender and taut as cord, outgrowing the warm cradle of Frankie's palm with a rapidity she has seen in no other species. It is as though each heart it devours is a growth spurt. Within a week it has outgrown the mice, swallowing the gnarled kernels of their hearts without chewing, though its teeth have finally emerged; they jut jagged and ugly from the bony shelves of its mandibles, chaotic as icicles clustered on frozen eaves.

Frankie has Jimmy drive her into Tunbridge Wells so nobody will ask questions when she emerges from the butcher's with two kilos of lamb's hearts, so fresh she swears they're still warm. The butcher eyes her briefly, studying her blue-streaked braids, her thick eyeliner and silver labret stud; he probably thinks she's a weirdo goth engaging in pseudo-vampiric rituals, but he smiles as he takes her money. She clutches the bag to her chest, hoping to disguise its shape, the raw meat odour. Jimmy swears to her it doesn't smell of anything, but she's too paranoid to believe him.

She hurried from the car, up the stairs to the first floor, holding the bag tightly. Jimmy rolls his eyes as he unlocks the door. In the kitchen, the angel - too big for its tank now, and housed in a second-hand parrot cage Frankie bought off the internet – presses itself against the bars in silent delight, wings opening and closing as if of their own accord.

"I think it can smell them through the bag," Frankie says, watching it squirm and paw like a dog enraptured at its master's return. She slips her fingers through the bars. Jimmy visibly flinches as the angel leans up, neck extended. "Relax," she says. The angel nuzzles at the pads of her fingers. It feels warm and dry, skin soft as old velvet. "It knows me."

"It's got *teeth*," Jimmy mutters, eyeing the creature with clear distrust. "It could bite your fingers off."

"It won't," she says. "I told you. It knows me. It recognises my scent. Sometimes at night it tries to make a nest in my hair. I think it feels safe there. It's actually kind of sweet."

His eyes grow large in sudden disbelief, mouth contorting into a grimace. "You let it sleep in your bed?"

"Well, yeah," she says. "Don't people let their cats and dogs sleep on their beds?"

"This is not a dog, Frankie, it's not even close." He looks over at the angel, now sat with outstretched legs in the corner of its cage, apparently musing over its own toes. "It could hurt you, you know that? Have you seen the way it tears mice open? Three seconds, tops. It's a carnivore, for christ's sake. It drinks blood and eats hearts and you're letting it snuggle in your hair?"

"Jimmy, you're overreacting," she says. "It's never even tried to hurt me. If anything, it acts really affectionate towards me. I don't know, maybe it thinks I'm its mother or something..."

"Enough," Jimmy says, shaking his head. He raises a commanding hand, palm towards her. "Just stop it. You sound fucking nuts. I've gone along with this because I haven't seen you this enthusiastic about anything since you came off your meds. I thought it was good for you but... look, we should've called a newspaper, or the zoo, or the bloody RSPCA because we literally have no idea what we're dealing with here. We've discovered a creature maybe no-one else in the world has even seen before, and you're keeping it in a cage and feeding it hearts, and..." he throws up his hands, sighing ostentatiously. "This is weird, Frankie. This is not normal and I should never have gone along with it."

A single syllable escapes her open mouth – "Oh?" – before she snaps it shut, afraid of what else might come pouring out. Everything about him right now is pushing all the wrong buttons: the awful, patronising paternalism, the rigid certainty of his posture, as though Frankie is a misguided child who has, through an act of monumental stupidity, let herself down. Because Jimmy knows what's best for her. He always has.

"Come on," he says, conciliatory now. He smiles, but his mouth is strange and thin and his eyes are flat, entirely without mirth. "Let's go back to where we found it. Let's head back to Wych Cross and let it go." His hand falls to her shoulder. Long fingers splay out over the curve of the joint. "Whatever it is, it's a wild creature. It's cruel to keep it in a cage." Fingertips caress, just once but it's enough; the involuntary shudder of her spine as he touches her bra strap is a red flag. She slides out of his grasp, aware even in separation of the slight clamminess of his skin.

"You're jealous," she says, triumphant, because here at last is the proof. "You're pissed off because I'll share a bed with the angel, but not with you. How pathetic is that? Do you think I'll be lonely if we take it back? Is that your plan?" He is bug-eyed, flushed with his own pent-up outrage, but she gives him no quarter; the anger flows out of her like poison from a rotten wound. "Did you think you could save me all over again, and this time you'd get your reward?"

"How can you—"

"I let myself believe you," she continues. "You told me again and again that we were friends, and that you were okay with that, and I pushed down the doubt because I didn't want to lose you. I'm bored of it now, Jimmy. I'm sick of you whining every time I tell you to get out of my bed because I *never* fucking invited you in. I'm sick of you thinking you deserve some kind of sexual reward because you're nice to me. And I am sick to death of you treating my friendship like a consolation prize."

"You're literally choosing a bloodsucking monster over me," Jimmy says. His face is still flushed, but his voice is dull, his shoulders slack; his traditional line of protest has been obliterated, and perhaps he can already sense the futility of the sympathy vote. "You're going to throw away two years of friendship so you can keep playing mummies & daddies with your weird pet."

"Two years of you chipping away at my patience," she fires back. God, it feels good to finally speak the unspeakable, and for him to listen, shamefaced at being found out. "Two years of you hanging around, waiting for me to cave in. That's not a friendship, Jimmy, that's a hostage situation."

"I'm your only friend," he says. "You can't afford to

push me away." His last, bitterest shot. It should be a gutpunch. It should leave her breathless and miserable, but she looks at Jimmy, at his sallow skin and the long, awkward features of his face – drooping eyes and bird-beak nose – and she wonders how this sad scarecrow of a man ever managed to hold her in his thrall.

She looks across to the angel, to where it sits placidly in its cage, gazing up at her with what she believes, deep in her heart, is pure canine adoration.

"I think you should go now," Frankie says.

❖

Later, when night has fallen, the totality of her loneliness reveals itself to her in every creak of floorboards, every whisper of branches against the window. Her phone taunts her from the bedside table: *who are you going to call?* She has systematically alienated everyone in her life. Even her parents burn with shame at the mention of her: three stints at the psychiatric hospital, each one more draining for them than the last. She can still recall the tired resignation in her father's eyes as they wheeled her away, for the third time, to have her stomach pumped.

She's doing better now. It's been four years. She sends them Christmas cards every year so they know she's still alive. No return address. She's done being a burden to them.

The angel is asleep in its cage. She hears the occasional hitch of its breath, the rustle of paper as it stretches out its limbs. It is rapidly outgrowing this enclosure too. She doesn't know what she'll do when it does: her sickness benefit doesn't stretch very far, and without Jimmy she probably won't get any more bar work to supplement it. Perhaps she'll have to let it roam the flat freely until she can afford a proper enclosure. It won't be so bad; it can sleep curled at the end of her bed, and if she closes her eyes she can pretend that the gentle depression of the mattress is from a real person, sitting beside her, watching over her as she sleeps. Keeping her company. Keeping her safe.

She switches off the bedside lamp. Her room is plunged into abyssal darkness, and in the moments before her eyes adjust she stares into the black, the hiss of her own respiration like an incoming tide, and imagines she is at sea beneath a starless sky, becalmed and utterly alone.

❖

Frankie doesn't hear from Jimmy for weeks. She expects passive-aggressive texts, or to see him cruising by her front window, ominously slow in his car; she's always thought him the type. But she doesn't hear a word from him, doesn't bump into him in town, and her insides are a roiling mix of relief and sadness. Did he care so little about her that this has been easy for him? Has he written her off as a mere failed conquest? The possibility stings far more than the pervasive dull ache of her loneliness.

Without Jimmy's car she finds herself frittering away increasing amounts of money on buses and cabs, ferrying herself back and forth in search of fresh meat; heart is not especially expensive but the angel is hungry, and growing, and she finds herself eating beans on toast or stale cereal to stave off her own hunger while the creature devours her offerings with its flytrap teeth, strips of gristle caught between long, thin incisors.

But it's worth her efforts. The angel grows bigger. Its body thickens; the taut bulk of its muscle grows visible beneath skin the hue of old parchment. It adopts a strange, simian gait, scrambling excitedly around the flat after Frankie like a large, hairless capuchin; wings fold neatly along its spine, dormant. She's not certain it could ever fly. It seems too substantial now, too bulky.

And yet despite the uncanny ugliness of it, she feels a surge of affection whenever it clambers onto the sofa beside her, gripping the cushions between the cleft of its crude, cloven hands; she delights in the velvet of its skin, warm beneath her palm. The angel follows her everywhere. For the first time in her life, she has something that needs her. For the first time, she is able to *give*.

It is three weeks after her last angry confrontation with Jimmy when she returns home to find him sitting on her sofa, comfortable and relaxed, as though the last few weeks have been a figment of her disordered imagination. The angel is sitting in the centre of the room, a fleshy blotch on the balding faux-Persian rug. It takes Frankie a few moments to realise it isn't looking at Jimmy but past him, at the blonde woman standing in the kitchen doorway with a lit cigarette dangling from her fuschia-painted lips.

Frankie drops her keys on the side table. The angel looks up. Its face is as smooth and sparse as always, blank gaze unreadable, but she senses its recognition of her. It gallops over, pressing itself against her calves; its wings flex periodically as if preparing for flight.

"What are you doing here?" Frankie demands.

The pink-mouthed girl smiles, exhaling grey smoke. She's tall and athletic, sporting an authentic and somewhat raw-looking mahogany tan. Long, sleek caramel hair. Frankie knows her vaguely from the drunken parties Jimmy used to take her to. "Jim wanted to show me your pet," she says, plucking the cigarette from between her lips. "I thought he was bullshitting, but..."

"I wasn't talking to you," Frankie says, a little too sharply; this girl probably has no idea she's being weaponised. "How did you get in here?"

Jimmy grins, languid. "I've got spare keys, silly," he says, patting his pocket. The angel seems to flinch at the sound; the nub of one wing presses sharp into Frankie's leg. "Jesus, what are you feeding it? It looks like a bald Pitbull. It'll be bigger than you soon, if this keeps up, and then what will you do? You can't feed it lamb hearts forever."

"It eats hearts?" The pink-mouthed girl grimaces.

"It's not your business anymore, Jimmy. You shouldn't even be here." Her muscles are tense, her voice shaky. She cannot comprehend Jimmy's complete lack of reaction to her anger, and there is a small voice in the back of her mind asking paranoid little questions: were the last few weeks a weird, extended dream? The argument is still fresh and vivid in her mind, but can she trust that memory? Is she going insane again?

"Tamsin said you should send a picture of it to the papers," Jimmy continues. His arms stretch out across the top of the sofa, spanning it in its entirety. Frankie thinks she can see track marks, but she's not certain; he always said he'd never go back to that, and she'd always believed him. But things have changed, haven't they? "They'd probably never believe it, but it'd give them a good five minutes of speculation. You might even get a bit of money for it. How *are* you doing for money, Frankie?"

Frankie breathes shallow, trying to still her trembling; she feels strangely brittle, as though she might splinter and shatter if she moves too quickly. "Just go, Jimmy. Please, leave the keys and go. I don't want you in my house anymore."

"You wouldn't believe how small it was when we first found it," Jimmy continues, oblivious. Across the room Tamsin is listening to him intently, puffing away on her cigarette as though she breathes nicotine instead of oxygen. "Like a little doll. I mean, it didn't even look real. Frankie's put her heart and soul into looking after it and it shows, doesn't it? Look how strong and healthy it looks." He looks directly at her now. The spite in his smile is unmistakeable. Her throat burns with angry bile. She hates him then. She hates him a hundred times more than she ever might have loved him.

Beside her, the angel tenses. A strange sound emanates from its open mouth: a thunderous rumble, the clatter-click of teeth vibrating against one another. She realises, with some surprise, that it is growling.

"Get out," she says. Her voice trembles but she does not cower. This is the last time he will ever have power over her. "Leave me alone. I don't need you, Jimmy. If you ever set foot in here again I'll call the police."

He gives a sharp bark of laughter but straightens up,

getting slowly to his feet. "I haven't done a thing to you. You gave me the keys of your own free will."

"More fool me," she says.

The angel bristles as Tamsin approaches; Frankie can sense the power in its muscles, the tension in its hunched body. She puts out a hand, runs placatory fingers over the ridge of its half-folded wings. The girl pauses at the door, scanning her with kohl-smudged eyes. Taking in Frankie's heavy thighs, the roundness of her belly. The shabbiness of her clothes. "He only wanted you so he could say he'd fucked a black girl," she says, with a casualness Frankie knows she has practiced. "I hope you know that."

Frankie turns to him once Tamsin is gone. "This isn't a zoo, Jimmy. Don't bring your friends over to gawp and expect me to be happy about it."

"You don't have any special claim," Jimmy says, glancing down at the angel. Up close, he smells unwashed, his clothes rumpled. She can see he's not taking care of himself; his spiteful bravado is a poor cover, but the lank tangle of his hair and cracked lips tell a different story. She might have felt sorry for him once. "It's as much mine as it is yours."

"No," she says, as he slinks past her into the hall. "It isn't."

❖

The sky is turning bruise-black at the edges when Frankie returns home from her second shift on the Asda checkout. She's got a plastic bag full of meat past its sell-by date – not hearts, but she's learned that the angel will eat it if it's hungry enough. The streetlights aren't on yet, and she hurries from the bus stop, head down, willing the sky to stay light until she gets home.

The Asda job is a small triumph. It is the first time in her 24 years that she has felt strong enough to approach the world alone – to turn up with her braids shorn and her hair springy-short, her makeup sparse, a hastily-ironed blouse and charity shop shoes and walk away with a job. The shadows around her lengthen and deepen as she approaches her block of flats, conspiring with the rapidly darkening sky. It's strange, she thinks, as she searches her pockets for her keys. She almost feels better without Jimmy's constant presence. Perhaps she'd always had the potential to go it alone. Perhaps Jimmy was a comfort blanket she never really needed. He'd been happy to go along with it. Of course he had, because in his mind, all paths led to one eventuality.

She realises, raising her key to the lock, that the door is slightly ajar.

Frankie panics. Her brain sparks with frantic visions of overturned furniture, smashed windows; she has no valuables to steal, but the angel is uncaged and roaming free. Would someone think to steal it? She shoves open the door, stumbling into the darkened hall. The Asda bag drops from her hand, forgotten. She peers into the living room, hunting for shadows. Listening for movement, though she can hear nothing but the erratic bass drum of her own heartbeat. And as she edges sideways into the living room, step by tentative step, keys shoved between her knuckles like she'd do anything other than run, she realises she can smell blood.

Coherent thought abandons her. There is only fear, sharp as a swallowed knife. She stumbles into the room, wide-eyed, searching desperately for her angel. Is it hurt? Is it crying out in pain? *Oh god*, she thinks, *don't let it be dead, I don't know what I'll do if it's dead*. The carpet is dappled with blood, a Rorschach blot spreading from the sofa to the defunct gas fire; a red-black spattering fans out above the armchair, coming to an abrupt halt just shy of the kitchen door.

She runs into the kitchen. Her feet skid on the tiles, and she has just enough time to register a single, ludicrous thought – *I'll have to clean the blood off my shoes before work* - when she sees Jimmy.

He is crumpled beneath the kitchen counter, lolling boneless and empty on the floor. His face is bleached and bloodless, skin slack on his bones. Behind him, barely visible except as a flash of bright colour in the gloom, is Tamsin; her long blonde hair is pooled out behind her, matted to the tiles with half-dried blood.

Frankie is too stunned to scream, too appalled by the copper-penny smell, the way Jimmy's body has collapsed in on itself; he is a discarded piñata, torn apart and emptied. Frankie's shoes are glossy with blood. Her shell-shocked brain makes attempts at rational thought: *they'll blame you for this, you can't stay here*. She acknowledges the grimness of her situation with total paralysis, though her body is screaming at her to move, to go, to run.

Behind her, something is moving.

She turns on her heel, a sharp and clumsy motion; her hand reaches out, grasping the wall. Her ankle grinds painfully beneath her weight and she falls, arms flailing for purchase and finding only air. She lands heavily. A sharp pain lances up her spine, into her brain. It's a welcome shock.

The angel approaches entirely without fear. It's bigger than she remembers it, though she's only been gone since this morning. Wet slivers of meat nestle between its teeth; its flat, smooth face is tacky with gore. It moves towards her on its hind legs, hands cupped and proffering. Inside, resting in the crude cage of its fingers, is a human heart.

"Jesus, what have you done?" Frankie whispers.

The angel pushes the heart towards her, silent and beseeching; this is a gift, she realises, choking down a wave of nausea. The angel has brought her the heart of the man who hurt her, and it is proud, unmistakably proud of what it has done. She stares at the broad set of its shoulders, the thick capillaries of its wings, flushed with new blood. From her place on the floor it seems to tower above her, translucent in the blueish dusk filtering in through the open window. It reaches out one bloody hand, cradling the heart in the cleft of the other; gently, almost lovingly, it slips a digit between her whimpering lips, prying open her clenched teeth with ease.

"Don't," she pleads, but her mouth is open wide and the word has no form. The heart is too big to fit but the angel pulls, straining to wrench her jaw wider. The pain is excruciating, the sour taste of Jimmy's heart vivid on her tongue. She raises her arms, tries to push it away but the angel is strong; it must interpret her struggles as frenzied feeding because it pushes harder, shoving the heart against her incisors. Teeth scrape against meat. Tears stream down her face, into her open mouth. She tastes salt, bloody tissue; she thinks she might die here, choked to death, a human heart lodged in the cavity of her mouth.

And then abruptly, it stops.

The pressure on her jaw is suddenly relieved. Her teeth clamp down, hard against spongy gristle. The curve of a ventricle presses against her tongue. She claws at her mouth, pulling the heart away just in time. The bile in her throat rushes up, expelling violently all over the tiles. There are shreds of meat in there, she notes, with numb horror, wiping her streaming eyes with the back of her trembling hand. She breathes through snot-thick nostrils, mouth open and gasping, face wet with tears and vomit and fluids she can't bear to think about.

Frankie feels the warm velvet of the angel's face nuzzling against her arm. She straightens up, holding herself upright with slippery palms. The angel rises on its haunches, reaching out with great care to clasp her chin, bringing her close enough to see her own round, terrified face reflected in the hard black beads of its eyes. She can smell sweet carrion on its breath as it presses its cheek against hers, blood-sticky skin against skin. This is how she has taught it to love: to nurture, to feed, to protect. To fight for life against the odds. She has been a willing parent, a good mother, and now it is paying her back the only way it knows how. Eat the heart. Grow stronger. Eventually, she might even be able to protect herself the way the angel has protected her.

The angel lets her go. It clambers up onto the kitchen

counter, extending its wings as it nears the open window. Nicotine-yellow net curtains billow out into the chilly night. It sits crouched on the sill for a moment, scanning the jagged black line of the treetops; in this low light, seen through tear-blurry eyes, it could almost be human.

Somewhere in the distance a siren bursts into life.

They must have heard screaming, Frankie realises, clambering slowly to her feet. The walls are paper-thin, the window wide open. The police will be here any minute and they will find her, bloody and shell-shocked, scraps of heart stuck between her molars. The angel hears her as she stands. It turns one last time, pale against the night sky, wings fluttering in the breeze. She wonders what it will do if she follows it. She wonders how far she would get if she tried.

It leaps. Wings extend like skin umbrellas, wide as sails; two powerful beats and it is up, buoyed on the wind, a black shape in a moonless sky, heading for the trees. The sirens are loud in Frankie's ears as she climbs onto the counter, trailing wet red shoeprints. She clings to the window frame with cold fingers, leaning out into the wind. She can't fly, but she can run. She can run a long way if she needs to.

The Castellmarch Man
Ray Cluley

Atop Raiders Hill in Radnorshire stands a solitary stone that some believe resembles a weeping figure. According to folklore, the shadow it casts as the sun goes down points the way to a cave of hidden treasure, stolen goods hidden by thieves waiting for a safe time to sell. Whether the stone figure weeps because it was never able to find this bounty, or because it grieves some greater loss, nobody knows, though of course there are stories to accommodate both possibilities. There are certainly plenty of caves in the area and the hills and mountains make for rewarding hikes.

Geo-cache findings: a toy car, a single glove, and a tarnished silver ring.

The Hayward Stables Guesthouse was a converted farmhouse with similarly renovated outbuildings, sturdy stone structures with heavy wooden mantles and beams. The door frames forced you to duck and the sash windows rattled in their frames when the wind was high, but it was cosy. All of the rooms were tidy, with instantly forgettable décor. Upstairs was carpeted thick enough to muffle footsteps whereas downstairs was all stone floor. A wide parking area extended around the back, and further down the track was an old stable that had been converted into a large storage shed, or barn, Charlie supposed. In the year since his last visit very little about the place had changed. Even the weather was the same: rain, rain, and more rain.

The food, though. That was different. Then again, perhaps the food was exactly as it always had been and he simply couldn't remember right; most food tasted bland to him these days, although he would have expected farmhouse fare to have been hearty and full of flavour, whatever his mood. The wine, of course, was fine. He'd worked his way through most of a bottle of red already. He'd probably order another.

It appeared there were only two other sets of guests staying at The Hayward Stables, judging by who had come to dinner. Maybe others had opted for bed and breakfast only (and maybe there was someone bedded down in the old stables – ha!). A large stone-floored dining room had been set with rows of mismatched tables and chairs, each piece of furniture up-cycled from something tatty to something deliberately dishevelled and shabby-chic. A young couple were trying to coax one child into eating and another into settling down, and they weren't doing a bad job. Another couple, middle-aged, sat only a table away from Charlie and bickered in hushed tones. The focus of their altercation was hidden beneath the noise of the nearby children and the persuasions of the parents, but the man seemed to be taking most of it, drinking his dark ale and listening, interjecting whenever moved by a particularly forceful point. The woman was a stern kind of beautiful, but maybe that was unfair. Maybe that was only because of her current mood: maybe she was usually more serene. Charlie used to get quite aroused whenever Lyndsey was angry, he didn't know why. He'd never told her that. Perhaps he should have.

Occasionally the husband caught sight of Charlie noticing and smiled politely, embarrassed by the quiet argument. They had bonded earlier over a complaint about the slow service, though neither party had voiced their concerns to anyone else but each other. While they'd waited for their food the man had joked, "Shame the stables are empty, I could eat a horse," and Charlie had laughed far too much. The man had noted the half empty wine bottle while Charlie raised a glass to toast his agreement, and to excuse his own reaction.

He pushed a piece of sausage around the gravy on his plate and loaded it with mashed potato but found he was no longer hungry. He never really had been. He laid the fork down just as the bickering woman wiped her mouth with a napkin she cast down like a gauntlet before excusing herself from the table. Charlie admired her legs briefly. The man made a half-hearted attempt to call her back, his volume restricted by public company. He looked around to check if they'd caused a scene. The young couple were far too busy with their own family but Charlie had nothing better to do and he offered a tight-lipped smile in sympathy.

"She doesn't like the weather," the man explained.

Charlie looked at the window but the curtains had been drawn against the dark. He knew it would be raining, though. Or had just been raining. Or was about to rain. It had been raining for days. Mostly only brief showers and a pathetic drizzle that was more like mist, hanging in the air, but it was all still rain just the same. "Welcome to Wales."

"Is it always like this then?"

"I'm not from here," Charlie said, and remembered the man in the barn, though he tried not to. "I think this is fairly typical weather, though, yeah."

"We're having a bit of a stay-cation," the husband said.

"Ah."

Charlie didn't care much for conversation, but the new silence between them felt uncomfortable so he said, "Well, there's plenty worth seeing around here. Lots of interesting places if you know where to look."

"What brings you here?"

My wife, Charlie thought.

"Treasure-hunting," he said. The man tilted his head for more, so Charlie added, "Geo-caching?"

"Sorry."

Charlie waved the apology away. "Bit of a hobby," he explained, and took another sip of wine.

It had begun as a joke, a nerdy pastime to get them both out of the house, away from the sofa and the TV. It gave them weekends of fresh air and exercise that was more fun than the gym. It gave them a chance to get to know each other again as they drove around the country, looking for geo-cache 'treasures'. Charlie told the man some of this.

"There's a website that provides coordinates for wherever you decide to explore, and a GPS will take you to each concealed geo-cache," he said, pausing to refill his glass. "Just a Tupperware tub or something, filled with an assortment of keepsakes. You take something, you leave something, you sign the notebook, and then you look for the next one."

"And this is a thing? People do this?"

Charlie nodded. "It's fun."

It had surprised Charlie to discover how much he enjoyed finding these secret places. Lyndsey had admitted the same, so it was to their mutual amusement that what had begun as a joke became something of a more serious pursuit, with weekly jaunts up and down the country. There were geo-caches hidden everywhere. They found them in trees, under hedgerows, submerged in ponds and rivers. They found them hidden behind road signs, tucked beneath old stone walls and concealed in ruined buildings. And as they searched, so they came to know hidden areas of the land, beautiful places off the beaten trail. They became tourists in their own backyard, learning more about their country. It always surprised Charlie just how much there was to discover. Every nook and cranny of Britain held a secret, it seemed.

"There are these clues," Charlie said. "Sometimes just coordinates to follow but sometimes something more cryptic. Those were Lyndsey's favourite. She liked to figure things out."

She had *me* all figured out.

"Lyndsey? That your wife?"

They both looked at the empty seat opposite Charlie. The plates were clean, cutlery still napkin-wrapped.

"Yeah. We came here this time last year. This is sort of an anniversary."

"Well, congratulations."

Charlie smiled a thank you into his wine, thinking, *not that kind of anniversary*. He tapped the wedding ring he still wore against the glass. He'd recently had it engraved with GPS coordinates. It represented their lives better than dates. The place where they met and the place where they parted suggested a journey that was both literal and metaphorical. Dates, he thought, would have seemed too much like an epitaph.

Charlie took a pouch of tobacco from the pocket of his chair-backed jacket and excused himself for a cigarette. He offered the pouch but was glad when the man declined. He didn't want to know him any better than he did already, and he'd shared too much about himself as it was. He left his wine and jacket to make it clear he was coming back, but he hoped the man would be gone by then.

❖

The Church of Saint Brynach in west Dyfed, Wales, was founded in the 6th century. Its churchyard boasts the Nevern Cross, which dates back to the 10th century. Fashioned from dolerite, the cross stands 13 feet high and is beautifully carved, knotwork and ringwork and geometric patterns making it one of the most impressive carved crosses in Britain. The first cuckoo of the year is thought to land on this cross to announce the coming of spring. Also in this churchyard is 'The Bleeding Yew'. Its trunk bleeds a red resin believed to be the blood of a monk wrongfully hanged from its branches.

Geo-cache findings: a plastic bird, a colouring book of Celtic designs, and a packet of sweets (out of date).

It wasn't raining, but Charlie still sheltered beneath the small roof at the back of the guesthouse because the sky was thick with cloud. The moon appeared occasionally but only briefly. There was plenty of light, though, thanks to an automatic security bulb that had come on as Charlie stepped outside. It illuminated a vast puddled stretch of gravelled ground and four parked cars. One of them was a people-carrier which he guessed belonged to the young couple with kids, or maybe the owners of the guesthouse, though there was also a mud-splattered Land Rover that he thought might have belonged to them. The Audi was probably the bickering couple's car. The other vehicle was his. For a moment he thought there was someone sitting inside – on the passenger side, Lyndsey's side – but it was only the coat he'd draped over the seat. Not his new one, just his old waterproof, pale grey with bright orange reflective strips up the sides and arms, and absolutely hideous because those were the rules, according to Lyndsey, right up there with good hiking boots and a packet of mint cake. Every rambler, hiker, and apparently geo-cacher, had to have a vile waterproof jacket of clashing colours, preferably something that folded to the size of a handkerchief or packed itself away into its own pocket somehow. Lyndsey's had been orange and pink. It made her look like one of those sweets you used to be able to get from the corner shop, a rhubarb and custard. No, a fruit salad; rhubarb and custards were the other ones, the ones that lasted forever.

He rested the tobacco pouch on a nearby windowsill and set about rolling a cigarette. He tried not to look at the old stable but failed, glancing up at the dark shape of it several times between stages of the cigarette's construction. He would take another look inside before he left. He didn't particularly want to, but he was retracing his steps and the stable was a big part of that. Plus he needed to check if there was anybody in there.

He looked at the car again instead, hoping once more for that illusion of a passenger on Lyndsey's side, but the coat draped over the seat was just a coat.

Lyndsey didn't drive, but she was a fantastic navigator. Rather than rely on any conventional kind of sat-nav, Lyndsey used an app on her mobile phone with the volume down and provided her own range of voices, using outlandish, often terrible, accents, mimicking celebrities and sometimes people they both knew. Sometimes she made up characters, like Farmer Jones (*that be the wrong way, lad*) and Lady Wetherby (*oh, do be careful, driver*). She changed the voices whenever Charlie laughed. It was a game they had.

"Oh. No," she'd say, her voice overly robotic. "You do-not. Want. To-go. That. Way." Or she'd urge, "The other way, *the other way!*" in a voice filled with feigned panic, all the while calm as she looked out of the passenger window at whatever part of the countryside they were passing through.

"This is *not* the right way."

"It is."

"At the traffic lights, make a u-turn."

"There are no traffic lights."

"At the next junction, go off-road."

"In this car?"

"At the next dealership, purchase a new vehicle."

That's how she was.

"Warning: we are low on fuel."

"We're fine."

"Warning: we need coffee and chocolate or we will become annoying."

"*Become* annoying?"

"Advisory: coffee and chocolate will lead to sexual gratitude."

"That would be tempting if you weren't Stephen Hawking."

She'd laughed at that, loud and sudden and surprised, then covered her mouth with both hands. "Oh, that's wrong."

"I just don't find him attractive."

"You're not supposed to find *anyone* attractive."

"What about—"

"Anyone *else* attractive." Then, serious, "You do still find me attractive, right?"

Charlie smiled. He was standing outside, in the cold, smoking in full view of the stables that marked the beginning of the end, but he was also back in the car, back with Lyndsey who was asking, "Are we there yet?"

"Nearly."

"What about now?"

"Nearly."

"What about—"

"*Lynds*..."

He looked over at the converted stables.

It was a large but surprisingly squat building, with a sloping roof of corrugated metal. He remembered how it drummed with the rain. Inside was a vast open space. If there had ever been stalls for horses they were gone now. In fact, there was little to suggest they were ever stables at all, other than the name of the guesthouse, and he supposed that could have been a deliberate misnomer, something quaint and countrified to lure the tourists. The inside had smelled wet and warm, bales of summer-baked hay wrapped in plastic yet somehow releasing an aroma so that rain seemed to mix with sunshine. There was a metallic smell, too, and oil, from a vehicle that was not quite a tractor sitting guard in the open double doors, the tines of its threshing machinery like some medieval war machine to keep people out. It hadn't deterred them, though. If only it had.

Those doors were closed now, the machine tucked away inside, if it was there at all. Charlie exhaled a final stream of smoke with a sigh. If the fucking thing had been parked away properly in the first place, the giant doors shut, then they never would have gone inside. They'd have forgone the novelty of the setting and had sex back in their own room instead, only yards away.

Charlie dropped what remained of his cigarette and twisted it dead under his heel.

You look angry.

It sounded like Lyndsey's voice, but it was only in his head. Still, it made him smile. 'You look angry' had been one of their geo-cache clues last time they were in Wales. It had looked like a code at first – *Ydych yn edrych yn ddig* – but it wasn't long after crossing into Wales that they'd realised it was simply Welsh. *Ydych yn edrych yn ddig*, you look angry, became a game so that whenever one of them said it in the car, thinking aloud, trying to figure it out, the other would offer a reply. *It's just the way my face looks. You stole the covers last night. I'm trying to fart.*

Not all of the locations came with clues or riddles, but those that did were Lyndsey's favourites, and she never Googled the clues or read the message boards in the community forum, nothing like that. She never cheated, not when it came to geo-caching. They figured them out together, just like they did everything else.

'You look angry' was a clue for St Brynach Church.

"St Brynach Church, named after – *wow* – St Brynach," Lyndsey said. "Sixth century chapel, famous for the Nevern Cross or Great Cross of St Brynach, one of the finest in Wales, thirteen feet high…"

Lyndsey liked to research everywhere they went, but only after they'd arrived, to avoid what she called spoilers. While she read to him from her phone, Charlie used his to take pictures. He'd usually manage a few secret ones of Lyndsey before she spotted him, and then she'd strike ridiculous poses or give him the dreaded duck-face pout. At St Brynach's she hadn't noticed for ages, too busy searching among the gravestones, so after he'd taken a few shots of her bending over he turned the phone around for a secret selfie or two he'd send her later.

"You look angry."

As Charlie was contorting his face into an ugly sneer he'd assumed she'd caught him, but looking up, still sneering, he saw that she had her back to him among the graves. She patted one of them before turning to face him.

"You look angry," she said again. "Cross. Angry is

cross. Get it? The Nevern Cross, probably. And you is probably yew tree. The one I told you about, the one that bleeds." She pointed and said, "*Yew* lead the way."

Charlie gave her one of his pity-smiles.

"Shut up, I'm hilarious."

Among the gravestones, Charlie said, "Honey, I love doing this with you, but I'm not digging up a grave. I've got my limits."

Yet here he was, a year later, digging up what should probably be left alone.

He contemplated another cigarette but it began to rain again, so he went back inside.

❖

Dryburgh Abbey, in Scotland, stands as a remarkably complete set of ruins. It contains paintwork that dates back to its construction in 1150 and remains one of the most beautiful examples of Gothic architecture.

According to legend, a woman who lost her lover made a home in one of the vaults and swore never to look upon the sun again until her lover returned. Learning he had died, she only ever came out from the vault at night, living a half-life of loss and loneliness.

Geo-cache findings: a heart-shaped fridge magnet, a novelty pen, an ornate thimble.

Whatever the couple had been bickering about was either resolved or temporarily forgotten by the time Charlie returned to his room. He was reminded of how thin the walls were by the sounds of their passionate make-up sex. Or maybe it was angry sex. 'Fuck you' sex, Charlie thought, unamused by his own pun.

You look angry.

It sounded like good sex, whatever it was.

Charlie undressed and stretched out on his own bed. He matched his rhythm to the sounds from next door, masturbating to the squeak and creak of their bedsprings and looking at a photograph of Lyndsey he had on the bedside table. Eventually the woman's climax drew a scowling one from him and he was able, at last, to sleep.

❖

Croagh Patrick is a holy mountain that rises 765 metres above sea level and overlooks Clew Bay in Ireland. It is believed that St Patrick made his way here from Aghagower and spent 40 nights on its summit praying and fasting and casting out demons. Time has altered the legend so that demons have become snakes instead.

Geo-cache findings: none (not yet visited).

In the morning, Charlie skipped breakfast and went out to his car for the geo-cache he'd left on the back seat, a little of the secret life of Lyndsey and Charlie West. Deliberately awful poems Lyndsey used to leave for him around the house (*I love you like blue loves sky, oh me, oh my*). A strip of photo booth pictures, Lyndsey flashing her boobs (never breasts, *never* tits), pictures they used to keep on the fridge and had to remember to take down every time they had visitors (and forgetting on more than one occasion). A length of rope (look out for snakes!).

He'd considered leaving his wedding ring too but he couldn't bring himself to do it, not yet. There was no comments book inside either because this would be a geo-cache he never registered online. If anyone ever found it, it would be the owners of The Hayward Stables during some clean up or sort out. Putting it here was entirely for his own benefit. Like flowers on a grave.

The car was still wet from last night's rain. Puddles the size of small lakes blotted the gravelled drive and the early morning air held the smell of wet grass. Charlie took a deep breath of it and looked to the sky. Grey, but not raining, and somehow clean looking, as if grey was its usual colour and it had just needed the blue washing out.

Charlie hadn't bothered to lock the car – there was nothing left he couldn't bear to lose – and he was glad not to ruin the peace of the country morning with the electronic blip-blip of central locking. He retrieved the container from the back seat and closed the door again, its soft thump the only sound to disturb the quiet except for the crunch and scrape of gravel underfoot as he made his way to the old stables that might never have been stables.

The large doors were closed. Would they be locked, though? Were they more careful since the Castellmarch man? He doubted it. As he neared, Charlie looked out for a coil of chain wrapped around the handle grips or a large padlock clasped closed, or both, but there was no such thing. He tucked the Tupperware box under his arm, wedged high into his armpit, looked around for anyone who might see him, and gripped the door with both hands. It was a large one that slid across, essentially a moving wall more than a door, and he expected it to be heavy, but it moved easily and quietly, its bearings well-oiled. He opened it only enough to step inside and closed it again behind him.

For a moment it was pitch black dark. He heard birds waking up above him somewhere and smelled the damp sweet aroma of hay and feed and maybe manure, the sharp tang of petrol and machine oil, but he saw nothing. Eventually his eyes adjusted to the gloom, grey light filtering in through rusted holes in the metal walls and roof and through the sheets of newspaper that had been stuck over a large window. Most of the floor space had been taken up by a temporary holding pen made up of boards held between breezeblocks. There was no sign of any livestock, but as a veteran geo-cacher Charlie recognised the pellets of sheep droppings. At the back of the building, a stack of stored hay. That was where, a year ago, he and Lyndsey had enjoyed a private moment, a secret moment that turned out to be less secret than they had supposed. And over there, between the hay and a workbench cluttered with tools, that had been where the Castellmarch man had loitered. Unseen, at first, bedded down in a spill of hay and bundled blankets and tarp.

They'd been walking the grounds, exploring the fields just before dusk. It had been good to just walk together without searching for a geo-cache – there weren't any locations nearby, not then – and they had held hands and talked and made new promises to each other. To try harder. To do more fun stuff. She would be faithful, he would be more spontaneous. As they'd neared The

Hayward Stables, Lyndsey had picked up the pace, claiming she wanted to get back before proper dark and the inevitable rain but walking with an urgency that suggested something else.

"You need to pee, don't you?"

"Maybe."

They only made it as far as the stables or barn or whatever the building was before Lyndsey had to relieve herself. She squatted behind a plastic rain barrel and a leaning stack of wooden pallets.

"Watch out for ropes," Charlie had warned.

Back when they'd first started geo-caching, one of the treasure boxes had been hidden among the roots of fallen tree. Lyndsey had crouched beside the trunk, reaching for an opening in the soil, but before she could finish a feeble joke about *rooting* around she'd leapt away with a scream of "Snake!" and the two of them had fled. The 'snake' turned out to be a length of dirty rope, some coiled excess from what had been used to secure the geo-cache container to the tree stump. Charlie had teased Lyndsey about it forever since. This new teasing as she peed saw her hand come up from behind the water barrel to give him the middle finger.

"You look angry," Charlie said. An old joke by then, but one they still used occasionally.

"There aren't any snakes in Wales," Lyndsey said, standing and pulling her jeans up with her.

"You're thinking of Ireland."

She'd put her hand to her chest in mock distress, gave him another one of her voices, temporarily Irish. "You mean there *are* snakes in Wales?"

"Baby," he'd said, "Wales has fucking *dragons*."

Worse than dragons.

While Lyndsey buttoned up, Charlie joked that she shouldn't bother. At least, it had started as a joke. But because she'd stopped to 'joke' back – "Oh yeah? Why's that?" – instead of simply dismissing his suggestion, he'd taken her by the hand and pulled her towards the open door. Her only protest had been an unconvincing, "We can't," but it turned out they could, and they did, rougher and wilder and louder than they had been in a long time. Proof, if any was needed, that they still had something. Reassurance, for Charlie, that she was still interested in him beyond the comfort and companionship of a long term relationship. Reassurance for her, he supposed, that he could still be passionate and commanding.

Afterwards, panting from where she lay bent over a collapsed bale of hay, Lyndsey had expressed surprise and gratification with the exclamation, "*Fuck*."

"Again? Okay, five minutes."

She had made a pathetic backwards slap at him without looking, exhaling a laugh that had little sound as she tried to catch her breath, but Charlie had already stepped away from her to get dressed again. He swatted her behind, gently this time, and placed her clothes beside her. He kissed her back, and when she rolled over with an exaggerated sigh, he kissed her breasts until she sat up. They were criss-crossed with lines from where she'd been pressed against the hay and strands were stuck to her sweaty skin. He helped her brush them away until she brushed *him* away, slapping at his hands.

"If you want to help you can find my shoes."

They had been such a struggle to remove in the heat of the moment, stuck in her jeans, that Charlie had thrown them aside when they were finally off.

"Charlie?"

"Yeah, I'm looking."

He was peering into the shadows on the ground when Lyndsey called to him again, quieter this time, but with a new tone that made it sound more urgent; "*Char*lie." She had her t-shirt on but also held her arm across her chest while the other hand pushed her jumper and jeans into her lap, between her legs.

"Lynds?"

She didn't answer or turn to face him and finally Charlie saw what she was looking at. *Who* she was looking at.

The Castellmarch man.

He was wearing a hat, that fucking stupid hat with the flaps that came down over the ears. He was wearing an old army jacket, too, the type that was fashionable when Charlie was young if you wanted to prove how alternative or grungy you were. Army surplus with deep pockets, faded green (and if you were particularly rebellious or quirky, maybe you had a foreign flag stitched into the shoulder). His jeans were scruffy. Charlie couldn't see the man's boots properly but they were probably DMs.

"Oh, shit, sorry," Charlie said, "we just—"

"It was raining," Lyndsey said, slipping down from the hay bale to hide the lower half of her body. When that part of her was out of view she immediately stepped into her jeans, underwear be damned. It hadn't been raining, not quite, but it was now. It drummed loud against the roof.

The man exhaled forcefully from his mouth so that his lips trembled. Charlie couldn't tell if it was disbelief or amusement or anger or what.

"Sorry," Charlie said again, casting a quick look around again to ensure they had everything. He saw a pile of makeshift bedding, tucked away in the dark. A spill of belongings were spread across the ground nearby.

The man scratched at what he had of a beard and said, "Not from here." Charlie didn't know if he meant them or, judging by the rough bedding, himself.

"No, we're just... no. You? You staying here as well?"

Partly Charlie was trying to ascertain whether he and Lyndsey were in any kind of trouble. He was fairly certain the man was not one of the owners, and though there was a chance he was a farmhand or something, Charlie supposed the man was actually homeless, or a traveller, bedding down for a night out of the rain. Whatever and whoever he was, Charlie wanted to distract him from Lyndsey who was subtly trying to dress herself.

The man stamped one foot a couple of times and dragged it back across the floor as if trying to scrape something from his boot.

"I'm from *Castellmarch*. I *told* you."

Lyndsey shared a look with Charlie. It was a mildly judgemental look, as in she'd judged the man was mildly mental.

"I mean, I didn't tell you I was from Castellmarch," the man said, "just that I'm not from here. 'Not from here.' I said that."

"Right."

The man nodded. He looked at Lyndsey, dressing.

"So, is that in Wales then?" Charlie asked. "Castellmarch?"

"Castellmarch is in Abersoch, across the sea." He pointed in a direction that meant nothing to Charlie.

"Oh, right. Is it an island?"

The man laughed. "Abersoch's not an *island*." He looked at Lyndsey who had just plucked items of underwear from the ground, bunching them into a tangle of lace and straps and bra cups which she tried to hold casually. He grinned at her as if they shared a private joke or secret intimacy. "He thinks Abersoch is an *island*."

"He's not very clever," Lyndsey said, with a quick smile.

"Hey," said Charlie, "I'm right here."

"It's not an island," the man explained. "It's across the bay."

"Okay."

"I'm going to Carreg Castle."

"Okay."

Lyndsey was looking for her shoes. Charlie made a show of helping her so that he was too busy for further conversation.

"How about some music?" the man asked. He reached down to the array of things scattered on and around his bed. Charlie expected a radio but the man produced a flute, no, a whistle, a recorder or something, but surely he wasn't going to—

The man began to play.

The look Lyndsey gave Charlie was loaded with amusement, a smile in her eyes that acknowledged just how strange all of this was turning out to be. They would have fun, later, talking about it, the look said. She'd probably add this man to her repertoire of sat-nav character voices, Charlie thought.

The whistling was shrill but the open space of the large building seemed to soften it a little, lending a haunting echo that wasn't exactly unpleasant within the drumming sound of rain. There was a melody, and the man played with a burst of enthusiasm that made it lively at first, but his joy dwindled quickly and he stopped as abruptly as he had begun. "Do you know that song?"

Lyndsey shook her head. Charlie said, "No," and wondered if they'd been expected to sing along or dance or something. He wondered if they'd offended him somehow.

The man's scowl was only for his whistle, though. "That wasn't the song I meant to play," he said, pocketing the instrument. "I think it's broken."

Lyndsey laughed, partly in case it was a joke and partly because this was all just too weird. Charlie laughed a little with her, glad when the man smiled because it now it meant they were laughing with him instead of at him. Kind of.

The man withdrew a pouch of tobacco from his coat pocket. He offered it but they both shook their heads no.

"Don't smoke," Charlie told him.

"What are you looking for?"

Lyndsey said, "My shoes."

The man put his tobacco aside and crouched out of sight. When he stood again he had two hiking boots, one in each hand. He held them by his sides.

"Great," said Lyndsey, "Thanks."

The man made no move to offer them, though. "Want to hear a joke?" he said.

"We better get back inside," Lyndsey said. She reached for her shoes. The man made an underarm gesture with one of them. He did it a second time but didn't throw.

"Go on, then," Charlie said. He meant go on, throw the boots, but the man used it as an excuse to tell his joke, Lyndsey's boots held by his sides.

"Two men in a pub, right? One of them, he goes to find a table, see, and the other one gets the drinks in. 'Pint for me and my donkey.'"

Charlie nodded – clearly they had to listen to the joke as some part of an exchange – but when the man kept repeating the character's drink order, Charlie nodded again to hurry the man along.

"So this happens a few times, same one going to the bar and saying 'pint for me and my donkey', until eventually the other guy comes to the bar instead. Before he can order, the barman says, 'Your friend over there keeps calling you his donkey.' And the customer, he nods and says—"

Charlie knew the joke, he realised, but it had taken until now for him to remember the punch line. The man still surprised him, though.

"'Oh, *hee*-aw! *hee*-aw! *hee*-always calls me that!'"

The man brayed loud enough that each *hee*-aw! sounded like a scream, a shrill then guttural cry bouncing around in the confines of the barn. The sudden noise and volume startled both of them, as did the way the man thrust his head forward for each outburst, his lips peeled back against large slabs of teeth. Lyndsey had recoiled, pressing herself against a wall of stacked hay bales, wide-eyed. Charlie took her hand.

"Do you get it?" the man asked them, and without waiting for a response he said again, "He always calls me that. *Hee*-aw!" The final cry dissolved into laughter and Charlie laughed as well this time. Not at the joke, but in a kind of anxious release.

The man wiped tears from his eyes, still offering the occasional chuckle and sigh.

"Okay," Charlie said, "boots now, yeah?"

The man nodded. "You have a spirited filly," he said.

"Sorry, what?"

"Spirited," the man said. He looked at Lyndsey. "This filly likes a good ride."

"Hey," said Charlie, and, "Fuck," said Lyndsey.

The man laughed again. To Lyndsey he said, "Eager filly!" and to Charlie, "You ride her well," and then he tossed the boots. He threw them underarm, but he did it quick and Charlie had to twist and turn to try to catch them, missing both. Lyndsey gathered them up and pulled them on quick, laces loose, and Charlie turned her by the shoulders, guiding her outside and away, pushing her ahead of him. Behind them, the braying laughter of the man followed them out into the dark.

Charlie reported him to the owners. He did that much, at least. He gave them a slightly edited version of events in which he swapped post-coital surprise for seeing someone sneaking into the outbuilding and in the morning their breakfast was served with the reassurance that the man was gone. As to whether he'd been sent on right away or asked to leave that morning, the owners had been rather vague about that. 'It happens sometimes,' the wife had said, adding, 'we should really keep it locked, I suppose.'

Well, they still don't lock it, Charlie thought, and he was glad. He found a place behind the workbench where a metal brace and a supporting beam crossed (*x marks the spot*) and there, in a small nook close to the wall, he stowed his geo-cache of memories.

❖

Sadie's Lane in Dorset, England, is reported to be one of the most haunted roads in the county. It came by its name in the early 18th century when a farm girl called Sadie Young allegedly rode her horse to its death as she raced to meet a lover who had abandoned her. Pitched from the fallen animal, Sadie was also killed and is said to haunt what is now a busy relief road. The location has since attracted several other ghosts, each of them linked to tales of heartbreak and loss. It is now a popular suicide spot.

Geo-cache findings: a selection of pressed flowers and a chess piece (rook).

Leaving the outbuilding, stepping from the dark into a morning still fresh and clean and grey, Charlie was greeted by last night's couple approaching their car (the Audi). The woman smiled, the kind of polite smile you give to strangers with whom you share a certain level of intimacy, like those in the same train carriage or a doctor's waiting room. If she'd known just how intimate they were, now, after last night, she probably wouldn't have smiled, Charlie thought. Or maybe she would. Maybe she was well aware of how loud they'd been. Today she was dressed in a jeans and jumper ensemble that was practical yet still somehow stylish, more town clothes than country. Charlie admired how the denim fit her.

"Beautiful, eh?" the husband said to Charlie. "That fresh country air."

Charlie nodded, more in hello than as an answer. "Morning," he said, stepping to his own car.

"Thought we might look for some of those interesting places you mentioned," the man said. He waved a folded leaflet to support his point. Charlie had seen a limited selection of them fanned out on a table in the dining room.

"Be sure to visit Carreg Castle," Charlie said, slipping the name in with little fanfare. The man opened up the leaflet to look but Charlie gave him directions anyway, hearing in his head one of Lyndsey's wonderful sat-nav voices in echo. "Just heading there myself, but I recommend you try it around sundown. It's a bit spooky, but beautiful. Romantic."

"Thanks," said the woman, and this time her smile was a little warmer.

"Yeah, appreciate it," said her husband.

Charlie prepared a cigarette, concentrating on the task until he heard the double thunk of car doors closing, then he watched them for a moment, a silent movie behind the windscreen. They seemed happy now, but then so did many couples. Anyone could look happy if they buried their secrets deep enough. Charlie watched them reverse out of the parking area. For a moment, when she turned around in her seat, the woman looked like Lyndsey. That quick profile and final look at Charlie that disappeared as they turned away and were gone.

Charlie smoked his cigarette. He didn't smoke in the car because Lyndsey wouldn't have liked it, but seeing her waterproof parcelled up into itself on the backseat he leaned in to retrieve it, careful to hold the roll-up outside the whole time. He turned the coat out, unzipped it open, and shook it into shape. He draped it over his on the passenger seat. From the corner of his eye perhaps it would seem as if she accompanied his drive. It was a pathetic hope, but strangely soothing.

"Okay," he said, finishing the cigarette, and though there was no one to say it to but himself, added, "let's go."

For a lot of the journey the roads passed through open countryside, fields dropping into valleys or climbing into hills, distant sheep scattered like chewed lumps of gum. Tiny towns or perhaps villages passed so quickly that moments later Charlie wondered at their existence. Eventually, though, the hills closed in and the road cut its way through trees and shadow. The lanes became choked with mud and vast puddles made sections into shallow rivers. The hedgerows pressed close, sometimes scraping the car on tight corners. Charlie tried to focus his attention on the road, assessing when to slow down, when to speed up, balancing the risks of soft ground and floods by fluctuating between two speeds in a sort of compromise against getting stuck and losing control. He rushed through puddles in a shushed-thunder of spray that drummed underneath the car and spread in sheets either side.

On the back seat, another geo-cache container rattled as it slid left and right with the corners and jumped with the bumps and dips of the road. There was only one item inside.

He'd been hiding geo-caches up and down the British Isles for most of the last six months, building up to this moment. Little boxes of their life together, here and there. Their old GPS from back before they simply used apps on their phones. A half-eaten mint cake, which neither of them liked because it made their teeth feel funny but which they bought anyway because it was one of the rules, like the hideous waterproofs. He wondered how many people had walked past them, these secret geo-caches, never knowing what was there, and he thought, *well, life's like that, isn't it?* Everybody has a story you don't get to hear. Even in a relationship, there were things you didn't learn until far down the line together, or things changed, and maybe you didn't always like what you found. Lyndsey had thought she knew all there was to know about Charlie, and he used to think the same of her. For him, that familiarity brought comfort. For her, it was different.

He slowed the car just as an oncoming vehicle turned into the road ahead, blocking the entire width. The driver made a token effort to move aside, but there was no way they were going to squeeze past each other. Charlie checked behind and manoeuvred the car backwards.

"Attention: this vehicle is reversing."

That's what Lyndsey would have said as Charlie manoeuvred the vehicle back. "*Bleep! Bleep!* Attention: this vehicle is reversing." Then the warning again. And then the bleeps. And then the warning again, and then the bleeps, until—

"Lynds."

Her name sounded lost with no one to answer it. Charlie looked at the empty seat beside him but the waterproof there remained simply a waterproof, hanging like a thin corpse. An empty shroud, trying too hard to be bright and cheerful.

The other car followed Charlie, keeping close as if Charlie might change his mind, pushing him back. As soon as there was room, it pulled out and passed. If there was a thank you, Charlie didn't see it.

"You're welcome."

He changed gears from reverse to first and the car rocked in place. That was all. For a moment he thought he was stuck - "Come *on*" - but all he'd done was stall it. Overcompensating with the revs, he sent a fantail of mud spraying behind as he pulled away again. Better to lose control than get stuck in place, he thought, hurrying towards something he'd never find with nothing left to lose but himself.

❖

Carreg Cennen Castle can be found in the village of Trap about 4 miles from Llandeilo in Carmarthenshire, Wales. It stands on a limestone precipice and within its bowels there is a tunnel which leads to a well said to hold mystical healing properties, particularly regarding ear and eye complaints. Visitors to the castle often cast corks and bent pins into the water in order to be healed.

Geo-cache findings (four out of five caches): a novelty key ring, a decorative bookmark, a plastic toy knight, a packet of crayons, a rubber sheep, a deck of pornographic cards, a two-pound coin, 2 bottle openers, a candle.

The first time he'd seen Carreg Castle was between the stutters of the windscreen wipers, leaning forward to peer through the glass as if a few more inches would allow him to see it more clearly. Back then, the sun had barely been out all day and what there was of it was sinking behind the hill the castle stood upon, the sky taking on the deepening blue tones of early evening with some red shining behind and between the ruined walls. Part of the hill dropped away as a sheer cliff so that the castle walls on one edge seemed to merge seamlessly into the precipice.

"Spooky," said Lyndsey.

This time it looked postcard-picture-perfect. The sky had cleared by the time he'd reached the castle, the sun having burnt away the misty haze of the early hours to reveal a sharpening bright blue sky dotted with clouds that hung motionless in a panorama that was beautiful and all so completely wrong. It should have looked ugly. It should have been pissing down and miserable and the end-of-the-world.

There had been a sequence of geo-caches here. It happened that way sometimes, especially with popular landmark locations. Clues to one revealed clues to another, and so on, giving you a good walk while building to what usually turned out to be an anti-climax. But then geo-caching was never really about what you found at the end. It was the journey, as clichéd as that seemed. The spending time together. It was learning more about your own country, the secret spectacles of home. Learning more about each other, and hoping you liked it.

They'd found the first geo-cache easily. Some of a stone wall had fallen and tucked amongst the rocks was an ice cream container bearing a strip of masking tape across its lid that declared, simply, 'geo-cache'. Inside they'd found yet another Welsh key ring (this time a flat rubber oval with Carreg Castle in bas-relief), a decorative bookmark (or quitter's strip, as Lyndsey used to call them), and a plastic toy. The toy was an armoured knight. He held a lance before him and his legs were unnaturally bowed, a half-circle scoop as if there had been a horse below him as well at some point. They took the horseless knight and left the key ring and bookmark, adding a yo-yo for whoever came next. Take something, leave something, move on. Another strip of masking tape inside the container provided a new clue and they followed it to the next location, and then again, and so on, until they were at the castle. It had become something of a silhouette in the fading light, and a cool evening breeze tousled Lyndsey's hair as she looked down at the glowing phone in her hand.

"We better get a move on if we want to get the last geo-cache. It's in the castle somewhere and it'll be closed soon."

The castle was privately owned but still open to the public. "It has a tea room and everything," Lyndsey told him, scrolling through information on her phone, offering Charlie the highlights. She gave him details about the accidental sale of the castle, gave him particulars of its history and structure, its six towers, the drawbridges, the chapel, all of it, speeding through centuries.

"It's mostly limestone here," she said, "and there's an underground tunnel that'll take us to where the last cache is, I think. '150 feet of tunnel leads you to a well, believed to hold mystical healing powers'. That's what it says. You throw corks or pins in and make a wish. It's particularly good at healing ear and eye complaints, apparently. Which is why I think the cache is there, because of the clue. 'You'll do well to keep your eyes open'. Which is a crap clue but it makes sense."

"Why corks and pins?"

She shrugged. "Doesn't say."

Charlie wondered at what else it didn't say as he made his way towards the castle again. As he walked among the shake holes, sunken depressions in the soil and cracked stone, he also wondered how Lyndsey made her decisions about what to share and what to not, and would she have left him anyway if it hadn't been for the Castellmarch man.

At the castle, Charlie descended into a gloom that suited his mood. The stone stairs were slippery with old rain and the castle's outer wall close beside him seemed like it was leaning, as if it wanted to push him over the edge. He imagined falling. He'd imagined it lots of times. But he didn't fall, and soon he was standing before a long narrow gash in the cliff face. Hardly any light penetrated the passageway, especially with his body blocking what there was of it, and he didn't have a phone this time to illuminate the way; he'd never replaced his, and the police still had Lyndsey's. Knowing how much darker it would become, he didn't bother waiting for his eyes to adjust and simply plunged right in.

"Here we go."

He was swallowed into nothing by the darkness. Arms out at his sides, he used the walls to guide him deeper. The stone was smooth and dry but very cold. He stooped, remembering how low the passageway became in places, and sometimes he was more comfortable turning sideways, but eventually he came to the standing pool of water where Lyndsey had joked about Gollum. She'd hissed "My *precious*..." into his ear in the dark.

"I expected an actual well."

Charlie backed up a few steps and sat. He was wearing his new coat, which was long enough to offer him some protection against the cold stone. In one of its deep pockets was the Tupperware geo-cache he'd brought, shallow but long, perfect for what it held. He checked his watch, its light casting an eerie green glow that only seemed to make the dark darker.

He was early.

He waited.

Charlie had shone the light of his phone around the perimeter of the pool that first time. There were shapes floating on the surface and gathered at the edges. Corks. Some of them had pins pushed through them. Back then he'd had to psych himself up to put his hand in the water, and he'd gasped at the temperature. This time he merely reached out and caressed the surface of the pool, making small waves in the darkness. He felt a cork or two against his palm. He had stabbed himself last time on pins at the bottom of the pool, reaching for a geo-cache they never found. He'd dropped his phone, swearing. For a moment the light had stayed on at the bottom of the pool, and he'd grabbed it up again quickly, as if speed could stop it from becoming *more* wet. Tried to shake it dry.

"What?" Lyndsey asked. "What?"

"Dropped my fucking phone."

"Yeah, but why?"

"Well I didn't mean to."

"I mean, did you hurt yourself? Did something bite you or something?"

There'd only been the brief sting of pins. "I'm okay."

"How's the phone?"

It was fine, until he pressed a button to check if it was fine, and then the screen went black and the torchlight went out.

"Shit."

"Well done."

"Ssh."

"You shush." Lyndsey had lit the tunnel with her phone instead but Charlie took it from her and plunged them back into the dark. He found Lyndsey's arm. Her hand. He pulled her close and found something else and she'd said, "Hey!"

"We'll have to grope our way out."

"Funny man."

And they had kissed. He remembered that very well. Sometimes, when he couldn't sleep, he'd close his eyes as tight as he could to replicate the utter darkness of that moment and he'd remember the kisses they'd shared under the castle, buried in its rock. He couldn't tell any more if they only felt like final kisses now, in retrospect, or if he'd known it even then.

"We should pick up some rice when we get out," Lyndsey said, breaking away. "For your phone."

"Does that actually work?"

He felt her shrug. "Saw it on Facebook so it must be true. Absorbs the water or something. You remember Jenny from—"

"Ssh."

"No, I'm telling you a fascinating story."

"I think someone else is here. Listen."

They strained their ears to hear. Charlie turned his head and, for some reason, opened his mouth. He found that helped sometimes. This time it did.

"Hear that?" he whispered.

"Yeah, someone's coming."

And yet neither of them felt relieved. Maybe because whoever was coming did so without a light.

As if they'd agreed it between them, neither of them called out or made any noise, and though Charlie had Lyndsey's phone he didn't even consider using its light. He backed away, deeper into the passageway, pulling Lyndsey with him, keeping close to the wall.

It was the Castellmarch man, of course. For a while he was only the scrape of footsteps, but somehow they'd known. Why else would they have remained so quiet? Why else had they tried to hide, when the normal thing to have done would have been to greet whoever else had come to this special place?

He was singing something softly to himself. Welsh

words, unfamiliar, but Charlie thought he recognised the tune.

Lyndsey's breath was warm in Charlie's ear. Her mouth was so close that he felt her lips on him as she said, "It's him." He went to turn his head, to whisper back, but she held him still and said, lips to his ear, "It's the Castellmarch man."

The voice in the darkness with them was suddenly quiet, and though Charlie hadn't been able to follow the song properly he could still tell it had stopped mid-line.

"Somebody's there," said the man.

Lyndsey squeezed Charlie's arm tight but the two of them remained quiet. There was nothing to be afraid of, he thought. Not really.

"Who's there?" the voice called. "Why are you spying on me?"

They waited, silent, holding their breath and each other's hand.

"WHO'S SPYING ON ME?"

Charlie said, "We're *not* spying," and lit up the dark with Lyndsey's phone. Her grip on his arm tightened and they saw, together, the man crouching at the pool, that hat in his hands, and—

Charlie thought he saw... He thought, but he must have been wrong. He thought he saw the man's ears, long and pointed and furred, twitching at Charlie's voice. Horse's ears. Then everything was a chaos of movement and noise. The Castellmarch man leapt to his feet, literally bounding up and across at them on all fours. He knocked Charlie aside and into the wall, hitting him harder than he'd have thought possible for a man of such build. Charlie dropped the phone, but not into the pool this time. Its light stayed on, but the device was kicked several times in the to and fro of a scuffle. Lyndsey cried out, and swore, and Charlie yanked at her and pushed at the other, and they splashed through the shallows of icy water as the man cried out, "You saw me!" his voice bouncing around and back at them in the confines of the tunnel. "You *saw* me!"

Up close, Charlie saw the man definitely had horse ears. They stuck up from lank hair that swept from his head and down his back like a mane. He had one arm around Lyndsey from behind and then he leapt up so that he was on her back. Charlie tried to grab him, push him away, pull him down, and Lyndsey turned around, tried to run, tried to shake the man off. The Castellmarch man gripped her firm, though, fierce, his legs around her waist now. He reached down between her breasts with one hand, holding a bunch of her jumper in his fist, gripping at her ribs, and the other held a tangle of her hair, and he was laughing or he was screaming, it was hard to tell, all his noise coming out shrill and echoing back at them. His eyes were wide, and he frothed at the mouth, Charlie thought, and he rocked against Lyndsey's back, urging her on, pulling at her hair to guide her direction as she tried to run from him though he clung to her. Charlie saw her stagger the way they'd come and he pushed after them as the man's cries whinnied back and forth in the dark.

Near the entrance they became a hectic silhouette. Lyndsey was bent under the man's weight but still on her feet, ricocheting off the walls of the tunnel either side as the man held himself fast against her, upon her, one hand twisted in her hair and his groin rocking against her as if dry humping her back, playing giddy-up. In a panicked pirouette, Charlie saw his wife's head turn, saw her look at him a final time, the Castellmarch man leaning over with his cheek against hers and his ears, those stupid fucking twitching ears, and then the two of them were gone. They dropped away into open space and Charlie had to pull up hard to stop from following them over the edge and down.

Charlie had called out his anguish then, but now it was little more than a soft mewling sound in the dark as he remembered. Take something, leave something, move on, he thought. Lyndsey had been taken, he had been left behind, and if anyone had moved on then it wasn't him.

There had been no bodies down there, but in his dreams there were. Sometimes Lyndsey's, sometimes his own. Sometimes he saw her carried away, the Castellmarch man's bandy legs striding in great bounds. Sometimes it was Lyndsey who fled, carrying this strange man with her. The police found no trace of either person. They probably weren't even looking any more, but Charlie was. Leaving his geo-caches with clues only Lyndsey would understand, looking for her up and down the country. He wondered if she was looking for him. Just as he wondered, sometimes, about that final look she gave him. Sometimes he remembered fear. Other times, excitement. Occasionally what he saw, or thought he saw, was relief.

Charlie removed his wedding ring and, sitting on the ground, traced his finger over the engraving inside, the coordinates marking their life together. One of them was this one, Carreg Castle, where the water was said to hold mystical healing properties. The eyes and the ears and maybe, Charlie hoped, the heart.

He cast his ring into the water. There was barely any splash at all when really it should have thundered. Then, from his pocket, he took the final Tupperware container. He was wearing a new coat and the pockets were deep. From another he took the hat.

In that struggle a year ago he had torn the Castellmarch man's pocket and something had fallen from it. He had it now, in this final container. His wooden flute, or whistle, or recorder, whatever the fuck it was.

He took the instrument from its box and put it to his lips and played. It didn't take him long to get the tune right. Maybe it would call them back, isn't that how it worked in the old stories? Maybe *one* of them, at least, would come. Someone.

Anyone.

He played and he played until, finally, he thought he heard something. Voices, coming to him in the dark. He raised one of the flaps of the hat he'd put on and turned his ear to listen.

Yes. Voices. A man and a woman. He thought perhaps they were bickering, but that was okay. That might be better, actually.

He pocketed the whistle and the hat and stood. Take something, leave something, he thought. He pressed himself against one of the walls, hiding in the dark it made, and he waited.

❖

In Abersoch there is a 17th century mansion that goes by the name of Castellmarch. According to legend it was once the home of one of King Arthur's knights, March Amheirchion, who had the ears of a horse. He kept them hidden, but occasionally someone would discover his secret and March (whose name means horse in Welsh) would be forced to kill them. He hid the bodies in a nearby bed of reeds. His true nature was finally discovered when a boy made a flute from one of the reeds and the only song the flute could play was 'March Amheirchion has horse's ears'. Nobody knows what became of March Amheirchion, but it is believed he had several children and that his line continues to this day.

Ostrich
David Moody

We had such a beautiful home.

I still remember that buzz of excitement on the day we got the keys and the place was finally ours. I was pregnant with Sophie, so Norman did all the heavy lifting while I sat there with my feet propped up and my big belly sticking out, telling him and the removal men what went where. All that time and he's never let me forget it!

Twenty-six years we'd been there, and I still loved the place. We stretched ourselves to buy it and it took a long time to get everything just as we wanted it, but it was worth all that effort in the end.

I was the envy of my friends. Jacqui was always telling me how she wished her house was the size of ours. I met Jacqui in the playground when Sophie started school and we just connected. We remained friends long after our kids lost touch. Though she, Phil and the kids seemed happy enough with their lot, I always thought it was a shame they were so boxed-in when we had all that space going spare. It wasn't anyone's fault, just the way things work out sometimes. Phil owned his own business but got into trouble when the stock market crashed (or something like that... I can't remember exactly what happened). It was just after the last of their kids left home. So when Jacqui should have been taking it easy and enjoying herself, she ended up back at work instead. Poor love. Norman didn't want me having to work like that.

I always said I wanted two children, maybe even three, but Norm was happy to stick at one. That meant we always had plenty of room. Sophie had a playroom as well as her bedroom, and we still had a spare bedroom in case anyone came to stay. Not that people stopped regularly, mind. Mum stayed with us on a couple of occasions before she passed, but I reckon I could count on one hand the number of times Norm's folks visited. It didn't seem to bother him. *Funny buggers*, he used to call them. I always got on with them okay, but he was more cautious. There was a big falling out in the family before he and I got together, but to this day I don't know exactly what happened. He didn't like to talk about it, and it upset him if I asked.

Sophie never came back after university, and that left the two of us rattling around. I left her bedroom as it was in case she ever needed it, but she'd always been an independent girl. She has a good job now and is in a strong and stable relationship and I couldn't be happier for her.

I didn't used to see Sophie as much as I'd have liked. She was more than an hour and a half's drive away, and her place was a pig to get to by bus or train. There were no direct routes and I used to hate having to change at stations. I always got so het up and flustered having to get off one train and find another.

I should have made more of an effort and driven over

there. Truth is, I never liked driving Norm's car. We sold my Mini when he was between jobs and cash was tight and we never replaced it. He didn't think there was much point, and I tended to agree. We had one car between us, what was the point of having another? It would have just sat in the garage most of the time. We usually went out together and he put me on his insurance for emergencies so I could drive it if I ever needed to. Truth be told, I never fancied the idea of driving any of Norm's cars. Too big. He always had huge, powerful cars – Land Rovers and the like. I missed my little Mini. I used to love zipping around town in it.

I worked hard and kept the house nice, but the garden was Norman's domain. The front and back lawns were like putting greens. Absolutely perfect. At the height of the summer he'd be out there with the mower three or four times a week, sometimes even daily. He liked to get it looking just right. The stripes were always perfectly measured and dead straight, and the grass was the lushest green you could imagine. It was when the weather turned particularly hot and dry that you could really see how much care he put into his lawns. I used to notice it most when I was walking back from the shops. The neighbours' lawns would all be dried-out and yellowed around the edges, parched-looking, but ours would still be deep, deep green. Sometimes I'd see the neighbours looking, and occasionally one of them would pluck up the courage to ask Norm how he kept it looking so nice. "It just takes a little effort and commitment," he'd casually tell them, making it sound like it actually took no effort at all.

I'll be honest, though, Norman did obsess over his grass. I remember him hitting the roof one time when I wanted to go away for a week but he didn't want to leave the garden. I'd booked it all up as an anniversary surprise, but I hadn't thought it through. We usually managed a couple of long weekends away each year, but rarely anything longer. I didn't mind, though. It would have been a shame for all his hard work to have been undone just because I wanted a few days in the sun. We toyed with the idea of going out of season, but as he pointed out, it didn't make a lot of sense. "Might as well just stay at home and save the money," he'd usually say when I mentioned it.

It did become a bind, though, him not wanting to go anywhere. It stopped me seeing as much of Sophie as I'd have liked.

Despite everything, I had to remember Norm's feelings. It was easy for me. I wasn't the one with the high-pressured job who worked long hours. He said if he could do without a fancy holiday abroad, then so could I. It was difficult to argue with that.

From time to time I did find myself running out of things to do, though. I toyed with the idea of going back to work after Sophie went off to uni just to keep myself busy, but I didn't know what kind of job I'd be able to do. Norm was dead against the idea from the outset. He said I didn't need to work (which was true) and that I'd been out of the job marketplace for so long that I'd have struggled to find anything worthwhile (which was also true). He said he didn't want me stacking shelves or sitting on a till somewhere but, you know, I think I would have been happy with that. Norm thought the neighbours would have got the wrong impression. He didn't want them thinking we were hard up or anything like that. He used to regularly remind me how lucky I was. He said "do you want to end up like your friend Jacqui?" Jacqui always looked stressed-out, like she had a million and one things to do and no time in which to do them.

For what it was worth, Jacqui said herself that she thought I was mad to even consider working if I didn't have to. She said I should have joined a club, but hobbies have never really been my thing. I used to like badminton but I hadn't played for donkey's years. I collected teapots (unusual, I know) but that was hardly the most social of interests, and I'd long run out of space for them anyway.

I've always loved clothes shopping. That was a real weakness of mine. I could never resist a bargain. I used to get such a buzz picking up a new dress then trying to find an occasion to wear it. Norman used to say I wasted his money, but I'd just tell him it wouldn't be wasted if he took me out more often. He always promised he would, but he was under such a lot of pressure at work and whenever we made plans, nine times out of ten we had to change them. Half the outfits in my wardrobe I'd probably worn only once or twice, if at all. Such a shame. It was usually only family dos I got dressed up for. I'd go over the top when I had the chance, even though it didn't always go down well. Norm said I showed him up when I'd turn up at his brother's house in a fancy new frock when he and everyone else were wearing jeans.

He had a point, I suppose.

My immediate family was my real hobby. Between keeping the house nice and looking after Norman and Sophie, I always seemed to have more than enough on my plate.

Like I said, we had such a beautiful home. If I close my eyes and think back, I can still remember every little detail of every room. I remember the smells and the way it sounded; the creaks and pops at night when the heating switched off, and the rustle, rattle and clunk when the postman would deliver our mail.

I used to get a bit obsessive looking after the place, I'll admit. But I was no worse than Norman with his bloody lawns.

I've always been a tidy person, but I started taking things to the extreme. I'd spend ages dusting and cleaning and arranging and rearranging. I use to like my teapot collection to look nice, so I'd leave a few of them out on show on the sideboard. I regularly changed them and moved them around, but I always had the big yellow one Mum left me out on display. It meant a lot, that teapot. Mum inherited it from her mother, and it reminded me of when I was growing up.

I did like everything to be just right, though. I used to line the handles and spouts of the teapots up so they were all pointing the right way. Norm used to take the mickey out of me something rotten. He used to joke I'd got that obsessive compulsive disorder thing. He might have had a point. I hadn't realised how obsessive I'd become until I put the TV on one lunchtime, then started fussing with my collection. By the time I sat down to watch the box, the one o'clock news had finished and *Doctors* was halfway through. I'd spent more than half an hour trying to get everything just right.

Looking back now I realise I'd let things get out of perspective. You often don't realise until someone else points it out, do you?

It was my friend Mandy who first made me aware. She called around one day and we were having a good old natter about something or nothing. I made us both a sandwich, and it was only when she pointed out that I'd just thrown out half a perfectly good loaf of bread that I realised something was wrong. It was going out of date the next day, but I'd got it into my head that I shouldn't let food get anywhere near its 'best before' date. I realised I'd been throwing milk out when it still had a good couple of days shelf-life, and I'd got into the habit of doing the same with meat and vegetables too. Mandy asked me what was going on and she was like a dog with a bone, refusing to let go. I remember feeling really uncomfortable, because it's not nice when someone's putting you on the spot like that, is it? But Mandy and I had been close friends for a long time, and if there was anyone I trusted to be brutally honest with me, it was her.

She was asking me all kinds of questions about cooking and cleaning and whether or not I was happy, and then she asked me what Norman thought of it all and the question floored me. "I don't tell him," I remember answering. "He doesn't need to know."

"But it's because of him you do it, isn't it?"

I remember struggling to answer that. I was stammering and umming and ahhing, and then the penny dropped. You see, one time a couple of months before, I'd made Norm a sandwich and hadn't realised the loaf had started to turn. There was a little bit of blue mould on one of the slices. I couldn't see it, but he could sure taste it. You'd have thought I'd tried to poison him, the fuss he made. He gave me such a hard time. He was justified, mind. It can't have been nice.

So Mandy started asking if everything was all right between me and Norm which, of course, it was. I did tell her he'd started staying at the office later and later, and the things she said and the way she was looking at me got me thinking. She called me an ostrich because she said I had my head buried in the sand. I didn't agree. Mandy had divorced her husband years earlier, and she came across as being bitter. She said it was obvious Norm was having an affair, because this was how it started with her Peter, and that I needed to do something about it sooner rather than later. Much as I didn't want to believe her, the more I thought about what she'd said, the more convinced I became that she was right.

Mandy really fired me up. So much so that, a couple of days later, I found myself sitting in the middle of town waiting for him. *Watching* him. I put on a dress I'd bought a couple of weeks ago that he hadn't seen before and that I felt good in and I set myself up in the coffee shop opposite. It was the perfect location. Norman's office was directly across the road and the seat in the coffee shop I chose was so good I could see right inside and watch him at his desk. All afternoon there were women coming over to see him and ask him questions about this, that and the other, and every time I saw someone new I was thinking *is it you? Are you the one? Are you the hussy trying to tear my marriage apart?*

Norman never left the office before six (or so he told me), and as the clock crept past the hour I started to feel more and more nervous. I knew that any minute I'd see her.

What if she's younger than me?
What if I know her?
Was she at last year's Christmas party?
What if she's better dressed?
What if she's prettier?

You think all these pointless thoughts when you're nervous, don't you?

The clock was ticking and more and more people were leaving the office for the night. The light had started to fade and the electric lights coming from inside the office just made things even worse. It was as if someone was shining a spotlight on Norm so I could see his every move, and it felt like they were doing it to make me suffer. I didn't know what I'd done wrong. Had he strayed because I hadn't been paying him enough attention? Was the house not clean enough? Was it because I'd tried to poison him with that bloody sandwich?

It got to almost half-six and my mind was running overtime. Why was she late? What kind of games was she playing? Sounds crazy now, but I actually found myself getting angry thinking about this phantom woman messing Norman about. Ridiculous, I know.

And then, around about seven o'clock, he packed up his stuff and left.

Luckily I managed to jump on a bus before he emerged from the office, and on the way home I realised something that made me feel a thousand times worse than I already did. Norman wasn't having an affair after all. He just didn't want to go home.

I felt like such a failure. What kind of a wife was I? I decided two things that night. First, that I'd try harder to keep Norm happy. Second, that I wouldn't ever speak to Mandy again.

❖

A week later was my birthday.

I was still feeling awful, so I resolved to make the day as enjoyable for Norman as I hoped it would be for me. We went out to dinner that night – the first time we'd been out as a couple in ages – and we had a lovely time. We went to one of his favourite pubs (we always got a good meal there – *stick with what you know* was one of Norman's mottos) and it was super. Just like the old times.

He spoiled me rotten. Flowers, chocolates, and a new vacuum because I was always moaning about the old one. It was top of the range. Practically lifted the carpets from the floorboards, it did!

Things turned a little sour soon after.

It was a Saturday afternoon, I remember it clearly. Norm had been working in the garden all morning, and I'd taken the opportunity to run my new vacuum around and do a spot of tidying up. Dinner was almost ready. I always tried to time it carefully because I knew he didn't like to lose his rhythm when he was working on the lawn.

If I knocked him off his stride and the stripes weren't quite right, it would take him twice as long to correct and the dinner would be ruined.

I'd just finished mopping the floor when he came in. I told him his food was ready and he asked if he had time for a shower first. I told him he didn't but he went up anyway, telling me that whenever I said it was five minutes to dinner, it was always closer to ten, and this time he was actually right. It took me a while to clean up all the grass clippings he'd managed to tread into the house.

We'd barely started eating when the phone rang. He went out to the hall to answer it, and I knew straightaway who he was talking to. I couldn't make out what was being said, but I could tell from the way Norman was speaking that it was our little girl on the line. I also sensed that something wasn't right.

"Who was it, love?" I asked, just to be sure.

He ate a few more mouthfuls of food before answering.

"Sophie, of course."

"Is she okay?"

More food. More chewing.

"She's fine."

I didn't want to push him too hard because he and Sophie often didn't see eye to eye and he'd have just said I was nagging him, but I knew something was up. Sophie didn't often phone the house. She usually texted.

"What did she phone for?" I asked, keeping my voice as light and airy as I could.

He seemed reluctant, but he eventually answered. "Her friend's been in an accident."

"Oh no. Which friend?"

Norman spat out his answer. *"That* friend."

Now I should say at this point that Sophie's gay. It's not my cup of tea and it's not what I'd have chosen for her, but she's happy and Kerry, her girlfriend, is lovely. She's nine years older than Sophie and very sporty and not particularly feminine, but we've always got on and Sophie thinks the world of her.

"Poor Kerry. Is she all right?"

"She's in hospital. Got knocked off her bike, apparently."

"Is she badly hurt?"

"A couple of broken bones. Nothing too serious."

"It sounds pretty serious to me. We should go and see her."

Norman put down his knife and fork and looked across the table at me. "When, exactly?"

"I don't know... one evening perhaps?"

"Visiting hours would be over by the time we get there."

"Next weekend, then?"

"I was thinking about going into the office next Saturday morning."

"But you never go into the office on Saturdays."

"I've got a deadline coming up."

"When were you going to tell me?"

"I'd forgotten about it. Do I have to ask permission now?"

"No, I'm just saying it would be nice if I'd been consulted, that's all."

"I told you, I'd forgotten about it."

"What about tomorrow, then?"

"Too short notice."

"Well if you're going into work next Saturday, can I borrow the car?"

"Seriously? You haven't driven since you got rid of the Mini."

"I'll be okay..."

"I don't have time to take you for a test drive or anything like that, not this week."

"I'll catch the bus, then. Or the train."

"You do that. Ease up on the questions, love. I've told you everything I know. I'll find a way of getting you there if that's what you want."

I called Sophie back later. It turned out Kerry had almost died in the accident. Norm booked me a ticket and I caught the train to see them the following Tuesday. I stayed overnight, but I'd have happily stopped longer if he'd booked me an open return (he said he'd wanted to be sure I got a seat). Sophie gave me such an ear-bending when I was about to leave. She said her dad was a bully, and that he sulked if he didn't get his own way. I stuck up for him like I always did.

A couple of days later I took a telephone call which shook me to the core. It was Jacqui. Phil had died. It was very sudden. Apparently he'd been at work and had dropped dead from a massive heart attack in the middle of a meeting. He knew nothing about it, so that was something, I guess, but my heart went out to Jacqui. It makes you count your blessings when you hear about something like that happening, doesn't it?

The funeral was a week later.

My Norman always got on quite well with Phil, so he took the afternoon off and we both went to pay our respects. It was a lovely service. The crematorium was almost full. Oak Hill's quite a big crem, so you're doing pretty well if you manage to fill anything more than the first four rows. Loads of people turned out to say goodbye to Phil.

Poor old Jacqui was in such a state afterwards. We didn't go back to her house for the wake because Norm wanted to get away, but I managed to grab a few minutes with her before we left. Poor love could barely hold herself upright. She looked exhausted. Her face looked hollow, like she hadn't slept for a month. I remember it clear as day. She looked up at me, tears rolling down her face, and she said 'how am I going to cope without him?'

It played on my mind for days afterwards.

Anyway, she coped all right, because next time I saw her she was a different woman. It was a week or so later, and we passed each other outside the shops. I didn't recognise her at first. I had to do a double-take. She looked radiant. She'd had her hair done and she was wearing a lovely outfit. I'd always thought she was a little too thin, but she looked just right. She looked *alive*. She was grinning from ear to ear, so much so that it made me wonder if Phil's death hadn't pushed her over the edge.

I asked how she was doing and she said "really good, thanks Sue." And then she paused and pulled me closer like she didn't want to be heard. "I feel guilty saying this, but I'm really happy."

Happy? I couldn't understand it. She and Phil had been inseparable like me and Norm. She could see that I was confused.

"I loved Phil more than anything," she told me, "and I miss him every minute of every day and I think I always will. I expect I'll probably crash at some point soon, but..."

"But what?" I asked.

"But right now I'm enjoying my freedom. I'm my own boss for the first time in almost thirty years. I watch what I want to watch on TV, I eat what I like when I like, I go out when I feel like it... I know Phil wouldn't have wanted me to mope around feeling sorry for myself, so I'm not. Honestly, Sue, it's given me a whole new lease of life."

I didn't say anything, of course, but I thought she'd completely lost her marbles.

That night I was sitting with Norman watching TV. It was his favourite programme (you know the one... that BBC sitcom about the Muslim councillor from Birmingham). He was howling with laughter, but for some reason I just couldn't see the funny side. I felt awful guilty, but I couldn't help thinking about how I'd be if Norman died. Worse than that, I found myself thinking about killing him. It sounds silly and wrong when I say it out loud like that, but I sat there on the sofa watching him watching telly, and I tried to work out how I could kill him and not get caught.

I remembered watching an old black and white horror programme when I was a little girl. I don't remember all the ins and outs of the story, but the gist of it was that a woman got rid of her husband by clubbing him around the head with a frozen leg of lamb, which she then cooked and served to the police officers who'd come around to the house to investigate hubby's disappearance. I remember thinking *it's a shame lamb's so expensive at the moment,* and I made a mental note to have a look next time I went to Waitrose (and I'm not even joking).

I thought about poisoning him. It wouldn't have been difficult to slip something into his food – he usually wolfed down his dinner so quick it barely had time to touch the sides – but I knew I'd never be able to cope with the police questioning. I know Mandy called me an ostrich that time, but there's a world of difference between shoving your head in the sand to avoid saying what you think and lying intentionally. I could never have done it.

I thought about sabotaging the brakes of his car but, if I'm honest, I wouldn't have known where to start. I could have put petrol in at a push and maybe put air in the tyres, but anything else was beyond me and it would have aroused more than a little suspicion if I'd started asking Norman questions about mechanics all of a sudden.

How about a trap? What if I left the gas on? How about if I slipped something in his drink and left him to drown in the bath? The possibilities were endless...

Of course, it didn't take me long to realise how silly I was being. I felt guilty as sin the next day. What a horrible bitch I was for thinking such things about the man who doted over me. The house, Sophie... if it hadn't been for Norman I wouldn't have had any of it.

He came home late from work again next day, but that was good because it gave me time to spruce up the house and cook a special meal. I made his favourite – beef stroganoff – and he ate every scrap. We dozed together in front of the telly, and this time I managed to keep my thoughts in check and stay focused on the screen.

❖

The weekend began like any other.

I had loads to do, and I spent Saturday morning working around the house while Norman groomed his perfect lawns. I finished just after midday and started cooking dinner, and while I was waiting for the vegetables to boil, I telephoned Sophie. It had been a few days since we'd spoken and I wanted to know how Kerry was getting on.

I couldn't get an answer. Strange.

I carried on with my jobs and tried calling their flat a couple more times. Still nothing. I couldn't get an answer on their mobiles, either. It wasn't like Sophie, and I was concerned. I had a horrible, sickly, nervous feeling in the pit of my stomach that something was very wrong.

When Norman came back in from the garden, he could tell that I was upset. I told him what had happened and how worried I was, but he didn't seem surprised. "Well you won't get through to her," he said, sounding almost aggressive.

"Why not?"

"Because she's not at home."

Norman walked deeper into the house, leaving a trail of grassy footprints on the recently mopped kitchen lino and the hall carpet.

I followed him into the lounge. He was already in front of the TV, grubby shoes still on and grass stains everywhere.

"What's going on, Norman? What's happened?"

"Her friend's taken a turn for the worse."

"What?"

"One of those hospital superbugs. MRSA, or something like that."

"We've got to go and see her."

"Why? It's not Sophie that's sick."

I just looked at him. "How can you say that? We're talking about Sophie's partner here."

"I knew you'd be like this," he grumbled. "That's why I didn't say anything. We'll go and see her tonight." And he turned up the TV to let me know in no uncertain terms that the conversation was finished.

I felt myself tensing up. I wanted to scream and shout at him, but I couldn't do it. I just shoved my head into the sand as I always did, automatically switching to full-on ostrich mode.

I went back to the kitchen to check on dinner, picking up bits of grass from the carpet as I did. Then I stopped and checked myself, because something was niggling at me. My legs felt like jelly, but I knew I had to ask him and I stormed back to the lounge. "How did you know?"

"Huh?"

"About Kerry... how did you know she was ill again?"

His eyes never left the screen.

"Sophie phoned."

At that point I probably should have shut up and gone back to the kitchen, but I didn't. I walked over to the sideboard and started checking the spouts of my teapots were in line, my hands shaking with anger and nerves.

The words were stuck in my throat, but I made myself ask.

"When did she call?"

"Last night," he answered casually.

I couldn't believe what I was hearing.

"Last night? Why didn't you tell me?"

"Because I knew this would happen. I was tired last night and I wanted to get the lawns cut this morning. I knew you'd go over the top like this."

"Over the top?"

"Listen, love, I don't have the energy for this right now. It's been a tough week at work. You don't know what it's like, sitting here all day every day with your feet up."

I'd got the bit between my teeth now.

"No, *you* don't know what it's like. I only sit here all day every day because you won't let me do anything else."

I'd said it without thinking, without realising, and I waited nervously for his reaction. I thought he was going to explode, but he didn't. He just smiled at me and shook his head.

"You have a very funny view of things sometimes, Sue."

"I'm going to see Sophie," I told him. "Are you going to take me?"

"Later. I've got to finish the lawns first."

"Fine. Just drop me at the station, then. I'll get the train."

"Did you not hear me? I've got to finish the garden first. I won't get another chance. It's going to rain the evening."

"I'll go without you then," I said, and I meant it.

Norman just laughed. "You're not going anywhere. You can't do anything without me, love. You're bloody useless." And he kicked off his shoes and stretched out on the chair.

I had a moment of sudden clarity. It all made sense.

"Mandy was right," I said. "And Jacqui, too."

"What are you on about now?"

"It's my fault."

"Have you lost your mind?"

"I let you do this."

"Let me do what?"

"I let you control me."

In a single sudden move, I picked up mother's yellow teapot and smashed it over Norman's head. He yelled out in agony.

"Sorry, love," I instinctively said as he got up and lumbered towards me, blood running down his face.

"You stupid cow... what did you do that for? Jesus. Get me something to stop the bleeding."

"Get it yourself."

I felt awful, but I knew what I had to do next.

He walked towards me but clipped the corner of the coffee table and fell forward. He was on his knees in the middle of the room, one hand on the table and the other on the top of his head, trying to stem the blood flow. It was dripping everywhere, all over the carpet I wasn't bothered.

In for a penny, in for a pound.

I picked up the biggest crockery shard I could find and stabbed him in the back. And again. And again. And again. And again. And again...

I sliced him to ribbons then left him for dead in the middle of the lounge and went and had my lunch.

There wasn't much left to do outside, actually. He'd

finished the front lawn, and there was just a bit of edging to do in the back. It didn't take long at all. I didn't make as neat a job of it as Norman, but it didn't matter.

That afternoon I drove to see Sophie and Kerry. Driving wasn't so bad. A bit nerve-racking at first, but I started to enjoy it after a few miles. Norm's big car had some welly, that's for sure.

I had a lovely time, all things considered. Sophie asked where her dad was, and I told her I'd left him in front of the TV, which was as close to the truth as I wanted to get. Kerry's condition had stabilized, and Sophie and I had several cups of tea and a long overdue catch-up while she was sleeping.

I was tired when I got home, and the enormity of what I'd done hit me as hard as I'd hit Norm with the teapot. I sat perched on the edge of the sofa and I sobbed and I sobbed and I sobbed.

I think it was just nerves and shock, because then I stopped.

I poured myself a sherry to calm my nerves and slowly started to relax. It was almost eleven o'clock, the time we usually went up to bed, but I stayed downstairs instead. I watched a godawful film on TV – a soppy rom-com Norman would have hated – and had another sherry. By the time I went up I was half-cut and completely exhausted. I left the washing up from dinner to soak (it would still be there in the morning, I though), and I left my dirty clothes in a pile on the bedroom floor.

I felt heartbroken, nervous and terrified... but also strangely calm and relaxed. It was odd having the whole bed to myself. I slept like a log.

Next morning I made a half-hearted attempt to cover my tracks, but the grassy footprints and the massive bloodstain were a dead giveaway (pardon the pun). I got as far as dragging Norman's body out into the back garden because I had some stupid idea that I might be able to bury him. I knew I'd done a terrible thing, but there was no going back now. Funny thing was, I wouldn't have wanted to go back even if I could. The luxury of not having to constantly consider someone else all the time was blissful. I felt free. It felt good.

I tried digging a hole in the middle of the lawn, but I didn't get far. It was too much like hard work and after about an hour of trying, all I'd managed to dig was a hole about twelve inches square and the same deep. Anyway, Norman's body had gone all stiff and inflexible with rigor mortis, stuck in the same kneeling position in which he'd died. *Stiff and inflexible*, I remember thinking. No change there then.

I shoved his head in the hole and filled it in. There he was, right in the middle of his showpiece lawn: head down in the dirt, backside sticking up into the air.

'Now who's an ostrich?' I said to him.

I was going to phone the police, honestly I was, but Clive and Miriam from next-door got there before me. I'd have liked a little more time on my own first, but it didn't really matter.

And that's how I ended up here.

Any regrets?

They've said I'll never leave here but that's okay. I honestly don't mind. Most (not all) of the people in the unit are lovely and I enjoy keeping my little room tidy.

I've got a few things of my own to remind me of home, and I don't have to cook or think about anyone else. I'm free. Unrestricted. Uninhibited. I can relax and be myself for the first time since... well, since I met Norman, actually.

I've got some good friends here and my own TV I don't have to share so I can watch my programmes when I like. Sophie and Kerry try to drop in and see me every couple of weeks.

Everything's so much easier now.

Life is good.

Blue-Eyes
Barbie Wilde

It was a moonless night in the forest. Leaves were rustling in the wind. Tiny voles and mice scurried through the underbrush. The occasional shrill death cries of prey rang out as predators ruthlessly seized their evening meals. All the busy little noises of Nature's activities. An oddly comforting cacophony that had replaced the blaring and strident sounds of the city. However, anything was preferable to human company. Gazza had seen enough of humans to last him a lifetime.

Gazza Hunt ('wino or rhyming slang', as his more erudite drinking companions used to joke) looked about sixty, but he was really just thirty-nine years old. After he had lost his job, his wife and his house, things got to the point where he just gave up and opted out of the human rat race for all time. Life on the streets had been hard and Gazza's philosophy was the standard alcoholic's excuse for everything: "What's the use?" What's the use of trying to get a job? Some arsehole will only take it away from you. What's the use of keeping clean? Without a job, no sensible woman's going touch you with a barge pole anyway. Why stop drinking when it was the only joy in his life; the only thing that could take him away from himself for a few hours?

After several years on the cold, lonely and miserable streets of London, Gazza felt he needed a change of scenery. He moved out to the green belt and managed to snag a cozy spot in a little clearing in a quiet forested area near the bustling market town of Baggleswade. He'd nicked a kid's tent from somebody's backyard, a cheap barbeque from someone else's and then set up camp, surreptitiously combing the local scrap yard for enough jumble to make the place look homey.

Every other day, Gazza would manage to find the energy to tramp into the village, begging for change until he got enough to buy a couple of cans of beer. Food was just a necessary evil. He managed to rummage enough from the wheelie bins and skips behind fast food restaurants and supermarkets.

Hard to believe that Gazza had graduated from Uni, had once been a mechanical engineer, had a family somewhere up North. Well, fuck them. That was a million years ago. Fuck the world, he didn't give a toss anymore.

One night during one of the rainiest summers in living memory, he had to get up around 4 AM to spend a penny, as his Dad used to say. He moved away from his campsite to the bushes beyond, because it was always a bad idea to urinate where you lived.

After he'd done his business, he was turning around to go back when he spotted a strange bluish glow in the distance. He'd made sure when he'd first found his hideaway that it was as far away from human habitation as was conveniently possible, so he decided to investigate. Most likely some disaffected 'youfs' were on the razzle, mucking about sniffing glue, or quaffing Special Brew, or ingesting whatever the fashionable poison-of-the-week was to those clueless little nitwits.

Gazza proceeded with caution, because sometimes the kids got so drugged up that they thought kicking a homeless bloke to death was a whole world of fun and games. As he got closer to the light, the forest became almost eerily quiet.

He eventually entered a small clearing and was shocked to see that the bluish light was emanating from what looked like a shallow grave. He stopped dead and glanced around nervously. It certainly sounded and looked like he was alone, so he moved warily towards the source of the light.

He halted near the edge and peered into the grave. He couldn't figure out where the mysterious glow was coming from, but it certainly was strong enough to illuminate the body of a beautiful young woman – wide open blue eyes, blonde hair, red lips, naked... and very definitely dead.

Gazza looked around again. All was silent, empty – even the voles had stopped their squeaking. He should go to a phone box and call the police. He should tell someone. He should do something, but he was frozen to the spot, staring at the most gorgeous woman he'd ever seen in his miserable life. Even on telly. Even in pop videos or movies. She was perfect. Except, of course, for being dead, although in Gazza's scrambled mind, perhaps that wasn't such a bad thing.

Needless to say, sex for Gazza was pretty nonexistent. He was so low down on the food chain that not even the most drug-raddled tart on the street would've screw him for a pint, even if he could get it up. Gazing down on this pale-skinned, golden-haired goddess, his sad, pickled penis hardened and he became aroused for the first time in years.

The thought of a woman who wouldn't struggle; a woman who wouldn't slap him and say "no!"; a woman who wouldn't demand that he take out the rubbish first; a woman who would acquiesce to all of his demands was just too much for Gazza to resist.

No one was there. No one was watching. He could do whatever he wanted. He eased himself down into the grave. Some part of his brain was telling him that he should really check and see if the woman was actually dead, but another part of his anatomy was whispering something else to him – something nasty; something beyond the pale even for him.

Gazza lay next to the woman and gazed at her. She had such a lovely serene face, with amazing boobies and tiny adorable feet. He felt the pulse spot on her neck. Nothing. He bent over her face and sniffed. She was almost fresh. There was a whiff of some unidentifiable perfume, but underneath it she smelled a bit like raw hamburger that had been wrapped in cling film too long: a bit sour, but not unpleasant. Not that Gazza really cared. Not that his sex-starved penis cared either.

Gazza eased his trousers down and moved on top of the dead woman. Her limbs were pliable, even in death, as the rigor mortis stage had long passed. He stroked her smooth cool thighs and spread her legs. His penis tried to push its way into her, but it wasn't easy. Finally, he managed to penetrate his goddess and he began to make love to the most beautiful corpse in the world.

Then somewhere in the depths of his charred and miserable soul, a little voice shouted: *Gazza! Don't do this. What's happened to you? You used to be a human being. Call the police!*

Gazza stopped. His erection faded away. Tears of loss and frustration seeped into his eyes. He felt deeply disgusted with himself. No matter how enticing this woman was, she was still dead. Christ Almighty, was he really that desperate? (*Yes!* another little voice shouted in his brain, but he ignored it.)

Gazza gently lifted himself off her body, tugged up his trousers and climbed out of the grave. He stood looking down at this astounding lifeless beauty and sighed. He wondered what to do next. He couldn't take her with him, although he would have loved to. He didn't want to leave her here for the vermin and the voles and maybe some other fucked up wino to find. He sat down at the edge of the grave and tried to think, but it was no good. All brain cells of any use had been burned out years ago.

Gazza started to sob the big blubby tears of the hopeless alcoholic. She was so lovely. He didn't want to see her hurt. He could just imagine what a rat or an owl would do to that breathtaking face.

Feeling light-headed, Gazza stood up slowly. He needed a drink. Once he'd had a drink, his mind might be clearer. He'd already decided that he wanted to keep his corpse bride for himself. He just couldn't figure out how to do it at this particular moment in time.

Gazza staggered back to his tent and slept for a few

hours. After slogging into town the next morning, begging for a while, guzzling a few cans of beer, and finally eating a discarded, half-consumed, cold Egg McMuffin behind McDonald's, he felt a lot better. By the time he returned to his campsite, he had a plan.

Gazza knew he never should have left the woman (now affectionately known to him as 'Blue-Eyes') in the forest all alone. Indeed, her face had been at the forefront of his mind all day long. He had to protect her somehow.

It was dark by the time Gazza returned to the gravesite, once again guided by the blue light. He nervously peeked into the grave, hoping against hope that she hadn't been damaged by any beasts of the night.

Gazza was surprised and a bit perplexed. There was absolutely no sign of any animal or insect activity on or around her body, which seemed quite surreal in the circumstances. However, he was so overjoyed that Blue-Eyes was still intact that he chased the puzzling thoughts out of his head. He'd brought his sleeping bag with him, with the vague idea of placing her inside and then dragging her carefully back to his campsite.

The urge to continue what he had started the night before was almost overwhelming. Seductive voices were whispering in his head, saying that it was his duty to pleasure her, that she desired it. That it was important that he claim Blue-Eyes for himself.

Gazza slipped into the grave, pulled down his trousers and resumed his love-making. It felt strange, but whether it was because she was dead, or cold to the touch, or that he hadn't been inside of a woman for years, he couldn't tell, but he didn't care. He was making love to the most stunning dead girl he'd ever met and it was just wonderful. He almost could imagine that she was responding somehow. That there was some kind of cosmic exchange of energy going on between them.

Gazza finally came and he nearly passed out with the unaccustomed effort. He lay panting on top of Blue-Eyes for at least five minutes, trying to marshal his reserves. He withdrew and pulled up his trousers. He glanced at her face and was startled to see that her eyes were now closed, perhaps through the movement of their lovemaking.

Then he noticed that what he initially thought was some kind of choker-style jewelry around her throat was actually wide black gaffer tape. Gazza picked at the tape and was horrified to see that it hid a deep wound in her throat, almost as if she had been decapitated.

Icy cold fear congealed in his groin and Gazza hurriedly rolled off Blue-Eyes and stood up in the grave. He looked around again, fearing that someone had witnessed this damning violation of love, but the clearing was still empty and all was deathly silent.

Then he felt something snaking around his ankle. Gazza froze with terror. It took every fiber of his being to gather the strength to look down. Her eyes were open again: lifeless, sapphire blue and cold as the Arctic Ocean. They were like a doll's eyes: unblinking, unfocused, almost jewel-like. Gazza looked at his feet and nearly peed himself. Her hand was gripping his ankle tightly. He tried to raise his leg, but she held him down firmly. Gazza threw himself down at the edge of the grave and used his clawing hands to scramble out, but he couldn't shake off Blue-Eyes.

Gazza started kicking out at her, hoping to loosen her grip, but as he turned around and squirmed away on his back from the grave, he could see her body slowly emerging. Blue-Eyes was coming after him.

Gazza was making pathetic noises like a little girl seeing a spider for the first time. The more he distanced himself from the grave, the more his corpse bride was coming out of it. Finally, exhausted with the effort, he had to stop when her body was completely free of the grave and she was lying face down on the ground.

Gazza was hyperventilating with dread. Was he dreaming? If so, could he please wake up now? He bent over double and tried to pry her hand away, but it was as if it was glued to his ankle.

Gazza moved closer to Blue-Eyes and gently turned her over. Her face, although still beautiful, was dirty now and those icy blue orbs looked even more startling in the midst of the black soil that coated her face. Almost at his wit's end, Gazza pleaded with her in a crazed gush of words: "Please, please, please let me go. I'm sorry that I took advantage of you without your permission. I thought you were dead. Although that's not much of an excuse, I know. Please let me go!"

To Gazza's amazement, her hand loosened its grip. He scrabbled away from Blue-Eyes and then stopped, warily watching, wondering what was going to happen next.

Then Gazza began to whimper with panic. Blue-Eyes was moving. She flipped around onto her stomach. Her head lifted up and those crystalline, doll-like, dead blue eyes were like beacons. She stood up, smoothing the tape around her neck so her head wouldn't fall off.

Even though he was more scared than he'd ever been in his entire life, Gazza still couldn't believe how remarkable this creature was as she moved closer and stood over him.

Gazza lay on his back, looking up at Blue-Eyes, who was cinematically lit from behind by the bluish light coming from the grave. Stars circled her head like a diadem of precious jewels and he suddenly stopped being afraid. He didn't care what was going to happen next. He belonged to Blue-Eyes body and soul, and she belonged to him. If she wanted to kill him, that was okay. At least he was shuffling off this mortal coil in the most exquisite way possible, destroyed by something he loved, instead of dying of liver failure, or in a knife fight with another wino, or by being beaten to death by young yobbos. This was truly exceptional and he was at peace with it.

Blue-Eyes walked over Gazza, dropping down to her knees on either side of his body. She unzipped his trousers, stuck her hand in and fished around for his penis. Gazza's mouth hung open. He was expecting something unusual, but not this bizarre. Blue-Eyes found what she was looking for and he instantly got hard. He became scared again when she smiled – her face was now distorted by a crooked terrifying grin. Her teeth were speckled with dirt and grass. Blue-Eyes lowered herself down on him, placed her hands on his shoulders, and started to bounce enthusiastically, grinding her hips into his.

Gazza was gurgling with terror, spittle dribbling out of his mouth. Blue-Eyes smiled again and a slim noisome greenish stream of mucus gently tumbled from her open mouth into his. He gagged and that's when she laughed. It was a ghastly sound from the crypt: hollow, echo-y, buzzing, deep and too low for a female. Oh God, was he being raped by a fucking alien, or what?

The mucus hit the back of his throat and Gazza could feel it sliming its way down to his esophagus. It was if it had a life of its own – slithering and burning its infernal way into his stomach.

Blue-Eyes appeared to be having the time of her life – or death, as the case may be. She writhed on top of him in chilling silence and finally, she shuddered with a kind of otherworldly ecstasy. Gazza couldn't help himself. He came again and it was the most profound orgasm that he had ever experienced. Blue-Eyes flopped forward on top of Gazza, who lay gasping for breath under her body.

After a few minutes, Gazza tried to move away from Blue-Eyes, but it was as if they were melded together. He could push her body up and away to some extent, but his member seemed to be embedded in her vagina. He rolled them over so at least he was on top and could try to lift himself off, but something was very wrong. He was stuck.

Gazza noticed that the black gaffer tape around her neck had come loose. Concerned, he tried to stick it back on, but then saw to his astonishment that her neck wound had disappeared – miraculously healed somehow. Thoughts tumbled into Gazza's exhausted, booze-sozzled brain, but only one thing stood out as a viable possibility: did his semen have medicinal properties? Had her neck wound been healed because he had made love to Blue-Eyes? That was too crazy to contemplate, but then again, he wasn't exactly in the most normal situation in the world.

As he struggled once again to free himself from Blue-Eyes, her legs whipped themselves tightly around his waist. He looked down and those eyes, no longer dead, were focused and glaring right at him. Blue-Eyes smiled once more – the crooked, stroke victim grin now gone. She stuck her tongue out lasciviously at him in some kind of obscene parody of flirtation.

"No!" Gazza squeaked like a trapped vole and frantically tried to get away, but Blue-Eyes wasn't finished with him.

A grotesquely loud sucking sound emanated from her vagina and the sudden stabbing pain in his groin was excruciating. Gazza fervently wished he could black out, but he was surprisingly conscious, perhaps from the effect of the vile green mucus that he had been forced to ingest.

Slurp, slurp, slurp! went the corpse bride's vagina, accompanied by the screams and squeals of a dying, blood-drained Gazza. It was brutally plain to him that she was consuming him somehow – starting with his hapless penis. Gazza was melting away inside of her and Blue-Eyes was soaking up his life essence as if he was a fully grown fetus being sucked back into the womb.

The grisly process took a couple of hours and eventually the only things left of Gazza were his clothes and trainers, which Blue-Eyes threw into the grave. She briskly walked off into the woods with determination and renewed energy.

After traveling through the forest for ten minutes, Blue-Eyes came to another clearing, containing an identical shallow grave suffused by blue light. She stood at the edge and looked down. An apparently dead woman with raven hair and the same wide open blue eyes was lying at the bottom of the grave, no less a beauty than the blonde woman who stood above her.

Blue-Eyes jumped down and lay on top of Raven-Hair. She gently pried open Raven-Hair's mouth and appeared to be kissing her compatriot. Then, looking all the world like a mother bird feeding her young, Blue-Eyes starting heaving and undulating until a geyser of regurgitated Gazza flesh and blood poured out of her mouth and into the receiving mouth of Raven-Hair.

The flow of goop stopped abruptly. Blue-Eyes got up, wiped her mouth and pulled herself out of the grave, watching and waiting.

Raven-Hair, her luscious red lips smeared with Gazza's blood, blinked and smiled at her friend. She slowly stretched her whole body like a cat and then stood up and hoicked herself out of the grave. The two women sensually embraced and kissed, like long lost lovers. Then hand-in-hand, they marched deeper into the shadow-drenched woods towards a multitude of glowing blue lights throbbing in the distance... to awaken the rest of their diabolical tribe.

A Glimpse of Red
James Everington

At what point, she wondered, did it become okay to show your anxiety in this country? To show your panic? When did their old codes, the frozen prescriptions of their society become void?

Beyza didn't know. Her questions only added to her anxiety – Beyza's panic felt like the only heated thing under the grey English sky. She remained silent and frozen at the bus stop, fighting for calm. Around her were the people she was trying to impress – the other mothers, placidly awaiting the return of their offspring. Their presence helped Beyza keep her spine erect and her hands still – both by example, and by fear of their censure. Keep a motherly smile clamped to her lips. She refrained from jostling or craning her neck in the direction the bus should be coming from; she refrained from speaking in her own language to relieve her anxiety.

One of the mothers laughed, and the noise almost broke Beyza's control, for it sounded to her fake laughter, cold and superior, not the inclusive warmth of the belly-laughs of home. She knew it *wasn't* faked – that was an illusion caused by differences in accent and cultural mores. Being a foreigner here often felt like she was thinking two different things at once.

My name is Beyza, she said in her head, *and his is Altan*.

She was standing on the other side of an invisible divide from the rest of the mothers, whose eyes were blank with only the worries of the middle-class: that their child hadn't been popular, or not for the right reasons, or not with the right kids. Whereas she worried about far more terrible and fundamental things... The activities of the school organised adventure-day (abseiling, archery, quad-biking) were only a gloss on her real fear – that of Altan being away from her. She looked up, to where the shapes of the clouds seemed to divide the sky; Altan was on the other side to her. Anything could have happened.

Altan wasn't his real name, but the name the woman from the police had given him. When the devils had come out of the woodwork, and made it clear that she needed protection if she was to testify. 'Altan' – a pretty name at least, she'd thought, although she hadn't known why they couldn't have picked their new names themselves. 'Beyza' – very white. The irony was not lost on her, for Beyza and Altan seemed the only people without bleach white skin and starched accents in this town. This idealised cricket and gin version of England. It was a different country (or different decade at least) to the sprawl of the Northern city where she had lived when she'd first arrived in the country, with its multicultural estates, its twenty-four hour shops selling goods from all over the world, its restaurants and kebab shops selling nothing more English than french-fries. Her proud grasp of the English language had been book-born only and she'd found half the accents and slang incomprehensible.

Only the English sky seemed to connect the two places, seemingly slung over the landscape like a torn and dirty sheet, the same grey colour whatever the weather, the same claustrophobic closeness overhead.

In this small town they spoke (and lived) by the book, yet Beyza still couldn't understand all of their code: SAT tests, the removal of stains from uniforms, 'his little ways in bed', and the grey, grey sky. It was closer to the English she'd learnt, but still there was something about their talk that unnerved her, a sense that more was implied than was being said. There was a gap between the townspeople and Beyza, small enough for them to pretend it wasn't there, large enough to preclude any conversation unless they initiated it. Which they never did. So Beyza stood and wondered (she tried to think in English like she was one of them) when in this cold country she was allowed to *say something* and ask for help.

The bus appeared at the top of the high street and made its way towards them, past the butcher, the Post Office, the sweetshop. This isn't going to happen, Beyza thought; she looked up to the sky as if to orientate herself, and she allowed herself a moment's hope. The bus stopped by the group of mothers (and it was all mothers, their husbands at work, as if its secluded position in the gentle hills had sheltered this town from the tides of the last forty years). The doors of the bus opened and immediately there was a confusion of young faces with healthy smiles, and Beyza felt herself hopelessly lost. Her vision doubled as she tried to pick one face from the crowd; her ears couldn't distinguish individual voices in the hubbub. The other mothers were reunited with their offspring as if by some natural instinct, recognising each other's calls. Beyza stood to one side of the crowd, craning her neck and calling for her son. Was she defective, was she such a poor mother that she couldn't spot her boy among all these others? Especially as his pretty coloured skin stood out so! As did the cautious look of a foreigner that he carried in his eyes, his inheritance a wariness in every step, every syllable.

Already the rush of kids had slowed, the more popular and cocksure had barged off first, and now came the fat ones, the book-worms, the other kids who would never fit in. *Altan!* she thought; and blasphemously, his real name... But Altan wasn't even among these second-rate English, not even behind them, not even the last child to get off.

"Altan!" she cried, out-loud.

She had crossed the line.

He must have become scared and remained on the bus – Beyza ran forward to the door before it could close. The driver protested but she got onboard and ran down the aisle, checking the empty seats, calling in her own tongue despite the police warnings, for the devil that must have taken Altan was an *English* devil and maybe her own words would hold power... *This* was the time when it was okay to voice your panic, surely, and Beyza had the sudden feeling that if the other mothers accepted this, if she had *got it right*, then all would be well. They would advise her, join in the search. And indeed she heard them behind her, coming onto the bus.

She reached the back seats but couldn't see Altan, and

she beat on the rear window with her fists, looking at the road behind curving away under the low, cracked sky. Behind her someone tutted under their breath, she heard exaggerated noises of professed sorrow. Hands reached for her. They had come aboard, but only to restrain her – each of the hands gripping her was weak on its own; forceful when combined. She cried and twisted but she was pulled down the aisle, dragged out of the door, leaving the bus to pull away with a wrenching feeling in Beyza's gut.

When the women let go of her their mouths were puckered as if someone had said a bad word. They were all sick of this foreign woman, and didn't know how she had ended up in their town. Where had she come from? They were sick of things like this happening. After all, didn't everyone know that damned kid of hers wasn't *ever* coming back?

Released, it was all Beyza could do to keep from falling. She could hear the school children telling their parents excited stories about their day, and the sound called to her. She tried to take a step towards it, but she was unsteady on her feet and went sideways. "Just go," one of the other mothers said, angry and defensive. Beyza felt compelled to, and in the direction the woman had pointed, like she had been banished or moved on by the gesture. And so it wasn't Beyza's fault that she ended up outside the gates of a park devoid of children – it was their crude symbolism, not hers. She had played with Altan in this park over the summer, running around so much like a child herself that the other adults had stared.

Now it looked barren and empty, the grass bent and muddied, the trees gaunt. There was nowhere to hide; Beyza could tell at a glance Altan wasn't there.

She dusted herself down, tried to make herself look presentable. Her panic subsided somewhat, and she was able to stick to her rule about thinking only in English. *Of course* Altan wouldn't have been on that bus, for why would she sign a release form to let him do such a thing? You had to do that, in England, so that later you couldn't sue if the 'adventure' trip turned real – Altan bloody and crooked, Altan hugging a bright red wound in his belly, Altan shot through by another boy's arrow. She remembered the pink slip he had brought home, the way he had pleaded to be allowed to join in, but she would never have signed him up for such things! So where was he? Would he have had to go into school anyway, to sit in front of one bored teacher? Or would they have let him stay home for the day? She couldn't work it out. But the school was nearest.

It was also on the other side of the park, so Beyza cut through. In the centre was a large Victorian house, with two wings and a view of the duck-less duck pond. A blue plaque on its side told someone important had died or been born or worked there. Beyza had never heard of him; she must remember to ask someone. The house was owned by the town council now, and it intimidated her somewhat so she gave it a wide berth, taking the path which led through the gardens. Nothing was in bloom, the vegetation colourless and stunted. A man in a flat cap with his sleeves rolled up was raking some of the flower beds, and Beyza smiled as she walked past. "Keep off the grass," the man muttered, although she was on the gravel path and hadn't strayed. His quick glance up at her contained both mistrust and lecherousness, and she hurried on. His instinctive feeling that she was a wrongdoer made her feel guilty, despite her new name, new home.

The sky was now being divided down the middle by a rash of darker clouds, and it felt oppressive and close as she hurried from the park. The school was at the centre of the town, near the old railway cottages, the Conservative club, and a church with a tower but no spire: militant-looking, with its battlements and commanding views. She was fascinated by the fact that in England something so old had survived and was still used for its original purpose. All the English history she had read (and which Altan was no doubt being taught), the deaths of Kings, the wars and inventions and outbreaks of rebellion seemed unimportant, unreal even, when compared to the fact that people had prayed to the same god in this church throughout it all. Feared the same hell.

The school, in the church's literal shadow, was appropriately enough a C of E school. Another "multi-faith school" (by which they meant, faithless) was available for the poorer kids. She didn't know why Altan hadn't been sent there. She supposed the woman's group had swung her some kind of favour, for the C of E school was undoubtedly a *better* school. All the townspeople knew this without having to read any government league tables, even the children knew; those who went to the multi-faith knew some doors had already been closed in their futures.

The redbrick school was another building that unsettled Beyza: its smug sense of superiority perhaps, the old dates of its conception inscribed in its architecture. It didn't need any blue plaque to prove it had history, had Tradition. A Latin motto she couldn't comprehend was carved above the entrance – at least she assumed so, wasn't 'Albion' Latin? There was also a sign saying *All Visitors Must Report To Reception* and she knew she should obey the rules.

The receptionist looked at Beyza with the distaste of recollection, her smile kept its form but lost its warmth. Her eyes were cold and suspicious behind bifocal glasses. Despite the weather outside the air conditioning was on, and Beyza felt her skin prickle with cold, felt her nose start to itch. The English always looked at you with disgust if you sneezed and it wasn't the dead of winter, she thought. She said hello to the receptionist nervously, not sure what it was she intended to say. The receptionist turned back to her computer, pretending she had some important click of the mouse that she absolutely *had* to make before she could attend to Beyza. When she looked back, she had that air of assumed superiority that even petty positions of power seemed to grant in this country, and Beyza found that she couldn't remember Altan's name; not his *real* name (which she must never say aloud), not 'Altan' as she had to think of him now, but his (and her) assumed surname – Altan *what*? It was like the receptionist had wiped it from her mind, in order to prove right her unspoken assertion that Beyza shouldn't be present. Beyza tried to think back to when the police had first told her their new identities, but the memory was hazy, as if something else had been happening simultaneously.

"Well?" the receptionist said frostily; and Beyza saw she had a devil in her eyes.

Lots of people got the devil in their eyes, Beyza knew; and she knew here, in this damp and grey land, the devils were different from the hot, fiery demons of her own country. *Here* they were cold, malicious beings – unmasked she imagined them as no bigger than imps, snide and officious monsters who could chill your blood, freeze your heart. Their irises would be grey, their sclera the dull white of old paperwork, as would the blunt claws which sprang from their ink-stained hands. Now Beyza knew she must show no fear, or let her detection of the demon be noticeable.

"Altan?" she said, her voice cracking over the half-name.

The demon smiled. "Now we've been through this before," it said.

Beyza felt herself nodding in agreement, felt her skin prickle with the chill of déjà-vu. But she mustn't fall for the devil tricks of this lady; the school didn't organise adventure trips every day did it? She was sure of that.

"The day out today," she said, staring the receptionist right in the eye to impress on her the fact that she wasn't fooled, she knew what day it was. "Where are the children who stayed behind?"

"The years that didn't go?" the receptionist said, not in the least perturbed. "In their last class of the day of course."

"Not the other years," Beyza said, "the ones who didn't have permission to go. From their mothers."

The receptionist paused, but not out of confusion, only to emphasise her next words. The cold little demon in her eyes danced in a blue flame. "That all went," it said, "and they all came back; they all had permission."

They all came back, Beyza thought – why would the demon say *that*? It was nothing this receptionist could possibly know. But was it a foolish move, or one that she simply didn't understand? The blue-rinsed creature guarding the entrance to the school smiled at her, and Beyza felt very tired. She looked around seeking inspiration, another place than this one, but the blunt reality of school's foyer remained, with its list of past Headmasters and their dates of service, a notice board crammed full of memos, Harvest Festival pictures, and important dates. She remembered giving Altan some tinned food to take in for Harvest Festival, but she remembered also how she hadn't been able to explain *why* he had to take the food to school. *They* hadn't explained of course, they'd taken it as read that everyone knew; and her face had reddened as Altan had struggled to comprehend.

"Anything else?" the receptionist said testily.

Standing as she was, the periphery of Beyza's vision caught the entranceway. Where there was a sudden colour, a flash of bright red.

It was the colour more than the movement that caught Beyza's eye, and she jerked around, saw the quick retreat of the creature that had peered round the doorway. *Altan!* she thought – Altan had seen the bright red anorak in a shop one day, and although she'd suspected it was not the sort of thing the other boys at that school would wear, he had been so taken with the colour that she'd not voiced her fears. It had been a pretty colour, distinct and out of place in the high street store. And now she saw this exact same shade in her after-vision, blinking her eyes as if she'd seen something from a brighter reality overlaid on this one.

The receptionist was still attempting polite sarcasm, trying to distract her. Without saying anything Beyza turned away, thinking that in this chilly place the colour of flame should signify the opposite of hell. But outside was the same dismal, monochrome day. Which made the glimpse of red – running down the side of the road and darting down an alleyway – more distinctive, more of an impossible thing.

Impossible, but true – Beyza called Altan's name again, and ran after him.

❖

Beyza wondered when the devils had wormed their way into her life, splitting it in two. Had it started in that bar in her own country, where she had met the man who would bring her to England as his wife? (She refused to even think his name, now). He had said he was important in England, but then they had all said that, in that bar. It was known as one of the places foreign men went to meet local girls: the men all said they were rich and important and looking for a wife, and the girls all said they were young and childless. Except Beyza, although that hadn't been her name then. She told them up front about her eight-year-old son. If she was lucky they'd still buy her a drink before they moved on. But this man bought her more than one, and it had turned out he really was important, turned out he was the one in a hundred who really did want a wife. Or so she'd thought.

He was so important that, after what he did, the only way Beyza had agreed to testify was with police protection. A new life. She'd realised by then he wasn't the only devil in England, despite its chill and drizzle. The police had fallen over themselves to comply; they'd bagged a big fish and didn't want anything to go wrong at the trial. They contacted a woman's charity to help with her relocation, gave her a new name. Very white. Like the bandages over her wounds.

She was pulled from the court in raging tears before she'd halfway explained to everyone what had *really* happened that night of spilt blood, of split skies. But regardless, in the end the jury couldn't have been more eager to send the bastard down. Her man. Whom she had told she had a son, and who had stayed with her in that bar, and not even tried to fuck her. Who had asked to see her son before he brought both of them to his house.

After the verdict, which didn't make sense (he'd had a devil inside of him but he hadn't done *that*) the embarrassed police rushed her down south as quickly as they could, to some quaint town she'd never heard of. The woman's group had set her up with a cleaning job and a one bedroom flat on the cheaper side of town.

The first night she'd held Altan tightly and told him not to be afraid.

❖

Beyza pursued Altan down the alley, calling out his name. The figure continued to run away from her, and all she could see was his back. But it was definitely him – if that red coat wasn't distinct enough his thick hair was, curly, unruly, a deep black colour that seemed tinted by a hotter sun than this. *Why was he running?* she thought, *was he scared of something, was he being bullied at school?* The idea made her thoughts slow, indolent with a fiery resentment. She would allow no one to hurt Altan.

The alley cut through the centre of the small town, parallel with one of the main streets, crosswise over the other. It led behind the back of the tea room, and the local King's Head – from the other side of the wall Beyza could hear braying laughter, as if there were unseen spectators to her flight. Despite the weather she felt hot as she ran – the fleeing figure had her at full pace and she still wasn't gaining. The warmth and the sweat made her feel like she was really running in a hotter and more homely place. As if her surroundings were just a vision she could shake off with exercise. But they refused to fade. Birds lined the top of the alley wall, dulled from the dirty sky in which they'd flown, watching her, shuffling uneasily but refusing to take off. Their eyes were bright and predatory. Litter lay underfoot and graffiti was sprayed on the alley walls – nice, middle-class graffiti, spelt correctly and avoiding pictures of copulation. People marking their territory, and indicating those they wished to make feel unwelcome... She thought she saw a swastika in her rush, but wasn't sure. The townspeople barely used this alley, she realised, as if it were part of a reality they couldn't see. And yet it cut right through the centre of town, with its revealed and racist secrets which none of the town council's budget was spent on removing; which none of the irritable letters to the local newspaper complained about or even mentioned.

Altan burst out of the alley, and when Beyza followed the sudden sunlight was like she'd crossed some kind of divide. She was on the main street, near the deli and opposite the Christian Aid shop. An old gentleman, dressed up in a suit (and you could tell that he always made the effort) held the door open for an equally old and well-dressed lady. The sunlight came down through the rents in the sky, it gleamed around the church tower in the distance and Beyza had to shut her eyes. The afterimages she saw were the red of Altan's coat; the blues and greys of the town's graffiti. Both seemed like the pollutions of her own eyes – but no, there was Altan on the other side of the street. Beyza dashed across the narrow cobbled road after him.

There was the squeal of brakes – *but it's pedestrian only*, Beyza thought, outraged. This outrage was not at the driver exactly, but at the fact that yet again when she'd thought she'd known the rules she'd got them wrong.

She looked to her left, ready to curse, and saw it was a police car which had almost hit her – did the law have special dispensation, to drive up this street? Beyza felt uneasy; she might be the wrongdoer after all. But the policeman didn't get out of his car, merely shook his head angrily, gestured her away. Her legs shook as she obeyed. People were watching her; she could sense that sly English half-look that *pretended* to be getting on with its own business. Not that she cared about them at that moment. She looked up and down the street, saw only people in brown duffle coats, slick wax jackets. She started to run again, but aimlessly and too late. She had lost him.

She didn't call out for Altan, for the policeman was still eyeing her as he drove by. Not blinking. The street she had found herself on was one of the busiest in the town, its old buildings misaligned and not quite true. An uneven cobbled road that made your vision jerk as you walked it, although the locals strode it confidently enough. Beyza had already drawn attention to herself, and she now wished to remain unobtrusive, so that the eyes of the town grew bored, were distracted by something more unusual and worthy of censure than her actions. Because the street was pedestrian-only (or so she had thought) there were benches on which to sit, and Beyza did so. Breathless. The afterimages in her vision were so red they bled back into the town when she opened her eyes. She tried to calm down, to think of nothing. She watched a hanging sign swaying on the wall of a tea-shop opposite, and she wondered how it moved with no wind. Maybe it was flimsy, cardboard not wood; maybe what was around her was the falsity of a movie set. And there was something unreal about the way each of these shops occupied the ground floor of the old, black-timbered buildings.

Beyza felt her hands shaking, mocking her pretence of calm, a nagging reminder of Altan's vanishing act. Her hands were cold, fingertips numb, and she couldn't help but pinch at them for the short nips of heat – each hand in turn trying to warm its sister. *How can they live like this?*

she thought. *How can I?* She knew there was something wrong with her thoughts and memories; had been all day. Had been ever since. She felt clouded with a barren despair, with a feeling of maternal failure. Nothing around her felt like home, and she had tried so hard to make it feel so. For both of them. She knew it *was* real, knew this grey sky and cobbled street, the easy integration of age-old tradition and genteel consumerism was a reality as strong as her homeland's – but it wasn't one in which Beyza could feel real, in which the right action or words could come to her without a tiring effort. She was tired now, and irritable, and each of the people passing by was an annoyance to her: the young couple at the estate-agent's window, the mothers stood side by side with identical pushchairs, blocking the pavement as they chatted, the two school-kids coming out of the sweetshop wearing uniforms like costumes from black and white films. She had been feeling such annoyance more and more recently. The smug-looking old man in his blazer and tie – *why so smug*, she thought, *when underneath you're exactly the kind of person who travelled to my country to find girls to fuck?* But her home seemed a long way from where she was now; the route between the two places not quite clear. Not quite right.

I can't stay here, Beyza thought, *it's too much*. Her thoughts seemed to hover between her two languages, incomprehensible to either tongue alone. She decided she would head back to the flat – maybe that was where Altan had gone. He was a good boy. Her flat was in the one poor part of this rich town; the one estate they tolerated (for their cleaners came from there) but never mentioned. Beyza's head felt light as she stood, and she stumbled, like someone just stepped out into unexpected bad weather. In doing so she delayed for a second the progress of an elderly shopper – and this old lady, grandmother and one-time local councillor no doubt, gave her a look of absolute *hate*, her eyes cold and mocking, knowing in a glance that Beyza was a stranger.

It's in the eyes, it's all in the eyes, Beyza thought as she hurried home; *all the devilment is in their eyes*.

❖

The England her man had brought her to had seemed, at street-level, as colourful as home. The neon and the fluorescent had tricked her, dazzling colours of hot gas, flickering between existence and non-existence against a sable sky.

For having got the two of them into his house her new husband seemed to want to flee it every evening. His money had meant babysitters for Altan were no problem. She hadn't known what he'd been fleeing from, had assumed it was maybe just his own age. The bars he'd taken her to had seemed continuations of the one she had met him in. Filled with the same girls; she didn't know why he'd had to come to her country. But she'd tried not to question it too much.

Maybe, she'd thought, he regretted picking a wife with a child. Maybe he regretted it anyway, for when he'd finally made love to her it had been stilted, like an English conversation. Afterwards, he whispered words that he later amplified into "I love you" and although Beyza didn't believe him, she'd felt gratified by his lies.

Her own feelings had been equally ambiguous. He had offered her warmth and security, and she'd needed that – for her son as much as for herself. Maybe her lack of honest attraction, her business-like and almost cynical capitulation into the relationship had been the chink through which the devil had entered? She didn't know, when it came to English devils.

There had been no prelude, no forewarning. But one day when she had been coming back from buying some new clothes, Beyza had felt something that seemed to rip through the air. When she'd looked up the clouds had made strange rents in the sky, bifurcating it.

The nanny was off sick, but he'd stayed at home with Altan so that she could still go out. He'd been spending more time with the boy recently. Making an effort; and she'd been able to tell it was an effort, for whenever she returned, his face had been strained and he'd been quieter than normal.

The door had been open when she'd got back to the house, sucking in the cold British air. It was no warning for her, no hot and fiery presentiment in her belly. She went inside, shut the door behind her. There had been a chill in the living room, and neither her boy nor her man were there, which was unusual. The house was very quiet, which was unusual too. No taps running, no TV, no clattering from the kitchen, no noise of electronic children's toys.

Something guided her upstairs; and something kept her footfalls cautious too. She carefully pushed open the door to Altan's bedroom. And her gut clenched around a ball of ice.

After that, she'd told the police, things had been unclear. She remembered Altan, sprawled on the floor, actually *under* the bed, and peering out at her. He pressed his finger to his lips, tried telepathy with the frantic movements of his eyes and the gestures of his small hands. (But no, not Altan, that was what she had to call him *after*.) There was a funny smell too, like meat left out. Beyza didn't know why she didn't rush to him, crawl under the bed with him perhaps, whisper in their own tongue in that secret place about what was happening.

But she didn't; she looked around the room, looking for anything abnormal. It was like she was seeing the room twice, for it seemed simultaneously mundane and aslant in her vision.

Altan retreated further under the bed, gone from sight.

She called out the name of her man, and he came. As if summoned. He didn't reply or call back, just appeared silently behind her; his shadow fell over her and she turned around and faced a devil.

Not that she'd realised at first, for he still looked the same – there was no hint of that fiery unpredictability of demons, none of their hot and bright capering, the inferno behind the eyes. Even the steel of the knife hung impotently in his hand glinted but dully. Her first thought was he'd come from the kitchen making stew, but the knife was murky with more than supermarket meat. And his eyes – there was something in them after all, Beyza realised, something iced over and glinting with irony. Her man smelt not of brimstone but of the off-meat smell, as if the devilry and butchery were all behind and this was already the dull aftermath; something his limp and sated air reinforced – he seemed to be waiting for her to speak, to react to something she hadn't yet seen.

Devils – she knew from the past that it was always better to let their tempestuous and impatient natures make *them* act first – but was this the case, here, with this thing? It was undoubtedly different. And besides she didn't have that luxury, she had to stop it entering the room and finding Altan.

She took a step forwards, and the knife in the devil's hand raised a proportionate amount. She froze, looked in its eyes, looked at the bloodshot whites, the cold and dull irises. It was daring her forward she realised, she was doing what the devil wanted. But behind her! She must get it away from this room, in which Altan was hidden. She cautiously took another step; the knife moved further upwards – one more step and it would be against her belly. But the thing was confused, its red-rimmed eyes looked for the source of her strength, her unseen ally that made her so bold. Love and the higher emotions always baffled them; she had to be quick, so that it didn't work it out. She took another step, felt the point of the knife press into but not puncture her belly. She could feel the coldness, the weight behind it. She looked her man in the face, smelt the whisky on his breath. She was looking for his old self, for his habitual pretence of love. There might have been something she recognised... Any other time she would have taken the risk of reaching him with their love-words, their shared memories, but not with her boy to save. She felt a rush of terrified love for Altan as she pictured him curled under the bed, as if around a wound.

She had to get him away from her son. She looked at the point of the knife against her stomach, and back up. The devil looked her in the eyes and *dared* her.

She took another step forward.

The hand holding the knife slackened in surprise; but only partially, and the wound she pressed herself into was cold, the heat of the blood escaping from her not even registering against the chill. But it worked – the instincts the devil couldn't entirely keep down took over and her man took a step backwards. Despite the pain it caused her she took another step forward, and he retreated one more backwards. The knife fell from his hand with a clatter, and her eyes followed it, as if wanting something... but this was another hazy moment, as if the devil was in the knife itself, and one she hadn't mentioned to the police. And they had only found his prints on it, so she couldn't have picked it up.

He half-fell against the wall, eyes staring at nothing, then slumped slowly down to a sitting position, a puppet with its strings tangled by a clumsy hand. The pain of her wound deepened; the haziness from lost blood was coming on. But she knew she had to keep focused until both she and Altan were out the building. Her husband started moaning and crawling across the lounge floor away from her, as if he were the injured one. Back – she'd gone back into the bedroom, peered under the bed and felt a moment's panic that she'd lost him; but Altan, the boy who would become Altan, was already behind her. She took his hand; she knew she had to keep him safe for the demons took many guises, and could reappear at any time. Her thoughts were vague, detached from the scene they were fleeing – her thoughts were on the things she had seen at home, their hot and fiery manifestations in people, and how all things were different when you were in a foreign land, even your devils.

The sky still looked torn apart outside, and Beyza and Altan were running right underneath where it had split in two.

❖

Altan wasn't back at the flat. The dying of hope she felt at this was distant, at one remove. The flat was a bedsit really, just one bed... Her thoughts groped for something; lost it. Beyza peered under the bed; Altan wasn't there. As she straightened, she felt the pulse of her old stab wound.

Her bedsit wasn't small enough for Altan to hide in, but all around was the suggestion of his presence – his satchel, his crayons, and yes, hanging up was the bright red coat she remembered buying him – so he *had* been back. There was no need to feel the doubt she had been feeling. Calmer, she opened her freezer, which was full of ready-meals. While she was waiting for the microwave to complete its twelve minutes she read the paper – she always bought the most popular, the most *English*, of the tabloids. There wasn't a week went by when the Union Jack didn't appear somewhere on the front page, or the England flag on the back. She studied it daily, and it revealed more of the English than all of her dictionaries and guidebooks had back home. The news may not all have been objective or even accurate, but the slants and biases gave her an insight into the psychology of this, her new homeland. Every time she came across a phrase that was new to her or hard to pronounce, Beyza said it out-loud: "a traditional Victorian Christmas"; "fight fire with fire"; "benefit cheats"; "stuff it to the Aussies"; "cheap labour costs…"

The microwave did its stuff, and the resulting meal was so sloppy she needed a spoon to eat it. Rummaging in the cutlery drawer for one, she felt a sharp pain; pulling her hand out quickly she saw a deep cut on the pad of her forefinger. For a few seconds it didn't bleed and she saw the pinkish inner flesh; then it filled red and leaked, a trickle of blood turned to a steady stream. Swearing in her own tongue, she stuck the finger in her mouth and sucked at her blood. She pulled the drawer further open to see what had cut her, and saw the dull blade of the kitchen knife.

Her mind faltered, as two times came together – but that was police evidence, what could it be doing here? Had she bought another *identical* one, even with the memories associated with it? Impossible! But then how…

Why do you expect to be able to work it out, a chill voice in her mind said, *when you know some of your memories are of things that didn't happen*? Or hadn't happened *here*, this side of the torn sky. The wound in her finger felt cold as it throbbed, and in tandem the scar from where she had been stabbed throbbed too, not the dull ache of an old wound, but a fresh pain. Beyza shut her eyes, thought of demons in hell inflicting the same wounds over and over again.

My name is Beyza, she said in her head, and his name is Altan. My name is Beyza and his Altan.

But then it is my knife, she reasoned. After the trial, surely the police return evidence, if it's *yours?* All the English police shows she'd watched were no help in proving this, and she couldn't work it through on her own. But wherever the wretched knife had come from, it was too dangerous to leave lying in wait in dark drawers: Altan might cut himself. Beyza picked up the blade by the handle, felt its balance and deceptive lightness in her hand for a few seconds, and then put it safely in the inner pocket of her coat.

❖

The wounded sky was healed by darkness overnight, before it pulled back like a bandage undone to reveal the same scars as before. Beyza woke up and called out Altan's name. He wasn't in the bedsit – but his red anorak had gone. He'd come home then, slept and left without disturbing his mother. That was the type of kindly boy he was. Nevertheless, Beyza dressed quickly and hurried out the house to find him.

There was no little red figure leading her on this time, but she still felt drawn on the same tour as before, through all those parts of the town in their own scenic time-warps: the tidy park, the quaint market, the cobbled streets; those places Beyza found hard to think of as real, whose fakery she was now starting to think of as malicious, jeering. *My name is Beyza and his Altan*, she thought to herself each time the church bells rang the hour, their chimes a brash crowing. The bells seemed to be counting down to something. *My name is Beyza and his Altan*. Who had come up with such names?

She felt feverish and weighed down, for she was wearing a heavy coat and scarf because the grey skies of this country always made her think it would be cold; but it wasn't, it was hot and clammy. Everyone else seemed comfortable, they had read the signs correctly, they were adapted to this blue-plaque town. But she never would be – she knew that now. She called out Altan's name in the streets, drawing strange glances from the locals, who just heard the foreign syllables and didn't even know it was the name of her precious boy. She wished she could do something to wipe that knowing look from their faces – that *English* look.

She saw no devils, or she saw them everywhere – she wasn't sure.

Eventually, she emerged from the alleyway that bisected the centre of the town, with its hate-speak and smell of piss, and found herself near the school. The jeering church bells struck four, as if she'd subconsciously timed it so that she'd arrive at the hour when the children left for home. Why had she spent the whole day ignoring the one place Altan was most likely to be until now? The same crowd of mothers stood waiting for their brood outside the school gates, and she saw the cold and naked mistrust in their eyes, before polite smiles hid their real selves. Again, Beyza felt that everything in this town was two-faced. The townswomen didn't bother to hide from Beyza that she was the subject of their talk: her mysterious origins, her dreadfully *inappropriate* behaviour yesterday.

The school bell rang (minutes behind the church) and children tumbled out the front entrance, running and stumbling in a great mass. And *yes*, she saw the bright red figure, running towards her, like a glimpse of another, a *better* reality, which had the tang of the real compared to this chill and grey coloured town...

But not quite, he wasn't quite running towards *her*, had he not seen her? She called out his names, but he ignored her, and ran straight into the arms of another woman.

Beyza's vision became blurred with red afterimages, like blood.

"Altan!" this mother cried in greeting, making it sound as English as any other name in this twenty-first century England. Beyza saw Altan's face for the first time in what felt like months, and it wasn't like she remembered it – she felt a sharp pain in her side when she saw how white it was, how light his brown hair had become, how cold was the laughter in his eyes. When he spoke to the woman who was his mother, it was without accent.

What have they done to him, Beyza thought – *they are all devils*. The chill she felt was as if her entire body was still and cold.

She looked up. But which side of this cold and devil-split sky was she beneath? The side where she'd saved Altan or the side where – but she wouldn't think of that. She wouldn't think in that language, for all it had once been hers.

She reached for the knife in her coat pocket; fire with fire, she thought, like the English say. The knife was damp and warm with her sweat; it felt *familiar* in her hands. It felt like home. She felt a hot and rising anger in her belly.

As if in response, the sky darkened as the clouds knitted together overhead, solidifying. There was *one* reality, not two – or she could make it so for a minute at least. Long enough that she could cross over.

Devils in hell, she thought again, inflicting the same torment over and...

But she pushed aside the chill of her déjà vu. She stepped forward, took her hand from her pocket. She would reclaim her son from these English, one way or another. Hadn't she done so before, when she'd returned to that bad house under a torn and foreign sky?

Her devil was with her again, and it was ablaze and righteous.

Mr Denning Sings
Simon Kurt Unsworth

Hymn number 29:
Like the Murmur of the Dove's Song

Mr Denning raises his voice in praise and worship.

It is his favourite part of the service, the hymns. He likes the fact he can be free, be unconstrained. In a life that he knows is as tightly wrapped around him as his collar and tie are tightly tied around his neck and in which there are few gaps or spaces, singing is his one great passion. He can feel the words, feel the tune and the love it contains, and in singing of his love he himself feels loved.

Every Sunday, Mr Denning comes to church. He has a ritual: he rises and dresses later than usual, at 8.00a.m., and allows himself the luxury of television as he eats his breakfast (two slices of granary bread, toasted with bitter marmalade) and drinks the two coffees he thinks it is reasonable to have in any one day. He always wears a shirt and tie and neat trousers, but rarely a jacket; church is formal but it is not work and he feels that a suit should be worn only for work or for weddings and funerals. In winter he also wears a jumper, because the church heating does not work well and the wind seems to find a myriad of ways to enter the building, but in spring and summer he goes in his shirtsleeves. He chooses ties that are also not work ones, slightly gaudier. He has one with gold stripes and one with a houndstooth check, both gifts from colleagues. His work ties are plain.

Mr Denning walks to church because the walk helps him clear his head from the detritus of the week, the work problems and the bills and the tiny inconveniences, because church is God, and God deserves his full and unswerving attention. He always sits in the same place – the third pew back and on the left side, under the wooden panel with the gold-painted names of the fallen of various wars – unless someone else has managed to sit there first, in which case he sits as close as he can. He likes to think, in his more whimsical moments, that his buttocks have made tiny grooves in the pew over the years, worn a shape of himself into the wood. In this way, he says to friends, he is leaving his mark... two marks, in fact.

The opening hymn isn't a favourite, but he sings anyway, giving it his all. It is modern, and he thinks it lacks the gravitas of some of his preferred older songs, but it is a good way to bring everyone together. It is one of his favourite things to do, to look around at the congregation, see them singing together. It is when they are the most joined, he thinks, when they are closest. Some people sing with their eyes closed, he knows, but he sings with his eyes open as wide as his mouth and his heart because likes to see, to watch. Sometimes he imagines he can almost see the tune forming in the air as people's breaths shiver the dust or condense in the cold, and it makes him feel a part of something larger than himself, larger than everything in his world, larger than the world itself. They are singing words that people all over the country are singing, were singing years ago and will sing years into the future. *We are singing a history and a present and a forthcoming*, Mr Denning thinks, and likes that he is a part of this thing, this community linked by word and note and belief.

Mr Denning sings and, in singing, Mr Denning worships.

Someone is coughing.

He hears it when they are about halfway through the opening hymn, a baritone rumble of someone trying to clear their throat. It lasts through the second verse and into the third and, although it is not loud exactly, it is curiously piercing considering how low a noise it is. Mr Denning peers around, trying to see who is making the noise but it is difficult to tell because, although it's not a celebration day, the church is quite full. Is it coming from the back of the church, from somewhere near the door? Behind the family with the three noisy children? He thinks that maybe yes, that the cougher is there, hidden behind the family.

The hymn comes to an end, slightly ragged, the organ wheezing to a breathy halt as the singing fades. That is another reason Mr Denning likes this church; it is old, the building thick dark stone, and it has a proper organ, one with pipes and stops that sounds like voices calling out when it's played. Mr Denning's church is church as it should be, solemn and devoted and with defined spaces of silence and noise.

The coughing comes to a stop just after the organ, emphasising the quiet. "Welcome, everyone," says Father Peter (Mr Denning refuses to think of him as Pastor Pete, despite the man's repeated exhortations to do so), beginning the service proper.

❖

Hymn number 146:
Holy! Holy! Holy! Lord God Almighty

Father Peter brings the opening prayers to an end and the congregation prepares to sing again. Mr Denning is as amused as ever to hear the usual shuffling of feet and the counterpoint rustle of hymn books opening and people fumbling for pages underlying the organ's opening notes. He always turns the book to the next hymn at the end of the previous one to be prepared, and doesn't understand why everyone didn't do the same thing. *That's people*, he supposes; contrary and disorganised and fallible and frustrating but mostly with little harm in them.

Two lines into the hymn, an older song and much more to Mr Denning's taste than the opening one, the cougher starts again. The sound is a diesel gurgle, starting hard at the beginning of each line and then trailing to little more than a ratchet grind before what sounds like a painful inhalation and it all starts again. It trudges through their voices, disrupting the hymn's elegant tune, and is extremely irritating. Mr Denning looks around again, but this time he is less sure where the sound is coming from because it seems to have shifted, still coming from behind him but slightly closer, as though the cougher has moved forward a few pews and slightly more into the church's central space. Still he cannot tell who is making the noise.

Mr Denning turns back to face the altar, uncomfortable at having turned his back on the holiest of places within the church, and equally uncomfortable with allowing himself to become distracted from the singing. In some way he can't quite articulate, not concentrating on the hymn feels as disrespectful to God as turning his back. The words and the notes need his full attention, his full commitment, otherwise the conversation he is trying to have with God will become one-sided, because why should God reply if Mr Denning isn't fully immersed in what is being said? He feels his shoulders tense, pull up, his chest tighten as the coughing carries on, as the coughing breaks apart the hymn and remakes it into something fractured and incomplete.

Mr Denning sings, and the cougher does not stop until the hymn is over.

❖

Hymn number 344:
I Will Sing of My Redeemer

Another old hymn, stately and grand, one that Mr Denning has sung only infrequently but that he likes. The author had died trying to rescue his wife from a train crash, Mr Denning remembers, and the words had been found in his papers after his death. It is a hymn that affirms faith, which is why Mr Denning likes it. He lifts his voice high, not really caring that he sometimes sings a little flat, that his musical ability is at best limited, because talent isn't the important thing, *being there* is the important thing.

And still, there is coughing.

It starts later this time, halfway through the refrain. Letting loose the opening verse of the song relaxes him and his chest opens, his shoulders dropping, and he is just beginning to find his equilibrium again, thinking that the problem, whatever it was, has resolved itself, when it comes crashing in with a noise like hoarse thunder. It practically drowns the first line before dropping away, phlegmy and wretched. It is louder now, more intrusive, but only Mr Denning seems bothered by it because when he turns to find the elusive cougher, he finds that he is the only one craning around and that everyone else is happily singing and facing the front. *How can they not be hearing it?* he thinks. It is so loud, so grinding, the noise of someone trying to clear their throat of a permanent blockage, choking around something swollen that is making their breathing wet and ragged. It conjures images in Mr Denning's mind of cancer wards, or things moist and swelling, of flesh that rebelled against itself and became discoloured and misshapen with bruising and pus. It is a noise surely being made by lungs that are no longer anything but stained black by cigarettes or other poisons, filled with mucus and slime. The coughs sound painful, raw and torn, and they fill the church and make the hymn something spoiled and bitter.

Mr Denning turns back around and tries to concentrate on the music, but that other noise fills his head with dank and slimy waves.

❖

Hymn number 357:
Oh Master Let Me Walk with Thee

The offertory hymns are Mr Denning's favourite part of the service.

They are sung as the collection plate is passed around, and whilst communion is taken, allowing people the time to reflect on the sermon and prayers and readings that they have just heard. Father Peter's service this morning is one of his better ones (he is sometimes be too metaphysical for Mr Denning's tastes, and sometimes interprets the Bible stories in ways that seem too modern and don't make enough moral sense, but this morning he had kept it simple and short), and the preparation of the wine and wafer is done with all necessary solemnity. As the first row of the congregation makes their way to take communion, the wardens helping the elderly and infirm, the organ starts up and the new hymn is launched onto the air. He is happy this Sunday, most of the choices (made by the organist, not by Father Peter, he knows) are older, and in their age they were less cheery and lightweight. Hymns, he thinks, should always be serious, a statement of the faith that underpins them.

Mr Denning opens his mouth to join in the singing, but before he can add his voice to that of his fellow worshippers, the coughing starts again.

His head whips around almost without instruction, his eyes scanning the crowd behind him. Who *is* it, this cougher? Can they not tell that their noise, unintentional though it may be, is causing a disturbance? Quite apart from the medical concerns it would raise in him, Mr Denning thinks that if he had a cough like that he would go outside, because to stay inside would be to draw the wrong kind of attention to himself. It would be embarrassing, surely, to be that loud, to sound that ill, to disturb everyone else's worship?

Only, no one else seems to be disturbed. They still sing without looking about themselves, without appearing to hear the sound. The offertory hymn is always calmer, more reflective and consequently quieter, so the coughing seems louder than ever, yet one else is reacting to it.

It sounds worse, somehow more ill, more decayed, as though the continual repetition has torn the lungs, making them into damp, torn strips, the air whistling from them through broken reeds. The cough has acquired an upper note now, a strained and breathy gasp that stutters at the edge of Mr Denning's hearing, a descant to the lower bass grumble. It sounds fevered, damaged and yet also, oddly, it sounds deliberate and makes Mr Denning think of gargoyles and imps, of carved stone glaring down at them, weathered and worn and cruel. It sounds gleeful and nasty.

It sounds closer.

This is beyond a joke, and it is spoiling Mr Denning's Sunday, the thing that gives his week structure. From Sunday, he feels, his whole week grows; he knows some people have their Saturday nights and their alcohol, or their dates and social media, that these have become the mainstays of the country he had grown up in but no longer really recognised, but they were not for him. Mr Denning has his week organised, and the highlight and the backbone of it is church on Sunday and the hymns he sings and the way the singing makes him feel.

Mr Denning looks at Father Peter and sings louder, and tries to ignore the wretched hacks that now accompany his every word.

❖

Hymn number 63:
Praise My Soul the God of Heaven

The collection and communion are taking a long time as the congregation is particularly large this week, and they go into a second offertory hymn. Ordinarily, this would make Mr Denning's day (especially as the congregation was large enough to hope that they actually make it into a third hymn), but now he is anxious.

How could nobody hear it? Why was no one else looking around? It sounds like a rusting set of ratchets turning and grinding, a string of guttural frictions that no longer have gaps between them. Mr Denning has a headache, his body is taut with frustration and it is the coughing, the *damned* coughing, and he is sorry for cursing even if it was only in his head and not actually uttered out loud, but he felt it was justified given the circumstances. It's getting even worse, which is terribly frustrating as this hymn is one of his favourites, a psalm set to music and given wings, and it feels as though someone is making it sordid, smearing it with something rank and sour. They are *spoiling* it.

Mr Denning actually turns, not just his head but his whole body, ignoring the looks from the people about him in the pews. He is not an especially tall man so he bounces up onto his tiptoes, the squeak and creak of his leather shoes near-inaudible under the singing and the awful, awful coughing. It has moved again, the centre of the sound now seeming to come from the block of pews he was in, and closer too, as though the cougher had jumped forward and over, but he still can't see them.

There! Was that someone bobbing down between Mrs Hargreaves and her husband (whose hand, Mr Denning suddenly recalls, is always wet when they shake during the Peace, wet and cold and slimy), a shadowed figure with its mouth open and its eyes wide?

It isn't even covering its mouth as it coughs, and Mr Denning has a vivid image of millions and millions of microscopic germs floating out on little puffed exhalations of sputum and disease, of them drifting up and then settling, coating everyone in the church like dust or light rain.

Or dandruff. Mr Denning reaches up and brushes his hair and shoulders, hoping to clear it away, and then stops, realising he is being silly. People are looking at him openly now, ignoring the hacking, ripping coughs and staring instead at him, as though he was doing something wrong, as though he was disrupting the service.

He turns back to face father Peter, *Pastor Pete*, who is

still going solemnly along the line of kneeling figures at the altar rail, either blessing or handing out the wafer. The line of those who haven't been done yet is still quite long, and Mr Denning realises that his own row has not yet been called.

They would definitely be going into a third Offertory hymn, and for the first time in as long as he could remember, Mr Denning doesn't want to sing.

❖

Hymn number 582:
Guide Me, O Thou Great Jehovah

There is a brief respite as the previous hymn comes to an end and the organist shuffles his sheet music about, and then the new hymn starts. It is another one that Mr Denning normally enjoyed, and certainly the rest of the congregation appear to like it given the volume that they're singing at and the passion they put into it, but as soon as the first word forms in the air, it starts again.

It's not even really coughing any more, more like a long bubbling string of noise, and it's coming not from behind him but alongside, from somewhere on the pew he occupied. Mr Denning turns and leans, trying to see past his fellow worshippers, but Mr Cottle's enormous belly is pressing into the back of the pew in front and blocking his view.

Is that the same figure, still bobbing low, at the end of the pew? Seeming to hide behind Mrs Cottle? *Because*, Mr Denning thought, *let's face it, there's enough of Mrs Cottle to hide behind*, before realising how rude he had just been, even in the privacy of his own head, and being shocked at his rudeness. *It's this coughing*, he thinks, *it's putting me on edge. It's upsetting me.*

It's scaring me.

Now why had he thought that? Surely he's not scared? It's just coughing, someone like Major Hardesty with bad lungs, moving around the church trying to find a place to sit, it's just noise, it's nothing to be scared of.

The cough is ahead of him now, in one of the front pews, and Mr Denning can almost see the person making the sound now, even though they're continually moving, slipping along the row in front of the singers, still putting barriers between Mr Denning and themselves. Whoever they are, they're small, and dark, apelike and hairy.

Hairy? No, surely not, but yes, apelike and hairy and *naked*, coughing and coughing, spraying their sickness into the church, into the *hymns* and suddenly Mr Denning can't stand it but he is trapped, hemmed in by the people around him and the fact that this is church and he can't make a scene but he wants to run, to run and scream but not cough, never cough, and now one of the wardens is at the end of the pew, indicating that they should go for communion. Mr Denning stops singing, places his hymn book (open, of course, to the next hymn) in the rack on the back of the pew in front, walks with the Cottles and the others in his row out into the main aisle and waits. The hymn carries on around him but the coughing has stopped, and when he gets alongside the rows in front and looks down them, there is no figure there, hairy and naked or otherwise.

The wafer is dry and catches in Mr Denning's throat,

but he refuses to cough, merely waiting for the wine to wash it down.

❖

Hymn number 610:
On Jordan's Stormy Banks I Stand

Father Peter brings the service to its end and Mr Denning breathes a sigh of relief. Through the final prayers and the dismissal there had been no noises that there should not have been, no coughs or splutters, not even a sneeze or throat clearing. *Everything*, he thinks, *is tickety boo*.

Until Father Peter announces the final hymn.

Mr Denning had forgotten, so happy was he that this was coming to an end, that there was a last chance to raise their voices to God, and even as the congregation start to sing what was usually Mr Denning's favourite moment of the whole service, the coughing starts again.

Only, it's not like coughing any more, it's like breathing, the soured breath of some hoarse and ragged thing, some godless abomination, wheezing and huffing as it takes in clean air and breathes out filth. Mr Denning keeps his eyes fixed on Father Peter as the priest leads the singing, his voice slightly flattened by the cheap amplification the church uses, and does not look about him.

Specifically, he doesn't look next to him and low, where the coughing, breathing sound is now coming from.

It's right by his side, at his elbow, so loud that it's almost a physical presence in itself. He doesn't look around, staring straight ahead, ignoring the feeling of dampness that fills the air, dampness and a fevered warmth and a smell of dirt and rottenness and oh God, what is happening to him? What has he done to deserve this? He is a good man, he *tries* to be a good man, and this is his one pleasure, these moments of song in the church of his faith, his weekly highpoint and it was being taken from him, and by what?

Nothing. There's nothing there.

But there is something there, because try as he might he cannot help but see the gibbering, gambolling thing in his peripheral vision, only now it's not low, now it's scampering up the pillar next to Mr Denning so that it is above him, implike, its head lower than its rump, and he knows its face is just by his and that it is staring at him and grinning and grinning and grinning. He will not turn, he will not look.

It coughs, and a cloud of warmth envelops his head for a moment. The cough is terrible, lodging in his ear like a worm, and he cannot help but turn because he cannot go on like this, he has to know, he has to understand. Mr Denning looks at the thing at his side as it grins wide, showing blackened stump teeth and a mouth that is dark and fetid and just by Mr Denning's own, and it coughs and it coughs and it coughs.

He Waits on the Upland
Adam Millard

Graham stared out at the dusky fields from the kitchen window, his hands wrapped around a mug of hot tea. Behind him, Jenny prepared a light breakfast of toast and crumpets at the grill. It never ceased to amaze him how noisy his wife was – by now, after thirty years of relatively miserable marriage, he should be accustomed to her incessant clattering and crashing around the house, her propensity to shower in the middle of the night, her somnambulism and the effects thereof, and yet every tap, every knock and rattle she made set his teeth on edge. In fact, every single clamour she made seemed to be complimented by a dozen more, equally as infuriating sounds. Even her voice – a shrill whine that couldn't have always been so irritating – drove him to the edge of madness. Much of the time he bit his lip, kept his vexation to himself where it would fester and eventually wane until it no longer seemed of import. And then she would make another noise, and the urge to murder her where she stood would return once again. Round and round we go.

"Do you have to make so much bloody noise?" Graham said, wincing as Jenny bothered the cutlery drawer with her arthritic hands. He continued to stare out to the fields, awaiting the rising sun like a man who had yet to see one.

"There's something jamming the drawer," Jenny said as she continued to yank on the thing as if it had wronged her during the night. Within, forks and knives and wooden spoons danced around, leaping from tray compartment to tray compartment, and still the drawer remained stuck.

I could get away with it, Graham thought. *I could do it right now. One swift clout to the back of the head. She'd be buried deep beneath the tractor shed by lunchtime.* Though the notion appealed to him in that moment, as she noisily fretted over the seemingly immovable drawer, he knew he could never kill his wife. Companionship was hard to find, made even more difficult if you were a farmer of dubious repute, and Saddler's Green was hardly teeming with willing replacements for Jenny. No, he would bite his lip, count to ten, round and round we go.

"Let *me* do it," Graham said, turning and slamming his mug down on the oak table so hard that the tea sloshed up over the rim, staining the wood almost as soon as it came back down. He marched across the kitchen to where his wife had relented and stepped away from the recalcitrant drawer. "You put too many damn things in these drawers," he moaned. "It's no wonder they stick."

"It's the scissors," Jenny said, somewhat faintly. "They're always getting stuck."

"Then why don't you find a new home for them?" It made perfect sense to Graham. How the thought hadn't occurred to his wife, if such things were becoming commonplace, was beyond him. But that was the thing with Jenny. She was absent common sense, content to let Graham do much of the thinking and then wonder why he was so irate when things went awry.

Groaning gutturally, more in anger than as a result of the laborious freeing of the drawer, Graham wondered how many years of Jenny's nonsense he would have to endure, for even though he could never strangle her himself or press a pillow into her face as she snored – *noisily*, of course – and dreamed in bed at night, a nice death by natural causes would be welcomed enormously.

The drawer gave an inch, and then another, enough for Graham to slip an open-palmed hand in to remove the obstruction. "There!" he said, straightening up and ignoring the terrible crack his back made as he did so.

Jenny leaned in and kissed him upon the temple – as she was wont to do whenever Graham proved himself useful – and it was all Graham could do to keep the grimace from his face. Breathless, he made his way back to the mug of tea and the dawn beyond the window. The day had gotten off to an unfortunate start. Graham just hoped that things quickly improved, lest he spend the rest of it in the stables, insensible on whisky and wishing for a better lot in life.

❖

Pleasant drizzle came down upon Graham as he descended the hillock toward the sheep fold. He had calmed somewhat since leaving the house; breakfast had been pleasant but hastened. He had waited for sufficient light before announcing his departure, and Jenny had informed him of her intended visit to the nearby village of Lacock, where she planned to pilfer the charity shops for knick-knacks of varying worthlessness until her purse was empty and her legs were no longer compliant.

So long as she's out my way for the day, Graham had unceremoniously thought as she'd climbed into her grey mackintosh. He had left her searching for an umbrella before she had had the audacity to ask him to help locate the damn thing.

A blackbird, tugging a worm from the rain-softened earth, seemed to watch Graham as he descended the mound. Its song – a congenial chirrup – ceased as Graham neared, and then it turned into a rather hostile *dik-dik-dik*. The noise, for some reason or other, reminded Graham of Jenny and the constant hullabaloo which accompanied her wherever she went. And then a ridiculous notion presented itself to Graham: what if the blackbird was not a blackbird at all? What if it was Jenny – his wife of *thirty* miserable years – who had somehow managed to conceal her ability to transform into wild animals and was now watching him when she should have been on her way to the village to spend his hard-earned money? It should, of course, come as no surprise to Graham that she should choose to rework her appearance so that she could continue to make as much bloody noise as humanly – or *inhumanly*, as the case may be – possible.

The blackbird waited until Graham was a few steps away before taking to the sky, the earthworm dangling from its beak like a limp and soggy cigarette. Graham quickly disregarded the preposterous idea that the bird was, in fact, his wife and continued on to the sheep fold, where he planned to spend the morning scrubbing the automatic waterers, trimming hooves, and cleaning out the ewe stalls. It wasn't a glamorous life, but it was all Graham had ever known.

❖

On approaching the field in which his sheep freely roamed, Graham immediately saw the three lambs lying motionless against the fence. Two ewes nudged at the prone corpses of their offspring with their noses, as if that might somehow bring them back to life, when it was quite apparent – to Graham, at least, who could now discern the puddle of blood surrounding the felled lambs and the crimson staining their otherwise pure-white fleeces – that there was no hope for the poor creatures. "Oh, no!" was all Graham could muster as he unlatched the fence and stepped onto the muddy field.

This wasn't the first time a predator had found its way into the fold; just last month he had discovered a mutilated tup at the rear of the barn, its eyes all but chewed out, several of its legs and its stomach eaten away. Graham had quickly discounted a red fox or badger as its killer. It was the work of something far more vicious, and Graham knew just what.

The pair of ewes stepped aside as Graham squelched through the mud toward the mutilated lambs. One of the ewes – *Gertie*, Graham thought – seemed to stare at him with wide eyes, imploring him to find her young's executioner and bring them to justice. The second ewe, Fredericka, keened plaintively, and a shiver ran the course of Graham's spine, for the sound was remarkably like that of a screaming baby and rather out of place out there on the rain-soaked field.

"You poor, poor things," Graham said softly. It was quite clear that the lambs had suffered greatly. Their necks had been broken – he could tell by their positioning – and, in one case, the throat had been torn completely out. Each of their stomachs had been hollowed out and were now cavernous, revealing not much other than gore and uneaten viscera. One of the lambs' mandibles had been removed entirely, as had its tongue. The predator had seemingly favoured this poor creature over the other two.

Much of what had happened that morning now seemed so trivial. The argument with Jenny over a stuck kitchen drawer, the anger he had felt at having, once again, been wakened in the night by the sound of the shower running and the racket Jenny made as she dropped shampoos, soaps, and various other implements and cleansing accoutrements into the tub. The semi-burnt toast Jenny had presented him with at the breakfast table. None of it seemed to matter.

All that mattered now was Mrs Wexler and those damned huskies she had the effrontery to call pets, for they were surely to blame for this massacre.

Graham set off across the field toward the public right of way at the bottom of the hillock, the anger burning inside of him like embers on a fire he had no means of extinguishing.

❖

He hammered upon the door first, and when that proved fruitless he moved away from the gravelled path and banged a fist upon the window. She was in there; she was *always* in there. Mrs Wexler only ever left the house to walk those infernal hounds of hers, and Graham knew her itinerary better than even she did. Three times a day she would lead her trio of beasties along the path at the bottom of Saddler's Green Farm. A public right of way though it might be, Graham had long considered the path an invasion of his own land, an encroachment which had no right to exist. It was seldom used by anyone other than Mrs Wexler and her huskies – except on occasion when the local bus failed to materialise, for it was the quickest way to the village, and on those occasions Graham made sure to stand down at the bottom of the hill, ascertaining no unsavoury characters were lingering.

Back at Mrs Wexler's front door (her first name often escaped him, though he was certain it was either Sara or Sarah or Sandra) Graham was growing increasingly incensed. "Mrs Wexler!" he said, hammering once again. "I need to speak with you this instant!"

There came a barking, and then something hit the front door on the other side, a commotion which could only be caused by three unruly piebald Siberian huskies. Then came the voice of Mrs Wexler, placating her 'babies', as she was wont to call them. "All right, you lot," she screeched in a voice which almost gave Jenny's irritating trill a run for its money. "Let me get to the door!"

Graham prepared himself, for this was not going to

be pretty. In fact, he had already resigned himself to an afternoon at the police station, either explaining his subsequent actions to the local constable or putting in a complaint of his own. Mrs Wexler was not a pleasant lady, and this was only made clearer as she flung open the door and leaned against the wall outside, a cigarette hanging from the corner of her mouth, the smoke trailing up into her narrowed and somewhat devious eyes. Had she been expecting him? It certainly seemed so.

"They haven't been anywhere near your damn sheep," the wretched woman said before Graham had managed to get as far as opening his mouth. She blew smoke toward him, and it arrived in a thick fug which made it almost impossible for Graham to speak, but speak he did, and with great vigour.

"Then why are three of my lambs lying with their insides on the outside? Huh? And if it wasn't one of your 'babies' that ripped the jawbone away from one of my poor flock, what the hell was it?"

Graham wasn't certain, but he thought the woman smirked. "Could be moles," she suggested. "I hear they can be very vicious this time of year."

"Is this a joke to you?" Graham couldn't believe Mrs Wexler's nonchalance regarding such a serious matter. That she should make light of his losing three lambs was revolting. He had a good mind to march back up to the farm and call the police, let the law deal with her and her apparently unmanageable menagerie. However, this was a matter he hoped to be able to deal with without involving the police. "Three lambs," he said, clicking his fingers angrily an inch in front of the woman's face. She didn't even flinch; simply wedged the hand-rolled cigarette back into the corner of her mouth and grinned thinly. "Shall we say fifty pound per beast? That's not unreasonable, and I—"

Her laugh cut him off mid-sentence. "You think I'm going to *pay* you compensation for something my dogs *didn't* do?" She shook her head frantically, as if the suggestion was the most preposterous thing she had ever heard. Within the house, her hounds began to bark and scratch at the door, as if they were trying to break free to protect their mistress from the ghastly man holding her to ransom.

"Now, Mrs Wexler, I have been perfectly polite regarding this matter, and I think it only right that my loss of three perfectly healthy lambs – at least healthy when I last saw them – be recompensed."

"That's all well and good, you old fart," said Mrs Wexler, "and when you can prove that my dogs had anything at all to do with the mauling of your flock, then I will have very little argument. Until such a time, I would ask you refrain from knocking upon my door. It gives me an awful headache, and as you can hear, the dogs aren't too keen on it – or you – either." Her words were harsh, but what she did next was far worse, for she flicked her still-burning cigarette into Graham's chest. It bounced off; orange cinders floating in the air for a moment before falling to the ground.

"You really are one of the most reprehensible women I have..." he trailed off, for the woman was already in her hallway, the dogs circling her legs for fuss, and then the door was slammed shut, leaving Graham incredulous of what he had just witnessed and unsure of what to do next.

"This isn't the end of the matter!" he yelled at the closed door. "I will not tolerate this, Mrs Wexler. The next time... the next time..." There wouldn't be a next time. Graham knew exactly what he would do; what he was well within his rights to do. To protect his flock, he would put an end to those pesky dogs of hers. All he had to do was wait, bide his time, and retribution would be his.

He turned away from the Wexler residence, no longer angry. It was amazing how the thought of bloody revenge could alter one's mood.

❖

"So let me get this straight," Jenny said as she unpacked the purchases of the day from her chequered shopping bag. A chipped china teacup here, a weathered flan dish there. It was all junk, as far as Graham was concerned; junk which would be discarded of at the first viable opportunity. "You are going to *shoot* Mrs Wexler's dogs? Is that what you are telling me."

Graham was sitting at the kitchen table, polishing his 22 RF rifle. He had already gone through the plan with his wife once, and so it was more than a little annoying that he now had to repeat himself. "The law states that, should a dog worry my flock or worse, I have every right to protect my livelihood. I shall do that very thing." He upended a box of ammunition onto the kitchen table; it was his turn to be noisy for once.

"Yes, that's all very well and good, but can you be certain that her dogs were responsible for the savaging of those lambs?"

"If you try to tell me it was *moles*," Graham said as he loaded the rifle and worked its bolt, "I shall save one of these rounds for you."

Jenny sighed and smiled, though perhaps she wouldn't have if she'd been able to read her husband's mind, where she would have discovered he was only half-joking. "All I'm saying, dear, is that you might be overreacting a little. You know how much those dogs mean to her."

"Precisely," Graham said. "I shall happily watch her deteriorate following the deaths of her precious 'babies', and don't try to make me feel guilty about it. This isn't the first time this has happened. That disgraceful bitch has had fair warning on several occasions. Do you think I *want* to shoot those dogs?"

Jenny's silence spoke volumes.

"Why anyone would want such predatory dogs in this country is beyond me," Graham went on as he stared down the rifle sight toward a mouse-trap on the floor in the corner of the kitchen. "Those dogs aren't built for England. They should be out pulling sleds in the northern hemisphere, not walked at a snail's pace through Wiltshire by some deranged cow with no idea of how to handle them." He was growing angrier by the second; visions of Mrs Wexler, smoking and laughing and mocking him, swam through his mind.

"Sounds as if you have already made up your mind," Jenny said as she unravelled another piece of jumble from its bubble-wrap and began to examine it intently. "Oh this one's a Wedgwood!" she said as she turned the saucer over to investigate its underside.

Graham placed the rifle down. "What do you know about *Wedgwood*?" he said, somewhat acerbically. "And I wouldn't get too attached to it if I were you. You know how you are with these things. I'll give it a week, maybe two—"

His words were suddenly stifled by the sound of breaking porcelain. He turned to find the saucer – *Wedgwood*, apparently – in about a hundred pieces on the kitchen floor, and his wife standing over it, one hand across her mouth and the other tugging at her silvering hair.

"Ha!" Graham said. "Told you so!"

Jenny all of a sudden seemed confused, as if she not only had no idea of what had just happened, but also had no clue as to who she was or how she had got there. She glanced around the kitchen, seemingly searching for something familiar, something to which she could relate.

"Jenny?" Graham stood and walked across the kitchen. Broken porcelain clinked beneath his slippered feet. "Jenny, what's the matter?"

She stopped scouring the room and allowed her eyes to settle upon her husband. Graham had never seen such confusion upon a person's countenance, and for the longest time they stood there, neither venturing to speak, neither moving; they simply stared into one another's faces as if they were strangers meeting for the very first time. Episodes likes this were growing in frequency; Graham was reminded of one evening, a few weeks back, when Jenny had called him 'Frank', the name of her high-school sweetheart, and had insisted upon using the moniker several times since. Whenever Graham brought it to her attention – correcting her somewhat angrily – she shrugged it off as a genuine mistake and one which meant nothing consequential. Perhaps she was, as Graham's dear old mother would have put it, going daft in her old age. That would certainly explain why she had taken to showering in the dead of the night, why she had grown so loud and inconsiderate, why she oftentimes got lost in the village, despite them neighbouring and subsequently visiting the godforsaken place on a weekly basis for the past thirty-three years.

Daft in her old age, Graham thought. The idea annoyed him more than it worried him. Keeping the farm afloat – what with the government interfering and the supermarkets driving down the price of milk – was hard enough without having to care for a wife on the verge of dementia. He would have no other choice but to secrete her away in some home, let her become someone else's burden, for love only counted if the woman you fell in love with remained.

"Frank?" Jenny said, so suddenly Graham staggered back a few steps. Broken porcelain crunched underfoot as he went. Jenny seemed to realise her mistake almost immediately. "*Graham*. Did I pass out?"

Graham shook his head. "Not unless you can faint on your feet," he said. Part of him was offended at his wife's indiscretion, while another part of him had already forgiven her. "Are you okay now?"

Jenny nodded slowly; Graham could see she was a little uncertain, though the life seemed to have returned to her eyes and she was no longer frowning. She turned her attention to the scattered pieces of Wedgwood upon the kitchen floor. "Oh dear!" she gasped. "I'd better get this mess swept up."

Graham returned to the table and to his rifle. For now, his wife had returned to her senses, though he watched her apprehensively as she went off in search of the dustpan and brush, and tried to recall the name of the lovely care home over in Chippenham in which his mother had spent her remaining days, drooling and rambling nonsensically about the Queen of England.

❖

After nightfall, Graham climbed into his wax coat, snatched up his rifle from the kitchen table, and headed out onto the mound. It was windy – something which he would have to take into consideration when firing the .22 from a good distance away – and though the rain had abated somewhat, it remained in the atmosphere like a damp fog. By the time he arrived at his spot, a perfect little upland fifty feet or so north of the sheep fold, he was wet and breathless, but he was ready for what lay ahead, for what he had to do to put an end to this unfortunate saga.

He settled there upon the mound, out of view of the public right of way at the base of the hillock and therefore the eye-line of that reprehensible Mrs Wexler, whose final walk of the day would take place in the next half-hour or so.

"I'll be ready," Graham muttered, staring down the sight of the rifle toward the sheep enclosure. Many of his flock had taken themselves into the barn for the night, as well they should in such inclement weather, but a few remained outside, peppering the muddy field. Graham had hoped for at least a dozen of his sheep to linger outside the barn after nightfall, and there certainly appeared to be that many, though he dared not count the ones which had, lest he fall asleep.

This made him laugh, which eased the tension that had been building up within him since settling upon the upland. But then he was hit by a terrible thought, one which he could have done without.

What if Wexler eschewed the final walk of the night for a nice warm glass of sherry and, in the case of her unruly dogs, a piss in the back garden. The weather was certainly off-putting, disconcerting to all but the most stoic of dog-walkers. Who in their right mind would be out in such damp conditions, other than a vengeful farmer sitting in wait?

She'll walk them, Graham persuaded himself. Mrs Wexler was nothing if not steadfast. She was, Graham thought, the type of woman who would continue to walk her 'babies' long after the apocalypse had destroyed most of humanity; she would just wear an extra layer as she did so.

As Graham sat there – the drizzle dripping from his coat – he thought about Jenny, lying in bed, for he had taken her up early in the hope a good night's sleep would do her the world of good. What had transpired in the kitchen that afternoon had made him realise how much he loved her, despite her annoying imperfections. She was not well, hadn't been well for quite some time, and he had been disregarding it as nothing more than old age and the effects thereof. If things didn't get better soon, he would have no choice other than to summon outside help. The farm was no place for a befuddled old lady. There were too many dangers, too much machinery into which she might fall, lodging there as the gears continued to move around and around, stripping the flesh from her skeleton and generally making it a bad day for all involved.

Claregate! That was the name of the care home. It came to him suddenly; he could picture the sign at the side of the road and the long bumpy driveway – almost a mile – leading down to the whitest of houses. His mother had certainly never complained about the place, at least not to him, and so he would feel quite relaxed knowing Jenny was safe there, a danger to no one, three square meals a day and a hundred percent less chance of becoming dog-food in the inner workings of a combine harvester. One day, though perhaps not in the near future, Graham would join her, spend his own infirm days in the care of someone else, someone paid to change nappies and wipe the congealed mashed potatoes from the corners of puckered lips.

"Something to look forward to," he muttered sarcastically.

An excited barking brought Graham back to his senses and he snatched the rifle up into position, his eye hovering over the sight and trained upon the fence at the bottom of the hill. Sure enough, Mrs Wexler came into view, her trademark roll-yer-own protruding from the corner of her mouth. The dogs circled her legs, entangling them with leads which she had to fight to escape from, cursing silently as she freed herself.

"There... you... are..." Graham whispered, never once taking his eye from the woman and her animals. She seemed to be in a bit of a rush tonight, the promise of a warm hearth and a tot or two of whisky an extra incentive to get back to the house as soon as possible, out of her damp clothes and into her tobacco-stinking nightgown.

As the woman led her dogs along the public pathway, she disappeared from view behind a row of firs and Graham sighed deeply and retrieved the hip-flask from his coat pocket.

She would be back. Ten minutes, fifteen, twenty, she would return, and that's when Graham would make his move. He planned to shoot only one of the animals and hope that was enough of a lesson to her, for he took no pleasure in the needless massacre of otherwise beautiful creatures. Mrs Wexler would no doubt take the matter to the police, though Graham knew she hadn't a leg to stand on. His rights were simple, and hers were non-existent in this matter. He had lost too many sheep to her 'babies' already. It was time to take a stand, to bring her to her senses and to teach her a thing or two about loss.

A panicked bleating suddenly filled the night. Graham dropped the hip-flask and snapped the rifle across to the sheep fold, where he saw the animals circling the enclosure, spooked by something or perhaps putting as much distance between themselves and an as yet unseen predator as possible.

"Got it!" Graham said, for it became clear that one of

Mrs Wexler's huskies must have once again slipped its lead. Through the sight of his rifle he could discern a low, shadowy form. It had already brought down one of the flock and was tearing into its flesh. The rest of the sheep were now bleating in unison, a rather hellish sound quite like nothing Graham had ever heard before.

From this distance, he knew he would be lucky to hit the infernal creature, and so he clambered to his feet and began to run down the hillock, slipping occasionally on the wet mud beneath. The rifle was always trained upon the fold, though; he was not going to let that little bastard get away, and though he knew he had lost another lamb – he knew just by the sound it made as the dog tore into it – he grinned, for retribution was finally to be his.

When he was close enough to be assured of an accurate shot, he dropped into the mud on one knee and raised the rifle, once again pushing his eye into the sight. Any closer than this, he thought, and there was a damn good chance the accoster of sheep would startle and attempt to escape, or even attack. Even with a rifle, Graham didn't feel an even match for a Siberian husky.

"Got you," he said, settling upon the feasting shape. Less than a second passed between his words and the slight kick of the rifle. A gunshot echoed around the field. If the sheep had been going crazy before they were absolutely wild now. Graham climbed to his feet and ran the remaining twenty metres to the enclosure, certain he had hit the aggressor with a clean shot, though he wouldn't know for sure until he entered the fold.

Pure adrenaline drove him on, and was the reason why he had the energy to climb the fence rather than work his way around to the gate on the other side. The felled beast lay motionless in the middle of the enclosure alongside what remained of the lamb it had been devouring. He laughed as he cautiously approached the shot animal, though his good humour soon disappeared as he saw the silver hair, now matted with mud and blood, and recognised the grey coat wrapped around its shoulders, for it wasn't a dog at all – how had he not realised – and had never looked like one.

"No!" Graham wailed as he rushed across the fold to where his wife lay, prone and bleeding in the mud. She was, he noticed, naked beneath the coat, which was wrapped around her shoulders rather than properly attached. Her entire body was covered with mud; the whites of her unflinching eyes seemed to glow in the dark as they stared out at Graham. The dead lamb's flesh hung from her mouth in uneven clumps. "No!"

Daft in her old age, his long-dead mother's voice said somewhere inside his head.

Graham sobbed, wiped the mud and blood from Jenny's face, made sure she was covered over properly with her favourite grey coat so that she didn't get any wetter than she already was.

Then he walked back up the hill, waited on the upland for the woman and her three dogs to return. Death would come to all of them that night, himself included. Once he had decided upon it, beautiful relief washed over him.

I'm coming, Jenny, he thought.

And he waits.

He waits.

He waits.

Misericord
A K Benedict

On one day every year, ants spread their wings and rise. Last year, Flying Ant Day fell in late July. It was one of those rare summer days when pavements are too hot for dogs' paws and barbeque smoke covers the suburbs. The kind of day that draws you outside, only to burn your skin and leave the texture of ant wings in your mouth.

"We could go for a picnic," Kate, my fiancée, said that morning.

"Or," I replied, buttering my fifth piece of toast, "we could go and see that church on Romney Marsh I told you about."

"No more churches," she said. "I've seen enough buttresses to last me a lifetime."

"This is the last church, I promise. This one has unique markings: it'll complete my last chapter. I told Mark I'd finish it by the end of the week." Mark Malone is my colleague in the Art History Department. We're writing a book on the semantics of church art, with him concentrating on the external features, me on the internal. At least we were.

"Do you really want to be inside on a day like this?" Katie asked. She took the croissants out of the oven. The top of one was blackened from being too close to the element.

"Do you really want me to miss my deadline?" I replied, flashing my 'you can't resist me' grin. "The church is only open once a month. Today's the only day we've got."

"Don't you try that smile on me," she said, laughing. "I'm not one of your students." She paused. "Anymore."

I kissed her, leaving red lipstick on her naked lips. We taste of pastries and last night's wine.

"Please?" I said, knowing I'd get my way.

"You always think you know how things are going to turn out, don't you?" she says.

"Aesthetically pleasing please?"

"How about a compromise?" she said at last. "A picnic outside the church in the sun, then you show me inside. Briefly."

"Deal."

An hour later, we were in the car. The back seat rustled and clinked with food and drink Katie said was absolutely essential for a successful picnic. I'd've been happy with a pasty but she liked to 'do things properly'. Doing picnics properly apparently involved at least three types of hummus.

The low road twisted through fields and marshland. Sheep looked up at us, then back down to the grass. Heat haze hung over the road.

"How can you have a church in the middle of nowhere?" Katie asked when the Satnav indicated we were nearly there. "I've seen only five or six houses in the last half hour. That's not much of a congregation."

"Probably why it's only open once a month," I replied.

"We're not actually going to a service, are we?" Katie asked, gripping my leg.

"God no. I wouldn't do that to you." I stroked her hand. Katie's experience with the church had not been a good one. "I rang the rector. There was a service this morning and then it's left open until dusk."

"And no one will be there?"

"Not unless there are some other art historians after the scratches in its walls."

The church sat in a shallow valley in a field crisscrossed with streams. The sheep looked like thought bubbles against the grass. We drove down towards it and pulled up at the side of the road.

"How do we get to it?" Katie asked, taking the bags out of the back.

"Over the fence then the bridge, I suppose. I don't know if there's any other way."

She didn't say anything. I didn't even need to look at her face to know what she was thinking. This had been the one Sunday I was supposed to concentrate on her and here I was working. I'd been writing the book for so long that our life and living room had been subsumed into piles of annotated pages. But it wasn't going to be forever. After the book was finished, I'd be free to plan the wedding etc. Etc.

I climbed the stile and held the bags while she clambered over to join me. We stumbled down the hill, bags bashing against our legs. Sheep jostled away, complaining.

Katie laid out a plaid blanket and started opening all the cartons and packages of food. The picnic took up nearly all of the blanket. I opened a bottle of wine and poured it into two plastic glasses. I drank my first glass quickly, looking over the bridge to the medieval church. Its door was open but no one was around. Apart from us.

Katie made up a baguette of goat's cheese, yellow-flecked tomatoes, basil, extra virgin olive oil, sea salt and black pepper. She offered it to me but I shook my head. I stuck with booze. It's hard to think on a full stomach.

After eating, Katie lay back on the grass. Her dark blue dress, the one she wore the night I proposed, rode up her legs. She closed her eyes. I stroked the inside of her right knee and up under the skirt. She grabbed my hand and pulled me onto her.

I held myself up in a semi-plank over her. Sweat ran down my temple. She looked up at me. The sun made her pupils almost disappear, like a stone dropped into a stream. By her head, a large ant, wings glinting, walked along the edge of the blanket. It was followed by another. And another. In the breezeless air, the grass was moving with insects. "Incoming ants," I said. "Flying ones. We should get inside before they swarm."

"Let's just stay here," she said, placing her arms up around my back. "They can't do us any harm. They're trying to fuck each other; I'm trying to fuck you. We're all here for the same reasons."

"*I'm* here to finish something," I said, shrugging her off. I rocked onto one side and stood up, brushing dirt off the heels of my hand. I regretted saying that almost straight away. It happened sometimes: that itch to say the hurtful thing tickled like an ant's leg against my throat. Sometimes I let it out.

The flying ants gathered on the blanket, roaming over half-eaten tubs of hummus, hovering over my wine.

"Let's get this done," Katie said, standing up. She walked towards the church.

Inside, it was so cool it felt like walking into water. The church smelled of the remnants of incense mixed with the sweat and perfume of those attending the service that day. The interior showed an interesting mix of adapted medieval and seventeenth century features, including six large wooden booths behind the choir stall and pews.

Katie opened the gate into one of the booths. "What're these compartments for?" she asked. "They look like cattle stalls." She walked in and sat on the bench inside.

"They were made for prominent local families. You could all be together, with some degree of privacy, while you prayed."

"And everyone else sat on a pew as usual. Charming," Katie said.

I didn't reply. I was too busy examining the apotropaic symbols that had been scratched onto the dividing walls.

Katie joined me, crouching by the door. "Are these your 'witch marks'?" she asked.

"I usually call them ritual protection marks," I said, tracing the markings with my finger. Excitement ran through me. I'd never seen so many in one place, and I had barely even started on the church.

"What do they all mean?" Katie asked.

I breathed in deeply and out again. All I wanted was for her to go away, to leave me alone for half an hour, an hour, so that I could interpret the markings in peace. "These ones," I said, pointing to one of the many hexfolds that ran around the booth, "are compass-drawn designs."

"It's a six-pointed flower," she said.

"Some think it represents Mary," I said, placing her forefinger on one point of the design, "others that it is a continuous line in order to trap the devil, or evil, in a loop." I move the tip of her finger around the shape, weaving in and out and back to the beginning where it started again in an endless circle.

"There's another mark behind the design," Katie said.

I looked closer. She was right. Behind the enclosing swirls of the circle were five wavy lines.

"I would've seen that but you're in the way," I said.

"There's some down here as well," she said, pointing to a row of joined up VV symbols, a common ritual protection mark thought to represent the Virgin.

"Would you get out of the way and let me do my job, for God's sake?" I said.

She flinched. Very slightly, but I saw it. She moved to the far edge of the bench, near the window and started drawing in her notebook. I thought about apologising for snapping. But didn't.

Footsteps echoed from the vestibule. "Hello?" a woman's voice called out.

Standing up, I could just about see over the walls of the compartment. A tall woman waved to me from the aisle.

"Is that Dr Arnett?" she asked.

I stepped out of the compartment and shook hands

with her. She was wearing a clerical collar and a trouser suit. "Yes, I'm Dr Arnett. You must be Reverend Sullivan. We talked on the phone."

"Call me Caroline," she smiled. I liked the way she looked me directly in the eye.

"And I'm Isabelle."

Katie coughed behind me. "And this is Katie. My fiancée."

Caroline took Katie's hand. "You're both very welcome here. St Mary's doesn't see enough people. I've come back down to make sure that you're OK."

"Is there any reason why we wouldn't be?" Katie asked.

"Of course not," I said.

Caroline laughed. "Turn of phrase. I thought you might like a guided tour."

"That would be very useful," I said. "As I explained on the phone last week, my research is targeted at medieval church graffiti, for want of a better word. The marks left by the congregation and masons."

"Listening to the lost voices," Caroline said. "Very commendable. And you started in the right place," She pointed into the compartment. "These enclosed sections are full of messages from family members going back six hundred years. You could spend hours just matching initials to the parish records."

"We don't have hours, sadly," Katie says.

"We have as much time as you can give us," I say to Caroline. I promised myself I'd talk to Katie about her rudeness later.

"Do you know what this means?" Katie says, showing

Caroline a drawing of the wavy lines under the compass drawn design and the VVs.

"Not my area of expertise. Sorry," Caroline said, checking her watch. "If you'd like to follow me, I'll show you some of the features of the church."

Caroline strode down the aisle towards the altar. She stopped at the baptismal font. "If you look closely," she said, "you can see that the stone has been carved into."

Katie stepped aside to let me go first. I looked into the shallow font. Every spare inch of stone had been etched with the same writing, over and over again. *Miserere mei deus.*

"'May God have mercy upon me'," Caroline said.

"That's a powerful message to have at a baptism," I replied.

Caroline stared at the writing, magnified by the water. "What?" she said. "Oh yes. Very powerful."

The graffiti continued on the outside of the font, running down to the base. The wavy lines were there, too, with Solomon's knots etched on top. I've found in my research that if a symbol appears behind another, it can represent a protection ritual against that which is represented.

"What are these?" Katie said. She'd moved away and was standing by the choir stalls.

"Can it wait a minute?" I said. I took pictures of the font on my phone.

"They're misericords," Caroline said, going over to her. "Shelves on the underside of hinged seats so that the choristers or the more frail members of the congregation can rest against them while standing."

"They're kind of weird. They've got faces on."

"Lots do," I said. "Caroline, can I talk to you over here?"

"Certainly," she said. Her shoes clipped against the floor.

"What's the history of this church?" I asked when she was standing next to me by the pulpit. The same wavy lines ran in a circle around that, too.

"Built in the 1300s," Caroline said, frowning as if trying to remember. "It's been extended since, of course, and augmented, but it remains the same simple Parish church." She reached out and ran her hand down the wall. "It's been here for years, against the odds, and it'll stay here."

"What do you mean, 'against the odds'?" I asked. I touched the wall too. It was cold. The stone seemed to vibrate.

"Oh, nothing," Caroline said, waving her hand as if swatting away an insect. "Just that being on marshland can be dangerous. This is, historically, an area that is easily flooded. There are still a few families left."

"Is that why the church is only open once a month?" I asked.

"Sacrifices have to be made," she replied. She picked up a chalice, wrapped it in a white napkin and placed it in a drawer beneath the altar.

"I hold a service here every month to keep up tradition," Caroline said. "It's important. The same prayer has been said for centuries to hold back the water. The longer the flood stays away, the better for our farmers, wildlife and remaining residents."

I looked around the walls of the church. There were no signs of tidemarks or water damage. "It seems to be working," I said. "Despite being in a valley."

"Someone's listening, then," she said, looking around the building. "Right. I need to go, I've got another service in a few hours. Let me know when the book's out, I'll buy a copy."

"Are we OK to stay here for an hour or so?" I asked.

I could feel Katie's reproving stare. It itched on my skin.

"Of course," Caroline said. "I'll be back after evening service to lock up so you've got hours. You may be joined by a curious visitor or two. The church usually attracts strays when it's open." She then shook my hand again, waved at Katie and left.

I took photo after photo, composing new paragraphs for the book as I went. Instinct, evidence and common sense, the research trinity, told me that the wavy lines represented flooding. They were all over the walls, the pews, the floor, sometimes covered with compass designs, sometimes accompanied by crude drawings of lambs, birds and insects. The church stood as a physical apotropaic symbol, warding off the water.

"Can we go now?" Katie asked after what could have been an hour, could have been more. "I'd like at least some of the day with you."

"You *are* with me," I replied.

"You know what I mean." She walked over and took the pen out of hand.

Irritation scratched at my throat. "You just don't get me, do you?" I said, grabbing my pen back.

"I do," she said, quietly. "I get that you said you'd spend time with me, but arranged during the week to come here."

"We only decided today," I said.

"No, you rang the Right Reverend Caroline during the week. You said so yourself."

I'd let it slip. Stupid. "Alright," I said. "Let's go and rescue the wine. Have another drink."

For a second, it looked as though she was going to go on about my drinking again. But she said nothing, other than, "Come on, then."

It was even hotter outside. Only a few ants were left on the blanket, picking over the remnants of the feast like aunts at the end of a wake. I picked up the wine bottle, and immediately dropped it in the grass. It was so hot it left a mark on my palm. I should've buried it in the stream or at least put it in the bloody cool box.

"Never mind," Katie said. "We can stop in one of the pubs we passed on the way. I saw one with a beer garden."

"As long as it's got beer, I don't mind," I said.

We started packing everything back in the bags. Somehow, there seemed more to dispose of than there was to begin with. Always the way when you're leaving.

Then they rose. The ants flew up, crawling through parched cracks in the earth, flying up around our faces. Their wings brushed my lips, their hard bodies pushed into my mouth and up my nostrils. I tried to blow them out but more came. I could hear Katie spluttering next to me, choking from them crawling into her throat. A dark haze surrounded us.

"The car," she shouted, her voice hoarse.

"Too far," I said, pointing to the church. She grabbed my hand and I ran, pulling her behind me. The flying ants surged and followed, more and more of them; their high-pitched chant screamed in my ears as they climbed over my face and through my hair.

I stumbled to the church, Katie not far behind, and tried to close the door behind us. It scraped against the stone floor, eking out its closure. The ants kept coming, flying past me. Katie joined in, pulling at the door with me until it was shut. The air was thick with them; I breathed one in and felt it dance in my tubes.

And they didn't stop. They came through the windows. They came in through cracks in the flagstones. They clambered, wings sticky, out of the woodwork. Ants rose out of the font.

I ran into one of the booths and crawled under the bench, my hands over my eyes, nose and mouth. I could feel them searching out my ear canal. I tried to swallow the one in my throat but it was stuck. The ants worked their way in between my fingers, flying against my eyes as if trying to push them inwards. I wanted to scream but if I screamed I would suffocate on the ants that wanted my mouth.

I don't know how long I was there. Maybe an hour, but it could have been more. I've told an officer that already. At some point, I realised that the scratching in my throat and at my neck and ears had stopped. Taking my hands slowly away from my face, I tried breathing in. I could. Easily. On opening my eyes, I saw the ant miasma had gone.

Scrambling out from under the bench, I called to Katie. I only heard the echo of my voice. I don't why I hadn't made sure she'd followed me into the compartment. I wasn't thinking. I've told them that.

"Katie," I called out. "Please."

I spent another hour looking for her. I searched in every compartment, under every pew. There was no Katie. And no ants. They'd gone, as quickly as they arrived. The door was bolted shut on the inside.

I called the police, of course I did. I phoned them as soon as I knew she wasn't there. They waited to see if she'd show up at home – "have you had an argument, Dr Arnett?" they asked. Again, and again – and then searched the church too. And then the fields around. And the streams. They found her dress in the stream, but not her. They never found her.

I did. The next month, I went to the service at the church in the marsh. There were a surprising number of people there, it was nearly full. I wondered, then, where they'd all come from. They had the look of people who had been going there for years, centuries even. Like they'd never left.

I sat in the booth we'd gone into first. I moved into the corner that Katie had sat in when I'd snapped at her. From out of the window, I could see where we'd had our picnic. Where the ants had come.

I looked away, down to the wall beneath the window and saw something scratched into it: K L-A. Katie Leonard-Arnett. It would've been our married name.

After the service, I waited for everyone to drift out,

including Rev. Caroline, I didn't want her eyes on me, then walked down the aisle. The church was cold, as if to spite the heatwave outside. I went everywhere that Katie had been that day, wishing I could play things differently, if only slightly. If I had that time again, I'd answer her questions; if I had that time again, I wouldn't have come.

I stopped by the choir stalls. I hadn't paid attention to the misericords before but every seat had one. Crouching down, I looked at the one that had caught Caroline's eye. On the shelf was a carving of a man's face, snarling out of the wood and underneath it, initials. The next one was similar, but the face was female, this time, with a look of frozen fear. The next one was a child, crying. I walked along the stalls, and then I got to the end.

The last misericord had a fresh carving, the marks still sharp in the wood, every detail of her screaming face preserved. I stroked her cheek, her hair, her nose and the initials underneath K L-A

I visit her every month when the church opens. The carvings increase every month, on the walls and in the pews, but I've lost interest in the book. The police won't believe me about the misericord but the case against me has stalled. I know the truth. In a winter in which it has rained non-stop since November, the valley hasn't flooded. And it won't.

Quiet Places
Jasper Bark

PROLOGUE

Sally reached the last cottage on Dundooan Road. It was the fifth house she'd visited that morning. There was a small silver birch in the front garden, its branches reached over the dry stone wall at the front of the property.

Sally was surprised to see a small sparrow on one of the branches. It was completely still, apart from its chest, which was moving rapidly. As Sally watched, it pitched forwards and fell from the branch, landing on the pavement in front of the wall.

Sally knelt and picked the bird up. It was still breathing but the rest of its body was completely limp. Its eyes were glassy, like a stuffed bird. Sally tried to stand it up on the wall, but it fell over. It would probably be dead by the time she came out.

Something brushed against Sally's calves and she jumped. She looked down to see a cat and felt a tiny jolt of excitement. Could there be one other conscious creature in the town? Might it have wandered in from outside?

Sally bent and picked up the cat. It went limp in her

hands, all the life draining from its muscles. It was half starved. She looked in its eyes and saw nothing there, they were totally vacant. There was no awareness at all.

Sally popped the cat back on the pavement and scolded herself for thinking it would be any different. The cat swayed, but remained on its feet and carried on along the cracked paving stones, moving from pure muscle memory. As she opened the gate, Sally felt a pang of guilt about the pets and other animals that were starving to death in the town. She couldn't feed them all, there wasn't the time. There wasn't even time to look after all the townsfolk.

The cottage was locked. This surprised Sally. Dunballan was a small, remote community, with almost no outside visitors. Everyone knew everyone else, so hardly anyone locked their doors. Sally examined the front door. It had a single Yale lock but no mortice. She'd learned a lot about locks in the last week or so, especially how to break into them. The Yale lock was over twenty years old, so it was very easy to open.

Sally reached into her bag and pulled out a credit card. She worked the card between the frame and the door, then slid it into the lock mechanism and released the latch.

The door swung open and a familiar stench greeted her from the hallway. It was in every house she entered – unwashed bodies, stale air and human waste. Sally still hadn't gotten used to it.

She found the first resident in the living room. A short lady in her mid-fifties, with dyed brunette hair, whose roots were beginning to show. She was sitting on the sofa, gazing at nothing, her jaw hanging slack. She didn't turn or notice Sally, they never did. Her only movements were the rise and fall of her chest and the occasional slow blink.

The TV was still on, tuned to a shopping channel. The presenter was chirping about incontinence pants. Sally looked at the yellow and brown stain that covered the sofa cushion and thought this ironic. She would clean the woman up in a moment. She didn't relish this, given how caked the stain was.

The woman's skin was flaking and her mouth and eyes were dry. She was dehydrated, having gone at least a week without any water. The first thing Sally needed to do was get her a drink.

She found the second resident in the kitchen at the back of the cottage. He was a tall man, with broad shoulders and wavy ginger hair that was grey at the temples. He seemed familiar to Sally, but she couldn't place him straight away. The man was holding something in his right hand, staring straight ahead at the wall. He was rocking gently back and forth from foot to foot. He didn't notice Sally, there was no thought behind his empty eyes and nothing but a vacant expression on his face.

There were mugs and a packet of teabags in front of him on the counter, next to a kettle and a rancid bottle of milk. He must have been making a cuppa when it happened. He would have been stuck in that position for over a week now. Sally came across them in the oddest places.

The front of his grey flannel trousers were wet and

there was a large brown lump in the back. Some of it had forced its way up and over the waistband, staining the hem of his cardigan. Another loose pile had found its way down his trouser leg and landed on the floor just behind his left foot. His heel caught it every time he rocked, making a tiny squelch.

Sally wrinkled her nose. She took one of the mugs from the counter, blew the dust out of it and filled it with water from the sink. She held the mug up to the man's lips. His lips parted and he began to swallow the water. It was an automatic response, his eyes gave no sign of consciousness. Some of the water spilled over his chin but he managed to drink most of it. Like the woman on the sofa, he was very dehydrated.

Sally put the mug in the sink and quickly checked the cupboards to see if there was any soup she could heat up for the couple. She didn't find any tins or packets, so she checked the fridge. It was full of raw meat that was starting to spoil.

Returning to the man, Sally was intrigued by what he had in his right hand. She took it in hers and tried to open it. His hand was rough and calloused but quite warm. The touch of it brought back a sudden memory and she knew instantly who he was – the local butcher.

Sally didn't often go into his shop, but the last time had been for a special reason. That was almost a fortnight ago. If she hadn't gone into the butcher's shop, he probably wouldn't be in this state, no-one in Dunballan would.

ONE

The butcher looked up as Sally entered. The door had an old fashioned bell which rang when you opened it. He greeted Sally with a smile. It was warm, but it had a proprietary edge.

Sally avoided his light brown eyes, but couldn't help noticing the freckles on his nose and his thick wet lips, which made her ill at ease.

"And what can I be doing for you?" he asked, modifying his brogue, because Sally was an off-comer.

"I'd like some steak," Sally said. "The best you have."

The butcher's smile broadened.

"Romance is in the air tonight," he said. "It's the big man's lucky night is it?" Sally demurred and looked down at the black and white tiles of the floor.

"As it happens you're in luck," he continued. "I have a nice piece of dry hung tenderloin for you. How thick would you like it cut?"

"An inch or so I guess."

"An inch and a half is best, keeps it nice and tender on the inside, just like me," he said with a wink.

"Okay."

"And how many will you be wanting?"

"Eight."

The butcher raised his eyebrows. "Eight?"

"No, ten."

"Are you having company? Visitors to the town perhaps? We don't get many of those."

"No."

Sally didn't want to explain herself to the butcher,

preferring to ignore his question. The smile fell from his face and he nodded, his manner became business-like as he went to cut the meat.

The smile was back as he laid the cuts down on the counter.

"Just look at that marbling," he said, pointing out the meat's thick veins of fat. "Best to grill these, make sure the pan's nice and hot mind. Couple of minutes each side and cover them with butter before you do, clarified is best. Don't forget the salt and pepper either, rub it in beforehand, use those soft little fingers of yours." He smiled again but it teetered on the brink of becoming a leer. Sally chose not to respond.

The butcher wrapped the steaks carefully and popped them in a large plastic bag. His fingers brushed Sally's as he handed the bag over, almost stroking them. "This'll put lead in his pencil," he said. "I can promise you that."

Sally flushed in spite of herself, hating the way her cheeks burned as she paid for the meat. How dare he touch her like that? She turned and left the shop without saying another word.

The meat was a cold, heavy lump in her bag as she strode up the tiny high street. She ground her teeth and breathed heavily through her nose, burning with anger at the butcher's presumption and his prying insinuations.

Sally got to the corner of the high street and looked up for the first time as she crossed the cobble stone road. She passed three middle aged housewives who'd gathered on the opposite corner. She tried not to catch their eyes, but they stopped their conversation mid-sentence and turned to watch her.

They smiled at Sally as she went by and on each of their faces she saw the same proprietorial look the butcher had. She turned away from them with her chin in the air. She wasn't going to give them the satisfaction.

She knew they were aware of what she was going through and, tacitly, they all approved. It was there behind their eyes and their expectant smiles, every time she met them, in the street or in a shop. They needed her to go through it, for reasons they would never divulge.

She'd mentioned this to David when they first moved to Dunballan. She'd tried to make light of it, turn it into a shared joke, but David had closed down on her as he often did. When she tried to push him, he told her she just wasn't used to living in a small town. They didn't get many off-comers, most people's families had lived there for centuries.

David's ancestors had once been Lairds of the manor. Though their estates had been sold off long ago, they were still seen as the town's first family, and David was the sole surviving heir.

Their arrival was seen as a big occasion by the townsfolk. Sally had thought it quaint, at first, when the older folk doffed their caps to David. After a while, it simply added to the claustrophobia she felt. She and David were under constant scrutiny. The townsfolk radiated a perpetual sense of expectation, and Sally felt herself slowly crushed by its weight.

She reached the foot of the long hill that led out of the town. There was a cut through between two terraced houses, an arched stone entrance opening onto a small alley that led to a set of steps. It was a short cut for Sally.

The steep steps were bordered by overgrown hedgerows. About halfway up, a sudden wind sprang up, causing the hedges to sway. Sally stopped for a moment. Dry leaves skittered on the ground and the trees overhead rustled. Was Hettie going to speak to her so near the town? She strained to listen but couldn't pick out any words.

Footsteps clattered on the steps behind her. "Sally!" a voice called out. Sally took a deep breath, she thought she'd gotten away. She wasn't able to hide her irritation as she turned to see Jane, the town librarian, huffing up the steps.

"Sally, I... oh goodness... just let me get my breath a moment," Jane said, resting a hand on the frail wooden railing. She was a tall woman, with brown, bobbed hair that framed her pinched face like a pair of old theatre curtains. Though probably in her late thirties, she was dressed like an old maid, in a tweed skirt and hand knitted cardigan.

"I'm sorry," she said. "I saw you coming up the steps and I ran after you." She paused for a moment, waiting for Sally to say something. Sally remained silent. Jane ran a hand through her hair and took a deep breath.

"Did you err, did you read the pamphlet I gave you?"

"Yes."

"Well that's what I... what I wanted to talk to you about." There was another pause. Sally didn't know what Jane expected her to say. Probably something about the pamphlet, a slim volume on local folklore.

"I thought you had a right to know, Jane said. "That's why I gave it to you. But I wouldn't want you... that is, I don't think you should do anything rash." Jane took a breath, weighing her words. "The people of this town, they're not... we're not bad people. I thought you should know there's a reason for everything that's happening, that's all. That's why I gave you the pamphlet. I... well, I don't want to be presumptuous, but I thought it might help. I... I thought you should know."

She looked up at Sally from where she was standing, several steps below. Her face was lit with a timid hope, she still wanted to connect with Sally. This irritated Sally more than anything.

The town library was empty most of the time, except for a few dozing pensioners. Sally was one of the few members who actually borrowed books. They'd become an important escape since moving to the town.

There was no phone coverage anywhere in Dunballan, and the remote cottage David and Sally lived in didn't have a landline. You had to drive five miles up the road before you got any signal on your phone, and there was no broadband either. Sally hadn't believed it when they first moved in, but after several hours of shouting at company reps from a payphone, she was told that no one in the town wanted it.

The town's only newsagent carried nothing but the local paper, the Sunday Post and aging copies of The People's Friend. Dunballan clung doggedly to its remoteness and refused to join the twenty-first century. Books not only became Sally's escape, they were also her only connection to the outside world. The library was surprisingly well stocked and even had a good selection of modern books.

Jane had remarkably similar taste to Sally, and began to recommend books and authors to her. Her recommendations were excellent, but her attempts to engage Sally in conversation were stilted and uncertain. Sally found them awkward and embarrassing. There are some people with whom, in spite of the very best intentions, you just never click. Jane was one of those.

Sally knew Jane was reaching out to her. She knew Jane wanted to be friends, and heaven knows she needed one, but not Jane. The longer she failed to connect with Jane, the more strained their interactions became.

Finally Jane had given her the little pamphlet on folklore. It was her last attempt to forge a friendship. It hadn't worked. After reading the pamphlet, Sally had come to resent Jane and the townsfolk more.

Now Jane stood staring earnestly up at her. It was her earnestness that Sally found most annoying. The flies from the hedgerow had begun to notice the meat in Sally's bag. She waved them away and pulled the top of the bag shut.

"Okay," was all Sally said. Then she turned her back and continued up the steps.

TWO

Sally opened her back gate and stepped into the garden. To her left was the allotment where she and David had planned to grow vegetables.

They'd been working on the allotment the last time the Beast appeared. Sally was busy sowing runner beans, pushing them into the loose soil trenches she'd dug. David was cutting bamboo canes.

Sally looked up from her work and saw David had stopped what he was doing. He was staring at the hills behind the cottage. Sally followed his gaze and saw the Beast among the trees at the top of the hill.

"I'm right here you know," Sally said. "I can see it too."

David looked away, suddenly sheepish, like a schoolboy caught doing wrong. He went back to cutting the bamboo.

"Is that it," said Sally, her voice becoming shrill. "Is that all you're going to do?"

David shrugged and continued making the canes.

"Well?" she practically shouted at him. "At least say something!"

David stared at the ground and avoided her gaze. Sally ground her teeth. How could he just keep on cutting bamboo and not do anything? She stood up and threw the trowel she was using at the ground. She'd very nearly thrown it at his head. He showed no reaction as she stormed into the cottage.

Sally shut the gate and glanced over at the allotment. The beans she'd planted had begun to sprout. The warm weather was good for them. The little row of canes was half-finished and the rest of the trench was empty. Sally was sorry now that they hadn't completed it. Like so many things in their relationship it was unfinished.

A sudden wind sprang up from the west. It bent the trees in the fields next to the cottage, but it was neither hot nor cold. It ruffled the grass, rattled the hedges and lifted Sally's hair and skirt but she couldn't feel it on her skin. Nor could she smell any of the scents that a wind such as this usually carried. It was almost entirely bodiless. You could see and experience its effects, but you couldn't feel them.

The leaves in the hedgerow made a dry, scratchy noise as they scuttled about in its wake. The hedgerow itself rustled, as though full of a thousand little occupants. The branches of the nearby trees creaked as they bent and strained.

The bodiless wind intensified and the sounds increased, like a discordant symphony. In the points where each noise overlapped and collided, new sounds could be heard, created by the dissonance. Sally tilted her head and listened carefully.

At first she made out the consonants in the discordance, plosive sounds like cracking twigs. Then she caught the vowels, low and keening like the wind moaning through the branches. A voice was coming through. A composite voice like a thousand voices talking all at once and not one of them human.

"You have the– have the– have the meat– the meat– the meat…" said the voice.

"Yes," said Sally, clutching her bag.

She sensed the presence behind the voice. She pictured it peering out from the shadows of the thicket. Something so primordial she could barely understand, let alone see.

"That is good– is good– is good. We can trap– can trap– can trap the Beast tonight."

Then, as sudden as a freak change in the weather, the

wind disappeared, the trees and bushes stopped shaking, and Sally was alone.

She felt, as she always did when Hettie came and went, that a shadow had lifted from the sun. That the unreal had withdrawn and the real had rushed back in to fill the void it left. More worrying was the emptiness she felt, and the craving for Hettie to return.

Hettie was what the townsfolk called the voice, and the inhuman presence that lurked behind it. Hettie of the Hedgerow. Sally knew that thanks to the pamphlet Jane had given her.

Increasingly, Sally felt her certainty wane whenever Hettie left. The sense of purpose Hettie instilled in Sally always seemed to ebb. For a second Sally wavered and wondered if she was doing the right thing. Then she thought of David, and why the house was empty, and she realised she had to see this course of action through.

Sally hurried inside the cottage to prepare the meat.

THREE

Sally dropped leaves and berries into an old stone mortar. She'd collected them in the dark places Hettie had shown her, in the forest on the hill that overlooked the cottage.

Sally pounded the mixture into a dense green pulp with a pestle. Then she laid out the steaks on the kitchen counter. She scooped out the pulp and massaged it into each of the steaks as though she were seasoning them, preparing a meal for the Beast, just as Hettie had instructed her.

It was less than a month since Hettie introduced herself, but Sally couldn't imagine how she'd gotten along without her. It had happened the last time David was away with the Beast.

When she heard Hettie speak for the first time, Sally realised that she'd been catching snippets of her voice for quite some time. Twigs would snap, rain drops would fall from branches and breezes would stir leaves giving the impression that there was a voice, or at least a higher design behind them.

Naturally Sally dismissed this view for as long as she could. She told herself she was just responding to the strain of the move and the isolation she felt, alone in the cottage for long periods. She was projecting her imagination onto natural phenomena as a way of dealing with her loneliness. She had better be careful or she'd end up having full blown psychotic hallucinations.

The noises persisted though, and at first she really did fear for her mental health. Then she read the pamphlet Jane had given her, and everything changed. After that she wanted to hear the voice.

That first time in the garden, she was so shocked to hear Hettie that she reeled, breathing so heavily she began to hyperventilate. It was happening, she could hear that, but it didn't seem real. Less and less seemed real to Sally with every day she spent in Dunballan.

"You are not alone– not alone– not alone anymore– anymore– anymore." Hettie whispered through the movements in the undergrowth. Sally shook her head, trying to banish the voices, but they weren't inside her mind. They came from a confluence of natural phenomena. No mind could construct such a complex hallucination.

"We're here to give you– give you– give you back what the Beast – what the Beast– what the Beast has stolen."

Sally's eyes misted up and she blinked away tears. She bit her bottom lip, took a deep breath and her chest shook with a barely suppressed sob. She was surprised at her reaction. An unearthly voice had addressed her. An inhuman presence, skulking beneath the bushes of the hedgerow, had reached out and made contact. Yet she didn't doubt her sanity and she wasn't afraid.

Instead, she felt something she hadn't felt since moving to the remote town. She felt solidarity. She had believed, for several months, that everything was against her up here. Not just the townsfolk, hemming her in with their ownership of David, but also the landscape and the ancient forest above the hill, where David now ran with the Beast. But here was a strange phenomenon all of her own. One that understood her predicament and wanted to help.

She could feel the hate emanating from the darkest heart of the thicket. A hatred of the Beast, the one thing Sally also detested most in the world. Suddenly she wasn't alone. She had her own dark magic, something that would scare the townsfolk, and it wanted to help her.

"We will school you– school you– school you little sister, and you will release him– release him– release him."

Hettie had come to Sally almost every other day since then. Sally had begun to seek out remote, wooded haunts where Hettie could address her. She came in her own time, and of her own choosing, and Sally could never anticipate when she would make contact. She just had to make herself open to it.

True to her word, Hettie had tutored and nurtured Sally's hatred. Sally learned many things from the strange multiplicity of voices. Mostly she learned what Hettie had planned for the Beast, and she was eager to help.

FOUR

Sally's relationship with David had always contained distances, both emotional and physical. They'd been together for over a decade, but until they'd moved to the cottage, they'd lived on opposite sides of London.

Neither of them made connections easily. Their circle of friends was small and they didn't have many significant previous relationships. It was one of the things that brought them together.

They were comfortable with one another's remoteness. They didn't cling to each other, nor did they make demands or depend on one another for anything. Days could go by without them contacting each other and neither of them would worry. They were happy being self-contained and their relationship seemed stronger because of it. At least in the beginning.

Looking back on their last year in London, Sally couldn't help but see a certain inevitability to their drifting apart. The one thing that had always seemed to be the biggest strength of their relationship was ultimately its undoing. They spent so long ensuring that they didn't need each other too much, that they came to wonder if they needed each other at all.

David's depression had been getting worse for a while. It didn't help when he was made redundant. His firm gave him a very generous settlement, and he didn't have any monetary problems, but he'd depended on work to keep the black moods at bay. He needed to remain active, and when that was taken away from him he went downhill rather sharply.

Whereas previously, when he took a turn for the worse, David had found Sally's presence comforting, now he found her a torment. He froze her out and sometimes went weeks without seeing her. Sally found this agonising and began to long for a way to strengthen their connection, even as their ties withered and fell away.

For all their remoteness, Sally still wanted David to open up to her. She felt like he was the key to some impenetrable mystery. Sally had wanted to unlock David practically from the moment she first met him. She was always afraid of what the consequences of that might be though.

Then, almost out of nowhere, he inherited what was left of the family estate. Sally had known that his family was once quite well to do, but she didn't know he was the sole surviving heir. There was one major stipulation, however. In order to benefit from the full estate, David had to return to his ancestral home.

Sally had thought this would be the end of them. So she was most shocked when David asked her to move up to the Highlands with him. It was the first time he'd reached out to her like this, committing to a major new stage in their relationship. Sally was overjoyed and, although this sort of decision would normally have sent her into a tailspin of indecision, she agreed on the spot.

Sally left David to dispose of his apartment and she set about selling hers. The cottage was stuffed with family heirlooms, furniture, silverware and such, so they didn't need to bring much.

David sold his property in a matter of months, but Sally found herself caught in a chain and negotiations dragged on interminably. She would have pulled out, but her buyer was offering her so much over the asking price that she didn't want to lose him. Sally had quit her teaching job to move up to the Highlands with David and, without the proceeds of her house sale, this made her financially dependent on him. This put a little pressure on the relationship, especially now they were cohabiting, but Sally learned to live with that.

They both hoped the move would lift David's spirits and, in those first few months, it did. In spite of the claustrophobia of living in a remote town under the constant scrutiny of the townsfolk, they began to build a new life together. They fixed up the six bedroom cottage that was now theirs, and they dug out a space at the bottom of their large garden for an allotment.

They took long walks together over the hills of the surrounding valley and into the forest just beyond their cottage. When the long winter nights came in, they drank Shiraz and stared into the freshly lit fire, trying to catch a vision of their future in the flames that leaped in the hearth.

Sally began to let her guard down with David. A few years before she met him, Sally had gone to see a counsellor. After spending many sessions talking about Sally's early life, and her mother's second marriage, the counsellor, a large, middle aged lady with iron grey hair and a weakness for silk scarfs, offered Sally a prognosis.

She told Sally that the lack of connection she felt towards others was a defence mechanism. Subconsciously she was protecting herself from getting hurt. Sally's father had suffered a massive cerebral haemorrhage when Sally was very young, which had left him completely incapacitated and unable to fend for himself. Her father became a shell of his former self. A slack-jawed, drooling lump whom Sally couldn't bear to be around.

Sally's mother became his full time carer, a task which left her emotionally and physically drained. She'd had no time for Sally when she was done with her husband. Sally grew up feeling totally excluded from her mother and father and bereft of their love.

After nearly a decade of dependency on Sally's mother, when Sally was in her early teens, her father died. A year later, her mother met and married a widower, several years her junior, a quiet and gentle man who had two young daughters.

Sally's mother had always wanted more children, but felt circumstances had robbed her of the chance. She also felt guilty that she hadn't been a better mother to Sally. She doted on her two new stepdaughters, seeing, in them, the opportunity to be the mother she'd always wanted to be.

This only made Sally feel more excluded, both from her mother and her new step family. She left for university when she was nineteen and never returned home. She had rarely seen her mother since, nothing was resolved between them.

The counsellor believed that Sally remained distant from others because she was scared of emotional intimacy, Her relationship with her mother taught her that intimacy led to exclusion and Sally couldn't bear to be excluded as her parents had once excluded her. Sally suspected the counsellor was perfectly right, but the pain of admitting this to herself was too great, so she never went back to see her again.

Instead she turned back to God. Sally's mother was not religious, but she sent Sally to a Catholic school and Sally had been very devout as a child. As an adult she was not devout, but she still turned to her Bible and prayer in dark times, and she attended church sporadically. It brought a little hope into her life.

It was replaced, in those first months with David, by a different hope, a hope for the future. There was still a lot of space between Sally and David, but they made many plans together. Plans to which Sally was integral. For the first time in her life she felt included in someone else's life.

Then the Beast turned up and ruined everything.

FIVE

It was David who saw it first. He always did. He was connected to the Beast on some deep, hereditary level.

Sally didn't realise what he'd seen, to begin with. She did spot the change in his mood though, since moving in with him she was acutely sensitive to that. David would suddenly go silent when they were outside together and look off into the distance. She wasn't one to pry, and simply let it go the first few times, but after a while she began to follow his gaze and ask him what he was looking at.

David would always smile and shake his head, in a self-conscious way, then try and change the subject. However, whatever was drawing his attention got closer, and eventually Sally caught sight of it.

They were coming back from a walk, approaching the garden gate, when David shuddered, as if from a sudden chill. He turned to look up at the woods on the hill. Sally looked too and there, between two trees on the edge of the bluff, she saw a huge, black feline creature.

The creature disappeared back into the trees so quickly that Sally wasn't even sure she'd seen it. If David hadn't been staring at the self-same place on the bluff, she might have dismissed it. His attention convinced her.

"What on earth was that?" she said.

"What?" David looked startled, guilty even, as though he'd been caught doing something he shouldn't.

"Up there on the rise."

"Come on, it's going to be dark soon. We should get inside." David turned and started back to the cottage.

"I know you saw it," Sally said. "I saw you looking at it. You spotted it before I did."

David continued to walk away from her.

"David..." she called after him.

"We need to get back," was all he said.

Sally tried to press the point with him when they got home but David kept evading her. She was puzzled by this behaviour. David could be secretive and self-contained at times, but she'd never seen such outright denial from him.

Sally was reminded of a girlfriend of hers who caught her partner coming out of another woman's home. When she confronted him, the guy refused, point blank, to admit it was him, even though he'd been seen and her friend could describe the clothes he was wearing. The guy was so persistent in his denial that, in the end, her friend came to doubt what she'd seen in the first place. That was how Sally felt. It would have been easy to dismiss what she'd seen if the Beast hadn't continued to make its presence felt.

They were foraging for chanterelle mushrooms a week or so later, something David recalled doing with his grandfather many years before. The idea of it really appealed to them, living off the land and filling their larder with wild produce.

The only problem was they were hopeless at it. After several hours they'd only found a handful of fungi and they didn't know if they were edible or not. The tiny pictures in the field guide they'd brought weren't at all helpful.

They were in the outskirts of the forest, and were about to call it a day, when they heard the sound of twigs cracking a little further off, where the trees were denser. They both looked up and saw a huge black shape pacing back and forth between the trees. It stopped, lifted its head as if scenting the air, then slunk back into the forest.

"There," said Sally, much louder than she'd meant. "You saw that didn't you? You saw it." David, who was crouching over a rotting trunk, just stared down at the leaf mulch in front of him.

After that the Beast, as Sally came to know it, became increasingly brazen in revealing itself, appearing closer and closer to their remote cottage. Each time she saw it, Sally was struck with how large it was. She guessed that its head would be level with her own and its length was that of a small pony.

Its body was all compacted muscle and moved with a grace that didn't seem possible. Almost as if it was reforming itself with every movement, sinews and bone becoming liquid every time it lifted a paw, only turning solid when it was still. The Beast's coat was jet black, darker than anything Sally had seen, light seemed to fall into it.

Sally's youngest step sister, Tina, was a bit of a flake, and they didn't get on. Her husband, Malcolm, was obsessed with weird fringe beliefs. A university drop out who liked the sound of his own voice, Malcolm had tried to lecture Sally on a number of topics over the years, from free energy to Rennes Le Chateaux, but he'd failed to convince her on anything.

One of Malcolm's favourite topics was alien big cats, or ABCs as he referred to them, strange wildcats seen wandering in the British countryside. For a short while, Sally considered photographing the Beast to send to her brother in law. Her phone was rarely charged these days though, due to the lack of coverage, and getting in touch with Malcolm would mean contacting Tina, something she was loath to do.

Within a short time, Sally became used to seeing the Beast, but David's refusal to speak about it made her very wary. Then one day, the Beast jumped over their garden wall, walked right up to the cottage and seated itself on the back stoop.

It looked patient and alert when David and Sally opened the back door to investigate. It was resting on its back haunches, its front legs upright and its tail curved around in front of them. In spite of its immense size, there was no sense of threat. The shape of its ears, its muzzle and its head gave the Beast an otherworldly air, like an infernal reimagining of what a feline would look like.

David did not look uneasy. He had the air of a man who has just confronted his wife and his mistress for the first time, and is relieved it's all out in the open. He actually sighed, and Sally could have sworn that a wistful, half smile played about his lips, just for an instant. He looked at the creature like he was greeting an old friend. There was an intimacy between him and the Beast that caused a sudden surge of jealousy in Sally.

The Beast opened its eyes wide, retracting its eyelids until its black, watery eyes were like two distended orbs. David let out a little gasp, and Sally saw that his eyes were also wide open and bulging. He rocked up onto the balls of his feet and leaned forward, towards the Beast, holding its gaze the whole time.

The Beast rose slowly to its feet, never breaking eye

contact with David. The two of them seemed to be swooning. David's breathing became shallower and more rapid. The Beast showed its formidable claws, digging them into the rough patio, scraping large grooves in the stone.

A low moan escaped from the back of David's throat. He was swaying as if entranced. The Beast stretched out its front legs, arched its spine and raised its hind quarters. Its tail stood erect, only the very end curled and uncurled as a deep, low purr rumbled from its chest.

Sally turned to David, appalled. "Stop it," she said, punching his arm. "Stop it! Stop it! Stop it!"

It did no good. David was oblivious to her. He leaned so far forwards he looked like he was going to topple over. His chest was rising and falling and his arms shook like he was in some kind of religious ecstasy.

Sally looked from the Beast to David and back again. The Beast's head was thrown back, and its body was tense, as though it was about to spring. Something about it was different though, something had changed.

It seemed to have something essential of David within it. As though his mind, and even his soul, had been transferred in that gaze. Had leapt from his eyes and poured themselves into the Beast's.

The Beast relaxed and stood still for a moment, all the tension drained from its body. It looked slowly about, getting its bearings. Sally could swear she detected some of David's manner about it, something indefinable in the way it moved. Almost as it if it was mimicking his mannerisms, in the way a huge wild cat would mimic the actions of a man.

Then the Beast turned from her and padded back down the garden. It jumped over the wall and bounded up to the forest, picking up speed as it went. Finally it was swallowed by the trees.

Sally turned back to David. His jaw was slack, his mouth hanging open and his eyes empty and glazed.

Sally tried to rouse him. "David," she said, "David", but he didn't respond. Sally passed her hand in front of his face. He didn't blink or show any expression. He was breathing through his mouth, deep, steady breaths that rattled the phlegm at the back of his throat. Sally checked his pulse and it seemed to be regular.

His body was fine but David himself appeared to be absent. Sally clicked her fingers next to his ear and shook his shoulders, but this didn't get any reaction. She raised her hand and slapped him hard about the face, hoping to shock him out of his stupor. She left a red mark on his cheek red but his vacant expression didn't alter a bit.

When she saw the mark, Sally regretted being so violent. She didn't want to leave David loitering by the back door, so she took hold of his shoulders and attempted to turn him around. He didn't show any resistance, turning compliantly. David's face was blank and non-responsive, but his basic motor functions were working fine.

Sally guided him back to the living room and helped him sit in his favourite armchair. She spoke to him the whole while, as if she were guiding him blindfolded but he didn't respond. He remained in the chair for the rest of the day, breathing loudly through his mouth and blinking slowly.

Sally fed him soup for supper, spooning it into his mouth, then took him up to bed. He had no problem with the stairs and was easy to undress, but he lay like an unmoving lump in the bed.

David stayed in this vegetative state for nearly three weeks. Every day Sally would get him out of bed, dress him, feed him porridge or broth, and bathe him when he needed it. At night she would undress him and put him to bed. Not once did he acknowledge her or anything around him. He was just a heavy sack of flesh that been left in place of her partner. David wasn't here with her in the cottage. He was out in the wild, inside the Beast.

This was a hard time for Sally and on occasion she felt utterly miserable. She tried all kinds of things to rouse David. She played him music and talk radio, tuned into the sports and current affairs he liked. Nothing worked. He didn't respond to any kind of stimulus.

Many times Sally thought of calling the doctor, or getting an ambulance out, but she always avoided it at the last minute, replacing the receiver before she finished dialing. She knew she was being foolish, but she also had no idea how she would explain what had happened to a medical professional. Not without sounding like she'd lost her mind. They would probably take her in for psychological evaluation along with David.

Sally could have lied, or simply told them she didn't know what caused David's condition, but they would have wanted to take him away and do all sorts of tests on him. Sally was sure that David would snap out of it and come back to her at some point. She was worried that taking him too far away would endanger this. That he wouldn't be able to find his way back from the Beast to his body if she let them take him to hospital.

As miserable as she was with the day to day drudgery of caring for David, it also brought her a masochistic kind of contentment. She was intimate with David on a level she had never been before. This included looking after his toilet functions, which wasn't fun. However, she got to fuss him a lot more, choose his wardrobe and touch him when she wanted without any pretext.

And, though she wouldn't have wanted to admit it, it brought her closer to her parents. When she was little, her mother never had any time for Sally because she was too busy with her father. Sally wasn't allowed to touch her father, who received all her mother's attention. Sally was excluded from the whole process of care, just as she was excluded by most of the other children at school. Now she had a man of her own to look after, she was stepping into her mother's shoes, fulfilling the role her mother had once played. And finally understanding it.

Sally was reminded of an incident in her childhood, when she was about eleven. Her mother had walked into the living room to find Sally, praying, with her hands on her father's head. She'd seen a film in assembly about faith healers and saints and she'd been inspired to try it on her father. She wanted God to reach out to wherever her father had gone, and pull him back into the hollow body he'd left behind.

Her mother was appalled. She slapped Sally's hands away and scolded her.

"But I was only asking God to help Daddy," she said between tears.

Her mother softened her manner, but she didn't relent. "I don't believe in God, darling, and your father is completely beyond His help, even if He did exist. Besides, you know I don't like you bothering your father, he's my responsibility, not yours. You're just a child, you shouldn't have to help."

"But I want to help Mummy, and so does God."

"God doesn't exist!"

"Mummy, it's a sin to say that, you mustn't say that."

"Don't be so silly, I can say what I like."

"But it's a sin, and Father Murphy told us that it says in the Bible that 'the sins of the father will be visited upon the children', and that goes for mummies too, because Susan Brown asked him if it did and he said 'yes'. And if you don't believe in God then I'll get punished."

"Don't be so ridiculous." Her mother's brow furrowed and her mood darkened. "Of course you won't have to pay for my sins! Besides it isn't a sin. There is no God in this world, not for me and certainly not for your poor father."

Sally's tears came harder now. "But Mummy, how can you live in a world without God?" She wanted to know if such a thing were even possible. Her mother really lost her temper then, and sent Sally to her room. Looking back on the incident, years later, Sally could see why her mother had no faith, especially at that time.

Sally's father had filled the space that God might have filled in her life. He was the closest thing her mother had to a substitute.

Sally had never lost her belief in God, but now, she had her own substitute in David. That was Sally's only consolation for the exclusion David made her feel, leaving her here for the Beast.

Then one afternoon, the light returned to David's eyes and he was back. Sally wasn't certain when it actually happened. She'd taken to leaving David in the cluttered conservatory while she got on with the household chores. She'd gone into the conservatory to collect the recycling she kept there. She glanced out into the garden and for the briefest moment she thought she saw the end of a long, black tail, just beyond the garden wall.

It was gone before she had a chance to properly look. Then she heard David clear his throat.

"Could I have a glass of water," he said in a soft voice that was barely a croak. Sally was so shocked she let out a cry of alarm and dropped the recycling.

David smiled apologetically. "I'm sorry, my throat's rather dry."

SIX

Sally knelt before the old dresser in the conservatory and pulled open the drawer where she kept all the tupperware. She lifted out the largest box she had and took it back to the kitchen.

Sally put all the all the steaks that she'd seasoned into the box. Then she put on her coat and made her way out of the back door, through the garden and up the hill towards the forest.

A large hedgerow ran up one side of the hill and Sally made sure to keep close to it as she climbed. She listened very closely for any breezes that might come. Twice she thought she heard something in the movement of the shrubs, but no presence made itself known. The hedge stopped about three quarters of the way up the hill. As she passed a corner where two rows met, Sally heard a sudden commotion.

The thicket shook as if someone had taken hold of it by force. The branches creaked and scraped each other and, in the darkest part of the undergrowth, something stirred up the dry dead leaves. From this cacophony of overlapping noises, a brittle, unnatural voice emerged.

"Nearly ready now– ready now– ready now. Everything is in place– is in place– is in place. The Beast will not last the night– last the night– last the night!"

Sally drummed her fingers on the tupperware box. Her certainty and sense of purpose surged at Hettie's encouragement. It was all coming to an end, the exclusion, the loss of David. She would have him back for good.

Sally left the hedgerow and trudged up to the top of the rise where the forest began. The trees were sparser around the outskirts and also more varied. There were native sessile oaks and silver birches, and the ground was covered with bluebells throughout spring and early summer. Deeper into the forest, where the trees were more dense, the Caledonian pines were dominant.

The earth was cooler up at this height and the air cleaner. Sally could never decide what the forest smelled like. The deeper you went, the more the resinous scent of the pines held sway. Further out, this was undercut by the rich loamy aromas of the forest floor and, just when you got used to that, there were sudden, sweet bursts of wildflowers.

The forest had been a haven for Sally when they first arrived. Pristine and untouched, it justified the whole move, and more than made up for the claustrophobia of small town life. Now it was tainted though. The forest was the Beast's territory, where it took David.

David had refused to speak about what happened when he came back to himself. Sally was desperate to know. She was gentle at first, trying to get him to open up with indirect questions. When that failed, she took a more direct approach and when that didn't work she sulked, threw tantrums and shouted at him.

The more she pushed him, the more David shut down and went into himself. Eventually Sally got tired of fighting and decided to make peace. She missed David. She missed the way they were together, before all this happened. She would learn to live with his secrets.

The closest he came to confiding happened one evening, about a week after the second time the Beast took him. David was more conciliatory this time around, perhaps sensing the lengths he put her to when he was gone.

It was a warm night, but they'd lit the fire all the same, and were enjoying a surprisingly good bottle of Merlot. Sally was making polite conversation, trying to stay away from contentious topics. She mentioned that the recent spate of downpours, followed by bright sunshine, meant many of the wild flowers in the forest had blossomed early.

"It's different in the heart of the forest," David said. Then he paused and a brief frown passed across his face. Sally and he had never gone into the heart of the forest, which covered nearly 4,000 hectares. They'd only explored the periphery.

Sally sensed an opportunity and reached out to him. "Is it much darker there? In the middle of the forest I mean."

"It's more primal and untouched. Very few people have ever gone all the way into it. Possibly a handful in living memory. There are parts of it that no human has ever seen."

Sally took a sip of her wine. She didn't want to pry too much or she'd frighten him off the subject. It was like coaxing a wild animal out of its lair with food. She couldn't make any sudden or threatening moves.

"They've always been important to your family haven't they?" David turned to her, he looked surprised at her perception and, for a moment, she thought she might have scared him off. He looked back to the fire though, and continued.

"My grandfather told me a lot about the woods. He was fascinated with them, like they were a part of him. It was the same for many of my ancestors, he told me. There was one especially, an 18th century Laird of the Manor, they still talk about him in the town. He's the one I get the family curse from."

"The family curse?" Sally had to repress a smile, she didn't want David to think she wasn't taking him seriously.

"My black moods, it's genetic apparently. He was 'much given to black moods' if you believe the local lore. He went to university in Edinburgh to study science and medicine, but his real interests were apparently far more occult. He got involved with some secret societies and then returned home under a cloud without completing his degree."

"Why?"

"He had some sort of breakdown, lots of rumours about it, all very melodramatic. There was gossip about him messing with dark forces, that sort of nonsense. That was the start of his mental health problems."

"Did he find the forest comforting, like we do?"

"He was fascinated with it. He even wrote a paper on the forest and published it privately. He mapped quite a lot of the territory and studied its flora and fauna. He proved there were species of plant in the forest that go back to prehistoric times, to the Paleozoic era even."

"Really?"

"Yes, that means it's pretty much untouched since before the ice age, before Britain was an island even."

"That's incredible, why don't more people know about this then? Why isn't the forest some sort of World Heritage site?"

"Well I'm afraid my ancestor had some rather, erm, colourful views about the forest that don't sit well with the scientific establishment, in spite of his proof."

"Occult views you mean?"

David nodded. "Yes, he had a lot of strange ideas it seems. He was very influenced by an ancient set of beliefs called the Qu'rm Saddic heresy. Its believers have been persecuted since before Mesopotamian times."

"And what does this have to do with the forest?" said Sally, with a slight air of nonchalance. She was careful not to reveal how fascinated she was with David's family history.

"He believed that the forest was one of the 'Quiet Places'."

"Quiet Places?"

"It's all rather complicated, I'm not sure I understand it myself." David reached for the wine bottle and refilled their glasses. He stared into his glass for a while, as if the answer could be found in its rich blend of tannins. For one awful moment Sally thought he was going to leave it there, but he took a deep breath and continued.

"Apparently, there are older worlds than this one, that came into existence before ours."

"I'm not sure I'm following you."

"Okay, let's call them higher planes then, you can follow that right?"

"I guess."

"Okay, so these higher planes also contain life, much older than ours, but not so corporeal."

"Like angels and demons, that sort of thing?"

"Erm... probably. Usually these beings can't... I guess you'd say 'manifest' here, in our world. But they can sometimes enter it through Quiet Places, like the forest, and we can even leave this world, if we want to, and if we know how."

"So these Quiet Places, they're like a portal or something?"

"I suppose so. It's because they're very old seemingly. They haven't changed in eons and they're the parts of our world that came into existence first, the bits that everything else grew from."

"Is that strictly scientific?"

"I don't think so, my ancestor was more of a mystic than a scientist."

"And he put all this in his paper, that's where you read it right?"

"Yes, but the paper doesn't cover all of it. He talks about it more in his journals."

"Wait, you've got his journals? You mean those mouldering old books you keep in your study?"

David furrowed his brow, as if in pain. His head dropped to his chest and he hunched his shoulders as he went into himself. In her excitement, Sally had overreached herself and now she'd lost him. Her heart pounded as she thought of something to say.

"I need to get some more wood for the fire," David said finally, and he got up and made to leave.

"Wait David, please," Sally said. "Come and sit down. The fire's okay, we don't need any more wood."

"I better get some more." He didn't even bother to look at her as he left the room.

"David... please..."

The closing of the back door was his only reply.

The next day Sally saw that David had fitted a lock to his study door, excluding her from any further family secrets.

SEVEN

It was only a few days later that Jane pressed the pamphlet on her. Sally had popped into the library to cheer herself up. A coffee morning at the community centre had emptied the place of pensioners. Jane was alone behind the desk.

"I have something for you," Jane said waving her over. Sally had conflicting emotions about this. She was reluctant to speak to Jane, but excited about the new book she'd got in. It might be an Audrey Niffenegger or a Jennifer Egan she hadn't read. Jane nipped into the backroom, and appeared a moment later with a thin, green pamphlet.

"I think you might find this very interesting," she said, handing it to Sally.

Sally found it hard to mask her disappointment. "Oh," was all she could say looking at the creased green cover. It had an old woodcut on the front, showing a hare by a riverside, looking up at a smiling moon. The title, printed in crude block letters, was Highways, Havens and Highlands.

"It's about local folklore," Jane said. "There's actually a couple of entries on our little town. Here, let me show you..." Jane flicked through to the relevant sections. The print was blurred and badly photocopied. "It's quite old now, it came out in the 80s, I think, but I really think you'll find it... educational. What with... what with living here and everything..."

Jane tried to smile. "You don't have to check it out. It's from my own private collection. Just get it back to me when you can." She was looking up at Sally with one of her awful, earnest expressions.

Sally put the pamphlet in her handbag. She glanced at the new arrivals shelf and the Recommended Reads, but she'd gone off the idea of browsing. "Thanks Jane," she said. "I'll look at it later." Then she left quickly, doubting she'd ever open the thing.

The pamphlet sat under a pile of old magazines on the dining room table for a couple of weeks. Sally hadn't bothered to go back to the library she'd found a bookshop in a neighbouring town. Finally the pamphlet got transferred to the recycling.

It stayed there for a couple of months, with the old newspapers and empty tins, until Sally decided to have a tidy up. David had been taken by the Beast for the second time, and Sally was in a righteous fury, purging the cottage of junk.

The pamphlet must have fallen from a pile of newspapers on the way to the car. It wasn't till Sally came back from dropping off the recycling that she saw it lying on the floor of the hall. She picked it up and stared at it quizzically for a moment, until she remembered where it had come from.

The thought of Jane irritated Sally, but flicking through the poorly produced pamphlet she found she was actually intrigued. She took it into the living room, where she wouldn't have to look at David, and began to flick through it.

There were chapters on hauntings, witchcraft and faery folk that were local to the area. The chapter that really caught Sally's attention was about hedgerows.

There was a story about the Gaelic Teine biorach, a series of Will o' the Wisp sightings, and finally her heart raced when she read this passage:

"The author has also collected several stories regarding a piece of lore unique to Dunballan, a small town in town in the Highlands. Several of the residents report hearing a strange voice haunting the thickets and hedgerows. The voice has variously been described as: "like someone crunching up leaves," and: "like lots of little pixies all talking at once". The voice is known as 'Hettie' to the locals, or 'Hettie of the Hedgerow', to use the full sobriquet.

Reports of sightings, or perhaps we should use the term 'hearings' in this case, go back at least a hundred years. Many have suggested they go back much further. Some reports claim the voice is drawn to those who have recently suffered a tragedy, or those who are about to suffer a great woe. Others say Hettie is more benevolent and warns those she addresses of coming tragedy, but you would do well to heed her warnings, for to ignore them is to court disaster. To cite an example of this, we need only look to the descendants of a certain Laird (see following chapter).

Sally raised her eyebrows when she read this last sentence and flicked through to the relevant part of the next chapter as quickly as she could. The chapter was on Phantom Black Dogs and the Gaelic mythological hound Cù-Sith. In the final part of the chapter, the author had noted a strange variation on the myth that was local to Dunballan.

"A Laird of the McCavendish family is said to have conjured a giant black Beast who stalks the Highland forest near the small town of Dunballan. Originally a promising medical student, and member of several scientific circles, in the mid-18th century, McCavendish was forced to leave the city of Edinburgh under a cloud of scandal.

The scandal arose out of McCavendish's membership of certain secret societies, similar in nature to the Hellfire Club and the Beggar's Benison. What most upset the good citizens of Edinburgh were the rumours of devil worship and occult practices that surrounded the societies. One society, Faith Before Man, was even rumoured to promulgate an ancient blasphemous heresy whose beliefs were so corrupting as to alter men's consciousness forever. It was considered, by the high personages of Edinburgh, that the riotous and sometimes orgiastic behaviour of these societies was excusable in a young and unmarried man. However, such savage and dangerous beliefs were deemed unfit for a man of science. McCavendish was expelled from the many scientific circles which he had worked hard to join, and was unable to find employment as a doctor when he graduated.

McCavendish returned home to his family estate, left to him upon the death of his uncle. It is said that he fell into a black mood and his lands fell into decline. McCavendish was allegedly prone to melancholy and lost days to its malaise, neglecting his many responsibilities in the process. So great was the affliction that his dark moods brought, that McCavendish sought release in the black arts he'd learned.

Deep in the forests that bordered his estate, McCavendish is reported to have summoned a huge black Beast to rid himself of his prevailing melancholy. Some versions of the legend cast the

Beast as a denizen of Hell, others have it cross over from the lands of Faerie. All agree that the Beast came from a race of beings to whom the misery of man is "like to food and drink". McCavendish had presumably wanted the Beast to consume the misery that plagued him, to free him of its burden. However, the Beast took more than just McCavendish's sadness, it also took his soul. In this instance, the Beast of Dunballan might be said to be similar to the Cù-Sith, in its role as a psychopomp – a spiritual guide who takes souls to the afterlife. The Beast did not take McCavendish's soul to the afterlife though, or if it did, it certainly didn't leave it there.

The following morning, McCavendish's absence was noticed by his few remaining servants, who raised the alarm. A search party was formed in Dunballan and McCavendish's lands were scoured the next day. After two days of fruitless searching, the party finally came upon McCavendish deep in the woods. He was alive, but utterly immobile, staring off into the distance at nothing at all. He could neither speak nor recognise anything around him. Nevertheless, they were able to lead him out of the woods and back to his family home without any difficulty, as it seemed he had not lost the ability to walk.

When McCavendish failed to rouse himself from this strange state, he was transferred to a sanitarium. A few months later, McCavendish had still not recuperated, so he was sent home. A week after his return, he came to himself and made a sudden and unexpected recovery. No one has ever offered a satisfying explanation of what befell McCavendish or why he fell into a fugue state, least of all McCavendish himself who, it is reported, refused to ever discuss it with family, friends or medical professionals.

According to the legend, McCavendish would fall into a

waking stupor many more times, sometimes for as a little as a week, other times as long as a month. On every occasion it is rumoured that Beast was to be glimpsed in the grounds of his house, both before and after McCavendish fell into this state. When McCavendish died, his house, and what was left of his estate, went to a cousin, who also developed the same affliction within months of moving into the house with his young family.

Every successive heir has fallen prey to this same affliction, and this has given birth to the legend of the McCavendish family curse. Whether, as some have argued, this is due to an inherited genetic flaw, or the continued presence of the Beast, is not for this author to say. Sightings of the Beast are said to continue to this day.

There is also an interesting coda to this tale. Around the turn of the twentieth century, the final heir to the McCavendish estate sold off much of the lands and the house, without taking up residence. Preferring to live in London, he kept only a large cottage and a small parcel of land for hunting holidays. Roughly six months after this last McCavendish heir sold up, mass hysteria gripped the little town of Dunballan.

It started when several women of the town claimed to have heard Hettie of the Hedgerow (see last chapter). They said that Hettie had told them that if the heir did not return, the townsfolk must kill the beast of Dunballan or they would all suffer an unspeakable fate. Apparently word was sent to the heir who refused to believe such superstitious nonsense. However, when more than a handful of the townsfolk suffered an unspecified misfortune, the heir was stricken with guilt and relented. He had not prospered in London and had lost a good part of the money he made from the sale of the estate. He returned home and the townsfolk suffered no further misfortunes. From that day forth, there has always been at least one member of the McCavendish family living in Dunballan.

That's where the chapter ended. Sally did not care to read any more. She let the pamphlet fall from her fingers to the bare floorboards. For a few moments she simply stared at the wall opposite.

Then she stood up and stamped on the open pages of the pamphlet, leaving dusty footprints on the torn pages.

She kicked the pamphlet towards the sofa and the rusted staples came apart, sending pages skittering all over the living room floor.

They knew.

All this time, the miserable, lying townsfolk knew. That's why they wanted David to come home. They knew what he was going through. They knew what Sally had to put up with and they approved. No, more than approved, they needed David to go through this for their own selfish ends.

That's why they could never hold Sally's eye when she met them in town. That's why they smiled and nodded and scurried away, clustering in little groups, gossiping amongst themselves. All complicit in the same guilt.

Right at that moment, Sally could have murdered every one of them for what they'd done to David. What they'd put her through.

A cold, hard plan was forming in Sally's mind. She was going to find the voice, the one that spoke to her from the hedgerow. She knew now that she wasn't losing her mind, that she really had heard it.

She was going to find Hettie, and then she was going

to learn, once and for all, how to kill the Beast and take back her man.

EIGHT

Sally wound her way through the woods where the undergrowth was densest. When she heard the bodiless wind push its way through them, she knew she'd chosen the right path.

The tiny branches rattled, the twigs beneath them skittered, and the many leaves moved in a flurry. The darkness at the heart of the shrubs seemed to throb, as the overlapping sounds of the thicket formed themselves into a voice.

"You're nearly there– nearly there– nearly there little sister. We will lure the Beast– lure the Beast– lure the Beast to its doom."

Sally stepped over a rotting, moss covered log. The silver birches were giving way to pines, which grew closer together and the temperature in this part of the forest dropped. The cool air brought a sudden flash of lucidity. Sally thought about what she was doing here in the middle of the forest and it suddenly seemed insane.

What if she hurt David in what she was doing? Was she fighting back against the Beast, or descending into worse lunacy? Was there a way to back out now if she was?

The low lying branches began to shake as if sensing her wavering, and Hettie's voice broke through.

"Hold on to your anger– your anger– your anger. Let

it guide you as it has done– as it has done– as it has done so far!"

Sally's anger usually subsided in Hettie's presence, along with her sadness and her other negative feelings. Now it rose up inside her, as if Hettie had given it back. The exclusion she felt from David, from the townsfolk, from everything in Dunballan had transformed into a purifying rage. It had focussed Sally and given her purpose.

After collecting up the pages of the pamphlet and dropping them in the bin, Sally had gone outside to the woodshed to collect the axe. She carried it up the stairs to where David's study was.

It had been locked since the night they chatted in front of the fire. He didn't need to do that. Sally had always respected his privacy, giving him all the space and time he needed. That lock was a slap in the face, one exclusion too many. Sally had wanted to unlock David, practically from the moment she first met him. She was always afraid of what the consequences of that might be though. She would have to content herself with his study.

Sally raised the axe and brought it down on the door. The old, weathered oak splintered, but the door didn't give. She brought the axe down again and again, gouging great chunks of dry aging wood from the door and the frame. Eventually she hacked all the way around the square, cast iron lock and kicked the door open. The lock remained in place as it swung inwards, the bolt still holding it to the frame.

David's study hadn't been dusted since they moved in, possibly even longer. His desk was hard to make out under all the paper, and Sally couldn't see his laptop anywhere. The bookshelf looked ready to fall apart under the weight of so many books. They spilled out into untidy piles all over the floor. Some of these piles were nearly as tall as Sally.

She hunted through the shelves and piles, picking up the oldest books and flicking through them, but didn't find what she wanted. After nearly an hour she came upon the chest. It was made of dark, stained wood and it was locked. Sally looked at the axe she'd left by door and wondered if she could bring herself to destroy a venerable antique.

Luckily she didn't have to, there was a tarnished brass key lying on a shelf just above it. Sally tried the key in the lock and opened the chest. It smelled of bitumen, fading leather and old musty pages. It was filled with journals.

Sally lifted them out and flicked through the pages. They were filled with a precise but florid handwriting, which took Sally a moment to decipher. After a while she got the hang of it and was able to quickly scan the contents, honing in on the volumes that were of most use to her.

This took her quite a while. The journals covered a period of roughly ten years and most of the daily entries covered multiple pages. The room grew dim from the setting sun and Sally's stomach growled. She hadn't eaten since breakfast, but she didn't want to stop till she'd found everything she needed.

Finally she returned to the living room with a small stack of journals and a light supper. She didn't feel like feeding David, she was too angry, so she left him where he was in the conservatory.

The first journal that really caught Sally's attention covered the period about six months prior to McCavendish leaving Edinburgh. It focussed most on his association with the society Faith Before Man.

As far as Sally could tell, most of the other societies McCavendish joined were mainly interested in drinking and hiring prostitutes. The diabolical and subversive beliefs they toyed with were just one more illicit thrill.

Faith Before Man was a different matter though. They were an elite society devoted to uncovering occult secrets in the forbidden texts they sought out and collected. They were particularly interested in an ancient set of beliefs called the *Qu'rm Saddic Heresy* or *The Faith that Came Before Man*, which is where they got their name. There was one passage, towards the end of the journal that really gripped Sally's attention:

"*JUNE 21st*____

It has been three nights now and I have barely slept. The laudanum does nothing for me. I cannot suppress the memories of that night. I close my eyes and the images rear up in my mind, in more terrible detail than when I first beheld them. They will not let me rest.

I am a disheveled wreck of raw nerves and wild fancy. I start at the slightest sound from the street. I have shut up the windows and closed the shutters, but the cacophony of the city finds me still. I have no appetite and even less wish to leave my rooms in search of food. I'm too distracted to read and yet I have nothing else to take mind off the events of that night. I cannot go in search of human company for I fear I am tainted, that my peers will read in my countenance some of what has come to pass, and will know the deeds to which I've stooped.

So I turn instead to my journal. I have neglected it of late, but now it is my one, slim comfort. I had such high hopes for it when I began. Was it really only two years ago that I wrote, in these very pages, of my ambition to chronicle my ascendancy into the loftier realms of science and my transcendence through the secrets of the occult. I had hoped to develop a new system of thought in which both could be synthesised to the benefit of the other. Now I fear that ambition must be abandoned. My sole hope is that, by setting down what happened, by capturing every memory that hounds me relentlessly, I can exorcise myself of them. While every word that was uttered is as clear to me now as when I first heard it, and every sight I beheld, or purported to behold, is carved like a stone relief onto my mind, I will endeavour to put it all down in these pages. I know there is little chance that this will relieve me of their burden, but I have no other options, this journal is my last resort.

My pen shakes as I try to gather my thoughts. I am procrastinating, I know am, trying to postpone re-living these events by putting them down in words. I know this is foolish and I must stop wasting time. Let me try a little laudanum and I will endeavour to continue...

The temperature was cold for the time of year, even for Edinburgh, with its arctic winter nights that barely improve in the summer. I arrived at Patterson's residence, in Hanover Street, a little later than I would have liked, but I had other matters to which I had to attend first.

I was greeted by Moran, Patterson's manservant, a slovenly and unkempt man for whom I do not care. He showed me, unannounced, into the drawing room, the largest space in

Patterson's residence. The spacious, high ceilinged room had been stripped of all its furniture and furnishings. All that remained were the drawn curtains and bare floorboards.

I entered to find McKendrick and Patterson eagerly awaiting me.

"What's this," I said, "Are the others not here yet? What of Stevenson, McGregor and Smythe?"

"I didn't tell them about our gathering," Patterson said. He was wearing only an unwashed shirt and a pair of breeches. He patently hadn't shaved that morning and his thinning blonde hair was plastered to his forehead with sweat. "We need a much smaller group for our first foray."

"To be honest," said McKendrick, who was leaning up against the mantelpiece. "I'm not sorry to be rid of Smythe, or her insistence we pay homage to an interminable litany of goddesses."

McKendrick was quick to disparage Smythe and her pagan beliefs, but he was happy to accept her patronage and the wealth she lavished on our society. He was as immaculately dressed as ever, in knee length coat, short double breasted waistcoat, and knee breeches, all perfectly tailored to his tall broad frame. He had also trimmed his large, military moustache since I last saw him. I looked around the room for the robes and artefacts Patterson had chosen for our ceremony, but could see none.

"Are we to draw a pentacle on the floor," I said. "Or did you have some other symbol in mind?"

"Actually, I wasn't intending to use any symbols in the ceremony," Patterson replied.

"None at all?"

Patterson shook his head. "Nor any wands, swords or other paraphernalia."

"The d____d fool doesn't even want to invoke the Four Watchtowers," McKendrick said.

"But without the Guardians of the Watchtowers, how will we open the way?" I said. "How will we call upon the elements for protection?"

"We won't need to," Patterson assured us. "The Rite of Adocentyn isn't that sort of ceremony. It's from a tradition that's much older than any of the Hermetic arts."

"So how did you find out about it then?" barked McKendrick. "Turned up some new scroll from your Uncle's collection?"

Patterson's Uncle, as I think I've mentioned before in these pages, had been an avid collector of ancient and forbidden manuscripts. These included original copies of the Corpus Hermeticum *and the* Picatrix *in both Greek and Arabic. When he passed away, he left his entire collection to Patterson. The rarest and most precious items from this collection had led to the formation of our society, and also helped christen it.*

Through means we had never discovered, Patterson's Uncle had procured perhaps the only surviving copies of the Codex Transfiguratio, *the* Codex Conscientia *and the* Vos Hokkumah Scrolls. *Among the most forbidden and blasphemous texts in the history of civilisation, this collection of writings comprised the only known repository of the heretical* Qu'rm Saddic *teachings, also known, in times before yore, as* The Faith that Came Before Man. *Each one of them had been copied by hand and translated from tongues so ancient that no record yet remains of them.*

"It was a game my Uncle used to play with me that provided the inspiration," said Patterson.

"Parlour games, you want us to find the Gate with parlour games?" McKendrick said with great derision.

"Not parlour games, I think my Uncle was secretly trying to train me to do the rite. He'd take my brother and I into a bare room, like this one, and he'd ask us where we'd like to visit. We could go anywhere in the world. We'd choose a place and he'd take us there with the power of his words. He'd start by describing the scene, then he'd walk around the space and begin to point out certain details to us. After a while he'd get us to join in with him and we'd start to point out what we saw, and describe our surroundings too. Eventually, matters would come to a point where we wouldn't need to describe things to each other in order for us all to see them. It became akin to a shared hallucination. What's more we could even verify this later."

"Verify it, how?" demanded McKendrick.

"When I was a child I was obsessed with the port at Alexandria. I'd read about it in my Father's library and I'd even written poems about it and drawn pictures of what I thought it looked like."

"I'll wager they were no better than the doggerel and daubings you produce now."

McKendrick was constantly deriding Patterson's work. He cared neither for the paintings or the poetry Patterson produced. Patterson ignored his barb and continued. "So, naturally, one of the first places that I chose to explore, in the game, was the Alexandrian port. I spent hours exploring it with my brother and uncle, we went everywhere, including a little stone archway for taking livestock into the city. The keystone on the archway had a very specific stonemason's symbol. My brother spotted it first and then he pointed it out to my Uncle and I. Years later, as a young man, I visited Alexandria by boat and spent several nights in the port. I was gripped with a sense of déjà vu, it all looked familiar, as if I had visited before, even though it was my *first time there. Then I remembered the game I had played with my Uncle, and realised that everything was just as I had seen it as a boy. It was as though I had been transported to the very spot where I now stood. I made a point of searching out the stone arch, and it was right where we'd seen it in the game, with the self-same symbol on the keystone. We'd never been to Alexandria when we played the game, yet we'd seen a unique landmark that years later, I could independently verify."*

"Well, that's all very fascinating," I said. "But what does any of this have to do with the rite of Adocentyn?"

"It says, in the third tractate of the Vos Hokkumah Scrolls, that to enter the city of Adocentyn one must think with the mind of God and see with the eyes of God."

"We've all read the blasted scrolls," said McKendrick.

"I know, it was me that showed them to you. So you'll also know that in the Codex Transfiguratio it says: 'the imagination is the Queen of all the senses, for she is closest to the thoughts of God.' *Imagination is the key to all magic, you know it is. Every occult ritual and symbol is merely a way of focusing the imagination, so we can recreate reality just as God once created it.*"

"You're not convincing me."

"*In the beginning was the 'word' and the 'word' was with God. He is the ultimate story teller, trapped within His own story. What better way to escape His story than with another story? The Rite of Adocentyn is a collectively shared story in which we're all storytellers. We counter the prison of Creation with a story of our own. That's how we enter Adocentyn and that's where we'll find the Gate.*"

Nothing in life had seemed the same to me, no part of my existence, or any other's, had remained untouched since I encountered this central truth of the Qu'rm Saddic Heresy. The pen still shakes in my hand as I recall each appalling revelation that confronted me while I pored over Patterson's scrolls by candlelight. Many times I had looked up from the parchment to see Patterson's grave countenance examining me, directing my attention to new passages that shook me to my very core and destroyed every certainty to which I had ever cleaved. Every ounce of my reason rose up in opposition to this one core truth, but my heart bade me believe it.

God is not just the breath of life that animates all living things, He is also a prisoner in His own creation. Just as a heavy cloud falls to earth as a thousand different drops of rain, God has entered the material world as a million different consciousnesses, each one perceiving itself as an individual entity. For this reason we never realise our collective divinity, never see the material world for the jail it truly is, and this ignorance is the greatest form of tyranny. Even Heaven is a part of this snare, for it is but a way station, a temporary respite from our journey back to becoming one with the source of Creation, from which we came and of which we were always a part.

We are not without means of escape though. However slim they are, there are stresses built into the architecture of the universe, tiny nooks and crannies through which our souls can slip and attain their true divinity. The scrolls had taught us such a Gate could be accessed within the city of Adocentyn. But Adocentyn existed on a higher plane now, within an older world than ours.

I had first read of Adocentyn, the legendary city built by the thrice great Hermes Trismegistus, in the Picatrix, that Arabic treatise on talismanic magic of which Marsilio Ficino, the Renaissance scholar who translated the Corpus Hermeticum, was so fond. Our study of Patterson's forbidden texts had taught us that the account of the city of Adocentyn in the Picatrix had a much older source. The Codex Transfiguratio described a rite that would allow the intrepid to access the ancient city and, once there, to search out the Gate.

Since discovering this, our elite society had become obsessed with deciphering the maddening clues within the text in order to enact the Rite. Now, it seemed, Patterson's Uncle might have known how to conduct the Rite all along and, furthermore, secretly trained his nephew without Patterson ever realising.

I could see, by the expression on McKendrick's face, that he was not unmoved by Patterson's argument. McKendrick fancied himself a hard headed pragmatist. A botanist by training, I knew that he supplemented 'his scientific studies with occult study not, as he claimed, out of a conviction that 'there was more to creation than can be found on a dissecting table'. Rather, I considered him a thrill seeker and, what may be worse, a man with a terrible will to power.

His family was part of the political class and there was a seat in some rotten borough waiting for him as soon as he tired of his studies. McKendrick had told me once that he believed true power, the purest kind of power over other men, was not found in the ballot box, but in the occult. His older brother, now a junior minister, had been an explorer when he was younger. He came back from Africa with stories of the Babalawo, Yoruba high priests who worship the Orishas, and the incredible sway they hold over their followers. When McKendrick spoke of this power his eyes came alive with a lust I found unnatural. To see him seduced by Patterson's logic swayed me also, I must confess.

Had I but had the prescience to cry 'desist' at that moment, to persuade us all to let go of such folly and bend our efforts to *another end, we might have been spared the terror that was to follow. But sadly, I lacked such essential precognition, and our dreadful tragedy played itself out to a most bitter end.*

"So, how do we go about commencing this rite of yours?" McKendrick asked, addressing Patterson with a newfound regard.

"We need to take ourselves out of this space, and into another. For a start, gentlemen, I suggest you remove your coats, the sun is merciless at this time of day in the east of Egypt."

The fire in the grate had fallen to embers and the room was large and given to draughts. Nonetheless, I took off my topcoat and, within minutes, I forgot the loss of it, as Patterson described our journey across the hot sands of Egypt in the most vivid detail.

"Up ahead of us, on the crest of that hill," Patterson continued. "Do you see it? A wall, fully twelve miles long. That, my friends, marks the perimeter of Adocentyn. Tell me how it looks to you."

I looked up to where Patterson was pointing. In my mind's eye the image was becoming clearer.

I pictured an ancient wall but not much else, as we drew closer I began to imagine more detail, then, as if he was describing the very thing I was picturing, McKendrick said:

"It's built in the style of the Early Dynastic Period, only it looks far more sophisticated, both in terms of its design and construction. The stones are so white, they fairly seem to glow as the sun's rays hit them."

We trudged on up the hill, describing to one another how the sand spilled into our shoes and the heat beat mercilessly down. I actually felt sweat break out on the back of my neck. As we reached the crest of the hill, we stood still and looked at each other in surprise.

"It's like an oasis," said McKendrick. "There's lush, fertile grass growing all around."

"And look," I said. "There's a lagoon, just ahead of us. The water is so blue, see how it fairly sparkles in the sun."

"Do you see the fish leaping?" said Patterson. "A fisherman would never go hungry here."

We walked around the lagoon and approached the city wall which reared up ahead of us.

"Look, there's an entrance," I cried, pointing to a large opening in the wall. "And look at that relief above it, it's so meticulously carved."

"It depicts an Ibis," said McKendrick, though I'd given him no clue, that's exactly what I also saw carved into the rock above the entrance.

"It seems to move," said Patterson. "To be watching us."

"That's an illusion," said McKendrick. "It's just the heat haze from the sun affecting the shadows."

"That's one explanation, but I suspect there are other forces at play."

Whatever the reason, we all saw the relief move, as if the Ibis was turning its head, with its long beak, to observe us. Though my body was still in Hanover Street, I no longer saw the empty walls and bare floors of Patterson's drawing room. I was wholly in Egypt, standing at the entrance to the city of Adocentyn.

Patterson kneeled and bade us do the same. He put his hands together as if in prayer and intoned: "Guardians of the Castle, Lord Bull, Lord Eagle, Lord Hound and Lord Lion, we humbly request your permission to enter Adocentyn and conduct ourselves without harm."

In brief succession we all heard a bull bellow, an eagle cry, a hound howl and a lion roar.

Each noise sounded incredibly near and yet seemed to issue from the depths of the city. There was something otherworldly in the echoing quality of each call.

Patterson stood. "I think we have permission to enter."

I will not exhaust myself by recording the many marvels we witnessed in Adocentyn. Suffice to say we saw a multitude of images and symbols graven onto the walls of the ancient buildings. In the wide open plazas there were many huge trees, all bearing multiple types of fruits. We continued to describe all of this to one another, stopping occasionally to marvel at one of the many stone or metal statues that populated the city. It was as if our words, and our shared perceptions of them, intensified every sight we beheld.

Not once did we see a single inhabitant. The whole city was deserted, and looked as if it had been that way for countless aeons. Presently, we came to a castle in the centre of the city.

"See here," said Patterson. "It is just as the Picatrix *described it. There are the four gates, aligned to the cardinal points of the compass, and above them are the guardians who granted our entry, the Bull, the Eagle, the Hound and the Lion."*

Huge stone statues of the beasts sat atop each of the gates, looking at once more real than life but also of another world entirely.

"And there's the tower," said McKendrick, pointing to the summit of the castle. "I'm no expert on the matter of ancient measurement, but I'll wager that's a full thirty cubits, and it has a rotunda on the top, just as we were expecting."

The rotunda atop the tower was glowing with an eerie light that changed from purple to deep blue as we beheld it.

We entered the tower by the western gate, beneath the Bull, and made our way directly to the base of the tower. There were only two doors in the whole of the base.

"One of these leads to the vaults, the other to the summit of the tower," said Patterson.

"Which do we choose?" I asked.

"Whichever one leads us to the Gate," said McKendrick.

"But which is that?"

"The third tractate of the Vos Hokkumah Scrolls *instructs us to think with the 'mind of God',*" said Patterson. "The Codex Conscientia *tells us that God descended to the material plane in order achieve the ultimate ascendance.*"

"We choose the vaults then?" said McKendrick.

"We choose the vaults," I said, with unexpected certainty.

The steps down to the vaults were on a steep spiral. Even though, in reality, we were doing nothing more than walking around in a circle in Patterson's drawing room, we were so immersed in our mutually induced hallucination that we squinted in the waning light, and wrinkled our noses at the dank odours that rose to greet us.

The stairs gave out on a long stone passageway that led to a low ceilinged stone chamber. As we approached, the chamber seemed to glow with an unnatural light. When we entered we saw the glow came from a mosaic of the moon, set into the floor of the chamber. What was causing the mosaic to glow with such a sinister luminosity I cannot say, but it drew Patterson, McKendrick and myself towards it as if we were moths drawn by a candle flame.

As we set foot upon the mosaic, a vision appeared before us. We saw a maiden arrayed in a shining silver robe, her skin was most delicate and pale, and her whole aspect denoted grace and an unmistakable devoutness. She smiled at us with the delicate *humility of one who is quite perfectly chaste. I found myself filled with awe and gratitude, that such an immaculate, apotheosis of divine femininity should bestow her attention upon us.*

"It's Monanom," said Patterson. "The dual goddess of the moon."

"And what would you travelers, so far from your homes, want within my chamber?" Monanom asked.

"We seek the Gate," said McKendrick.

"The Gate?"

"Yes, the Gate that leads out of Creation and frees us from the prison of this world."

"That Gate is not to be found in my chamber, or even this city."

"Blessed Monanom," Patterson said. "It is written that the way to the Gate is to be found within this city, and, we believe, also within your chamber."

"So you would find this Gate would you?" said Monanom. "Think carefully before you answer."

"Of course we would find this Gate," said McKendrick. "Why else would we travel all this way?"

"And this is the wish of you all is it?"

"It is," said Patterson.

Though I was reluctant to agree with my companions, for I knew in my heart it would grieve Monanom, and I could think of nothing worse than saddening her, I too said:

"It is."

At that, the goddess bowed her head, and folded her robes around her, then spun round with a sudden velocity. The temperature of the chamber plummeted and we saw that the reverse side of Monanom was the most hideous and repugnant crone I have ever laid eyes upon. I had forgotten that the dual sides of her nature sit back to back on the same body. The crone's breathing was hoarse, and came in long slow bursts. A stream of saliva spilled from her near toothless mouth, and a deep chuckle broke ominously from her throat.

"Are you sure you don't want to turn back?" she said.

"No, we want to press on," Patterson said, though I could see he felt as apprehensive as I did.

A tremor shook the ground at our feet and the mosaic rose six inches out of the floor, as though it were mounted on the head of a short column. All three of us fought to keep our footing.

"How about now, any second thoughts?" said the Crone.

"No," I said, though I hardly knew where the tenacity came from.

With that, the ceiling of the chamber collapsed and great chunks of masonry rained down all around us. It was a wonder that none of us were hit. The column beneath the mosaic rose up, with great speed, pushing through the hole in the ceiling and into the lower floors of the castle above us. Patterson, McKendrick and I fell to our hands and knees to keep from falling off the mosaic.

"Now will you turn back," cackled the Crone, a malevolent smile creasing her lined face, as she rose too, hovering in the air above us.

"No, God d__n you," McKendrick shouted.

The column rose again, and the ceiling above us fell in, and then the ceiling above that and every ceiling above us, until the column had pushed through them all and we were out in the open, level with the rotunda on the tower.

The crone circled us in the air. "Now will you turn back?" she said.

"No," I gasped, but my arms and legs were shaking.

"Hold firm," Patterson told us. *"She's trying to break our resolve. To keep us imprisoned forever in the material world."*

The column rose higher, at greater speed, taking us so far from the ground that first the castle, then the whole of Adocentyn disappeared from view. I became afraid to glance over the edge of the growing column. I pulled my knees up against my chest until I was curled into a ball, and dug my fingers into the mosaic's tiles, turning my knuckles white with the effort. The others did much the same. The Crone flew all around us, taunting us with her presence.

"Wouldn't you like to turn back now?" she called out.

None of us could muster speech, so we just shook our heads.

The column continued its ascent, but a fearful rumble passed through it. The outer edges of the column were starting to crack and fall away. The circumference of the mosaic, on which we crouched, got smaller and smaller, the column got thinner and thinner and we were all forced to our feet.

What was left of the column broke through the clouds and carried on rising. The column was now so thin, all three of us were standing, pressed up against each other, with our arms around one another's waists. The heels of our boots were hanging over the edge of what was left of the column. If one of us were to list even slightly to one side, he would have taken the others with him, plummeting into the vast expanse below.

We were now higher than the tallest mountain on the planet. The air at this height was too thin and we were all having difficulty breathing. Stripped to our shirt sleeves, because of the heat of Egypt, we were now numb with exposure. The column crumbled so much that, eventually, there was only room for us to place a single foot each upon it, and attempt to balance precariously.

The Crone swooped around us, her black robe flapping like the wings of some giant bat. "Do you want to turn back?" she shrieked.

God forgive me, I did want to turn back. I wanted to be out of this predicament and away from this trial. I had lost my resolve, I had failed the test and wanted nothing more than for it to end. I could see the same sentiment on the faces of the two men to whom I clung.

However, some indefatigable core at the centre of our being refused to let us give voice to our failure. We closed our eyes and trusted to our fortitude instead.

The column continued to climb and crumble at the same time. Finally we felt it fall away completely and there was nothing holding us up at so great a height. My heart lurched, and ice cold terror seized my innards. I felt something inside myself simply snap and give way. I surrendered myself to it utterly, expecting at any moment to plummet to my death.

Instead of panic, I felt transcendence flood through me. Instead of falling I found myself to be weightless. I opened my eyes and saw that I had been transported to another realm altogether, as had Patterson and McKendrick. We had come through our trial and we had succeeded. Whether we were in our astral bodies, or simply our incarnate souls, I couldn't say. We were experiencing a type of existence, and a form of perception, that we had never been aware of before. I could see, and even feel, whole new spectrums of colour and entire new modes of thought and movement.

Away in the distance, I saw two pillars of what seemed to be frozen fire, burning with a fire's intensity, but not dancing like a flame. The pillars had been carved into ornate posts, between the posts was a lattice work of what I can only describe as 'hard light' that glowed with an almost unbearable intensity.

Patterson gasped. "It's the Gate, we've found the Gate!" We were on the very edge of Creation, and we had found the way out. All things were easier and simpler on this plane and we only had to look at the Gate and wish to be near it, for us to move towards it.

As we got closer, we found the Gate to be resonating at some impossible frequency that we could apprehend only in the core of our being. It suggested to us that the Gate was itself a sentient being, capable of unimaginable thoughts.

Not one of us had the least idea what do at that point. We had found the Gate, as we had planned, but that was as far as our plans extended. Beyond that we hadn't the least clue how to proceed. None of us were certain if we had courage enough to take the final plunge and attempt to go through the Gate. To leave behind all of Creation and be utterly unmade so as to free the God within ourselves.

The Gate itself appeared to have some sort of gravitational pull. The closer we got to it, the more it seemed to draw us in, as though we were boats on an incoming tide. It remained closed for the whole of our approach and, I must confess, the thought of opening it terrified me. I had no idea what would happen if it were to swing wide. What might lie beyond it, or what would happen to all that lay before it on this side.

I had even less idea how one would go about opening the Gate. What sort of key would unlock it? More importantly, what key would lock it again, and keep it locked, if it were to swing too wide?

As we were silently deliberating, floating ever closer to the Gate, I heard McKendrick gasp. He was looking off into the distance. At first I saw not what had caught his attention. Then it became apparent. A small crowd of what I can only describe as entities was moving in our direction.

It is here that my powers of description fail me. I cannot adequately convey quite how these beings looked. They each appeared to be an intricate conglomerate of geometric shapes that were constantly folding and unfolding themselves into dimensions of space it was beyond my ability to perceive. They were golden in colour, but their surface seemed harder than any metal in existence, and yet also more fluid than any liquid I've known. The sharp, angularity of their surfaces were reflecting what seemed to be an ever changing array of objects. One moment it was a multitude of eyes, from creatures I doubt have ever existed, the next it was stars from no known cosmos, and in another moment, some black unfathomable gulf from the edge of time itself.

It was Patterson who recognised them for what they were. "Archons," he cried. "Run, for God's sake run, we mustn't let them get near us!" I knew instantly why he was so alarmed. We had all read of the Archons. They are mentioned not only in the Vos Hokkumah Scrolls *but also in the few remaining Gnostic texts that are passed between collectors of rare manuscripts.*

They are Lords of the outer realms of Creation, who patrol the very outskirts of existence. Their sole aim is to maintain the integrity of the material world and to keep every soul imprisoned within it, forever. They are Creation's last line of defence against the enlightened and the liberated.

They are also terrifying and hideous beings, capable of tearing apart and devouring a living soul for an agonising eternity of suffering. That is why, in spite of the ineffable pull of the Gate, Patterson and I turned away from it and willed ourselves to move as fast as we could in the opposite direction.

McKendrick was a different matter though. He remained where he was, as if transfixed by the sight of the Archons.

"Magnificent," he said, as the Archons bore down on us. "Such power, such incredible, undeniable power."

We called out to McKendrick as we fled. We begged him to join us, to get away while there was still time, but if he even heard our words, he did not heed them. He held up his arms in welcome to the Archons, mindful only of his overweening lust for power. The near unstoppably crushing power that the Archons represented had mesmerised him and that, as I always suspected, was his unmaking.

The Archons fell on him.

I cannot describe the agony of his screams, or the psychic emanations his suffering gave off. Patterson and I felt them most acutely though, in the very depths of our being. Even now my eyes fill with tears as I try to write this. My pen falters and my stomach rebels, I am going to have to set aside this journal, so I may vomit. I am sorry to be so course, but it is the truth...

—

I am back, for there is one further thing that I need to get down. The one thing that has haunted me more than any other part of the whole, lamentable experience.

As the Archons fell on McKendrick, a thick black mist sprang up beneath him, and swirled about his legs. It had the appearance of ink dropped into a glass of water, forming itself into viscous tendrils that ended in what appeared to be a cross between an infernal blossom and a tiny gaping mouth. As McKendrick screamed (dear God, let me forget those screams), the tendrils seemed to thicken and swell, as though they were glutting themselves, feasting on his terror and pain.

Patterson and I could bear no more of McKendrick's tortuous ordeal, and we fled as fast as we could, though we had no idea where we were going. Our own panic and terror grew with each *passing second and this drew more of the black mist to us, swirling around us as we tried to escape. It would seem that the mist and its tendrils was some kind of fauna, unique to this plane of existence.*

The mist grew many black tendrils, and many blossom-like mouths, that I could neither outrun nor outmanouevre no matter how hard I tried. They latched on to me and began to feed on my misery and terror. It was the strangest sensation, not unlike being bled by leeches to release the bad humour. In a short while I started to feel nothing. All the pain and fear that had gripped me was siphoned off and I was released of it. It was not a transcendent or a joyful feeling, but it was not wholly unpleasant.

In a little while I blacked out.

When I came to, I was lying on the floor of Patterson's drawing room, in a pool of blood. At some point in all the confusion I must have fallen and dashed my forehead on the corner of the mantelpiece. Being a head wound, there was a lot of blood, but it wasn't that serious, requiring six stitches that I later applied to myself. Patterson and McKendrick were not so unscathed.

I found Patterson a little while later, curled up in a foetal position beneath a bed in one of the guest rooms. He must have crawled there when he came to. He was quite traumatised by his experience and had lost the power of speech when I found him. All he could do was whimper whenever I addressed him, preferring to curl up in a chair with a blanket over his head.

McKendrick fared even worse. He was in the drawing room when I regained consciousness. He was still on his feet, staring vacantly in front of him, oblivious to all stimuli. He was in a totally vegetative state, he was breathing and was capable of movement but he had been stripped of any intelligence or cognitive ability. More than that, he was quite patently lacking a soul. I had witnessed what had happened to that essential and immortal part of his being and I still shudder when I consider its fate. What was left behind, on this material plane, was a hollow shell. A mockery of a human being, that brought only pity and loathing to all who looked upon it. A lamentable travesty stood in the place of the man he once was.

Moran was nowhere to be found, whether he had fled in the night, or what became of him, I know not. He has not been seen since, by anyone of my acquaintance. I summoned what help I could and made sure that my friends were in good hands, and receiving the best help available. Then I repaired to my own quarters to tend to my wounds. I have not left since, except to acquire laudanum and food.

This is all I have the strength to write. I have nothing more to say about the ordeal. All I have thought about since is the strange black mist I encountered that, for all its demonic qualities, may well have saved my sanity.

That and the Gate itself. I cannot stop myself from wondering what the consequences might be should it ever be thrown open, and how that might be prevented. What would one use as a lock, and what would be the key, for such an ethereal portal?

NINE

Sally put down the journal, rubbed her eyes and stretched her back. She realised she'd been reading for several hours solidly without a break.

Her bladder was uncomfortably full and her throat was dry. She was also more than a little light headed. Not just from sitting in the same position for so many hours, but also because of McCavendish's remarkable account. She'd been so invested in the handwritten pages that she felt as though she'd had an out of body journey along with him.

Before Sally came to live in Dunballan, she'd have considered McCavendish's account to be either pure fantasy, or the ravings of a deluded individual. With everything she'd seen in recent months, she was more inclined to believe it. It certainly answered a lot of her questions.

After relieving herself, and fixing a cup of peppermint tea, Sally read through the remaining journals. The entries became more sporadic and self-pitying, as McCavendish chronicled the events of his disgrace and downfall.

McKendrick never recovered from his vegetative state and died some months afterwards in his family's care. After an unsuccessful suicide attempt, Patterson confided what had happened to one of his doctors. The story spread, and more stories came to light about the Faith Before Man, causing a minor scandal that disgraced all the members.

McCavendish's return to the family estate was not a happy one. He complained a lot about the debt his uncle had left him, but didn't seem to be any more skilled at managing the estate himself. The gaps between entries got longer and longer as McCavendish suffered increasing bouts of depression. The prevailing theme of the last set of entries was the amount of time McCavendish had lost to his debilitating moods.

Contact with a rare bookseller seemed to lift his spirits for a while. Not only did the book seller buy several copies of McCavendish's paper on the forest, he also sold him an ancient grimoire, by an anonymous author, that fascinated him. This lead to an entry that Sally found particularly interesting:

November 21st____

Success! Sweet and blessed success. Finally I have the vindication I long sought. My heart is so light, I believe I could burst out into song, were it not for my awful voice and the shocked dismay of the servants, who already think my habits queer enough.

I have lost several days to poring over the Grimoire, a dense and obscure text to be sure, but not an unrewarding one, given careful study. Though I know nothing about the author's character, or any detail of his life, he could perhaps have been a brother of mine (or even a sister?), so closely aligned are our thoughts and ambitions. Today I chanced up on a bestiary of sorts, wherein the unnamed author attempted to categorise the many different inhabitants of the unseen, and rarely glimpsed worlds. In amongst the references to the Heolfor, the Byrgen-Beorden and the many other beings of whose existence I have already read, he mentions the little known Bréostwylmas.

Ulthar of Thoone, an Anglo Saxon monk from the 9th century, was said to have conjured up these entities, though they inhabit not this world, but a higher realm. They appeared to him as a viscous, black mist with many mouths on the end of tendrils.

He claimed to have witnessed them feeding off the negative emotions of lower lifeforms, draining them of their pain, their fear and their misery, which were like so much meat and drink to them.

These are the beings we encountered when we found the gate! Imagine my excitement to discover I am not the only one to have seen them and kept his sanity. The grimoire also contains an account of the ritual that Ulthar performed to summon the Bréostwylmas. It is complex, and most difficult to decipher, but I think I am up to it.

I recall, to this day, the blessed oblivion the Bréostwylmas brought when they drained me of my panic and terror. I think, with longing, of the release they might bring from the wretched melancholy that has plagued me ever since. A worse jailer than the Archons, it has robbed me of weeks and months, keeping me paralysed and a prisoner in my own bed. How free of it I could be if I were to offer it up to the Bréostwylmas as a feast. Let them suck the very sadness from the marrow of my bones and bleed me of this bitter, bitter humour.

I have one advantage that Ulthar had not – the forest. As one of the few 'Quiet Places' left in this world, it will be easier for me to open a portal for the Bréostwylmas to come through. My only concern is for the Gate. I will be exposing this world to its indefatigable pull. What effect might that have? What would happen to all the living souls nearby if it should swing wide? What is the key that would lock it? What? What? What?

The few entries that followed that were sketchy at best. Reading them, Sally thought that McCavendish was more intent on concealing than unburdening himself. The final entry of all was perhaps the most enigmatic.

I know! Oh dear Lord I know... Blessed Father help me, I finally know what the key is... It is... I am... I am beyond... I am... I am... I am... oh the key.

Sally let the last journal fall from her hands. Her eyes wandered to the gathering dusk in the sky. She slowly refocussed them, after the hours spent staring at the close handwriting of the journal.

A deep sadness filled her. She thought again of that childhood argument she'd had with her mother and the scripture she had quoted. *The sins of the father will be visited upon the child.* Her mother had vehemently disagreed, but then of course she would. No parent wants their child to pay for *their* mistakes.

Yet here, in the brown and musty pages of these two hundred and fifty year old journals, was proof of this edict. McCavendish's sins had been visited upon successive generations of his family for centuries. Now David was paying for the many mistakes that his ancestor had recorded in these journals.

Sally had always wanted to know how you could live in a world without God. If such a thing were even possible. If the strange and heretical beliefs McCavendish recorded in his journals had any truth in them, it wouldn't be possible to live in a world without God. Because not believing in God meant not believing in the most vital part of yourself, the part that was God, trapped in the material world. It would be like God not believing in Himself.

Sally wondered why she didn't take more comfort in this thought.

TEN

Sally followed the undergrowth down to the stream. The stream would lead her into the darkest parts of the forest and then to the clearing, where she was ultimately heading.

The undergrowth only lasted for a few more yards, so Sally lingered by it, listening. An invisible force seemed to move through it, shaking and rattling as it went. Sally smiled. Her stomach relaxed, like an addict who hears their dealer approach.

This thought struck her as a little strange She wondered how her mind had hit on that simile. Then she put the thought from her mind, because, in all honesty, she did know, she just didn't want to admit it.

"*You are sad– are sad– are sad little sister, and that holds you– holds you– holds you back.*"

"And yet that sadness always seems to disappear whenever you're around."

"*And why do you think– do you think– do you think that is?*"

"Because you're taking it away from me. You're feeding on it. You're *Bréostwylmas* too."

"*Very good, yet you've known this– known this– known this for a while now.*"

"Yes I have, but what I haven't worked out yet is why you hate the Beast, if you're also *Bréostwylmas* yourselves?"

"*The Beast has committed a crime– a crime– a crime against us– against us– against us all. The worst type of crime– type of crime– type of crime for our kind.*"

"So it escaped justice when McCavendish opened a

portal and summoned it. But you followed it here, McCavendish didn't realise he'd summoned you too."

Hettie remained silent, affirming all of Sally's suspicions.

"But why wait until now to try and stop it? Why bide your time for over two centuries?"

"Because now the time is right– is right– is right for the Gate to open."

The rushing amongst the bushes died down and Sally was alone again. Alone, but emotionally lighter. So that's what the Beast was doing, collecting the souls of the McCavendishes in order to open the Gate. There must be some critical mass or something. David must be the last soul necessary.

Opening the Gate was what McCavendish seemed to fear the most. It's probably what the townsfolk also feared, though they probably didn't realise it. Sally was going to make sure that it never happened and she had the most unlikely of allies, some of the Beast's own kind.

ELEVEN

The scents that came from the clearing were lush, primal and sharp. They had deep mossy undertones, like the bark of the ancient trees whose thick trunks encircled it. They had high fragrant notes, like the pollen and the wild flowers that grew all across the clearing. There were plants that had flourished here for countless millennia, plants that could not be found anywhere else on the planet.

Sally could not help but hold her breath when she entered. The forest was a noisy place. There were the calls of the birds who lived in the trees, and the other beasts who inhabited the place. There was the sound of the wind in the branches and the occasional rain on the leaves, and there were the thousand other unexplained noises that haunt such a wild and untamed territory.

The clearing was different though. Within this space all sound seemed to be suspended, as though a blanket had been thrown over everything. It gave the space a sense of reverence. It was a sign that it was among the most sacred of all grounds. This was a Quiet Place.

Sally opened the large tupperware container and was assailed with a different set of smells. The raw meat foremost, along with the blood that had leaked from it. There were the crushed leaves and berries that she had used to season the meat, and then there was the urine and semen she had collected from David. She had marinated the meat in his fluids, to give it his scent so it would fool and attract the Beast.

David was on the opposite side of the clearing, where Sally had left him last night, shortly after collecting the last sample of semen. He was spread-eagled against a tree trunk, his wrists and ankles held by ropes. He was completely naked and his skin was very pale from spending the previous night and day in the forest.

Sally could not resist a moment of tenderness. She walked up to David and ran her hand affectionately over his bare scalp. She'd shaved it the night before, along with his chest, legs and genitals. The raw, shaven flesh was puckering into little goosebumps. There was nothing Sally wouldn't do to protect David from the Beast.

She left David and moved into the forest surrounding the clearing. Here she laid a trail of meat that lead back into the clearing. When she was done, Sally returned to the centre, where she built a bonfire from wood she'd already collected. At the centre of the fire were McCavendish's journals. Sally had doused them in petrol, so they would burn more quickly. Around the firewood, she poured a large circle of salt.

As dusk came on, she stepped into the circle and, taking David's zippo from her pocket, lit it and threw it into the centre of the bonfire. The dry, brittle pages of the journals caught light straight away. She took everything she would need from her pockets and laid them out on the ground in front of her, then she carefully removed all her clothes.

Sally stood with her back to the fire and stared hard into the wood where she'd laid the trail of meat. In a strong, and unwavering voice, she chanted the old Anglo Saxon words that Hettie had taught her:

> "Under fot wolues, under ueþer earnes,
> under earnes clea, a þu geweornie.
> Clinge þu alswa col on heorþe,
> scring þu alswa scerne awage,
> and weorne alswa weter on anbre."

As she chanted, Sally heard movement and commotion just outside the clearing. It was working, soon the Beast would arrive.

But the sounds weren't coming from where she'd laid the trail of meat. They were coming from another part of the forest entirely.

By the light of the flames Sally saw a woman, in a bright orange waterproof, stumble into the clearing. She blinked about her, stunned by what she saw. She glanced first at David and then over at Sally, who felt a huge surge of anger when she recognised the woman.

"Jane, what the hell are you doing here?"

"Sally, oh God, it's worse than I thought. Stop, you have to stop this."

Even in the cold night air, Sally felt herself flush. She could have throttled Jane at that moment. How dare she stumble in here and embarrass Sally, still naked, with her unshaven legs and her cellulite on show. This was not for Jane, or anyone else to see.

"Get out of here Jane. Get out of here now. You're going to ruin everything."

"Sally, listen to me, please listen to me. You can't do this. You don't understand."

"No Jane *you* don't understand, there's so much here that you don't know about."

"But you don't realise how many people you're going to hurt if you do this."

"Again, Jane, it's *you* who don't realise how many people I'm going to save."

"I've seen, first hand, what can happen if we don't have a McCavendish in the town. My grandmother was one of the ones who was... affected the last time. I know you hate what's happening to David, but at least you get him back. That doesn't happen to the rest of us. That's why we need him. It's why we need the both of you. That's why I reached out, why I gave you the pamphlet. It was what I was trying to show you. You don't know how much I risked in doing that."

Sally was so angry, so protective of what she was doing, that she was ready to pick up a rock, or a flaming branch from the fire, and beat Jane senseless with it. Before she had a chance to do that, there was movement on the outskirts of the clearing. A huge, black form made its way into the clearing, raised its head, as if scenting the air, then bowed it, as if in sorrow. Jane froze, obviously terrified, and backed away, taking slow measured steps, to the outskirts of the clearing, never taking her eyes off the Beast.

The Beast padded up to the very edge of the salt and stopped. It could not cross the circle and it was groggy from the meat that Sally had enchanted.

Sally knelt and picked up a little figure of the Beast that she'd made, woven from all the hair she'd shaved from David's body. The Beast gazed at the woven figure, radiating sadness and apprehension.

"Sally, please, for the last time," Jane called out. "Please don't do this."

"Shut up Jane," Sally said, then began to chant.

*"Swa litel þu gewurþe alswa linsetcorn,
and miccli lesse alswa anes handwurmes hupeban,"*

"You and David aren't the only ones affected by this curse."

"And alswa litel þu gewurþe þet þu nawiht gewurþe."

"All of us are, all the townsfolk, we're not allowed to leave and neither are our descendants!"

Sally flung the woven figure into the heart of the fire. The moment she did, she was struck by regret. She didn't know why, but Sally was suddenly sure that she'd made a mistake. It was an almost physical sensation, like something falling away deep inside her.

The Beast arched its back, threw its head in the air, and roared with pain. David's body started to twitch and writhe in his bonds, his muscles twisting themselves into convulsions. Froth poured from his mouth, then he, too, let out a long, pain filled scream. She had torn him free of the Beast, plucked him from its breast with such finality, he could never return. Yet she felt no triumph in this, only a terrible and irrevocable doubt.

The Beast pressed itself up as close the edge of the salt circle as it could get. It fixed Sally with its deep black eyes, as if in remonstrance. Sally could not look away, the eyes seemed to grow larger and larger until they filled her field of vision. The Beast seemed to reach out and build a bridge between their minds, and across this bridge it sent an unconscionable truth.

Sally saw, finally, all that had occurred on that fateful night when McCavendish had summoned the *Bréostwylmas*. She saw what actually came through from that higher realm, and she began to weep. What really broke her spirit though, what tore up her soul into a thousand pieces, were David's last and final words to her, as he re-inhabited his body for the final time.

Sally heard wailing and sobbing. She turned from the Beast to see Jane, by the waning firelight, on her knees, her lips moving, her hands clasped in prayer. The words seemed to offer her little consolation, Jane was shaking uncontrollably with fear.

The Beast's body was seized by violent tremors, its limbs bent and cracked at impossible angles. Then its whole body began to fold in on itself, creasing and bending along dimensional angles that should not be possible on this plane of existence.

This was a Quiet Place, and such actions had greater ramifications here. A huge rent was appearing in the place where the Beast had been. A tear in the fabric of existence, through which another world could bleed. The rent had its own specific gravity, with an unbreakable pull, like a black hole. Not one that affected space or time, but something far more terrible. Only Sally was safe from it, inside the salt circle.

She felt Hettie rush through first, returning to her world of origin. In that moment, Sally was made aware of how deeply she'd been tricked, how despicably she'd been manipulated.

Jane screamed then. Sally was pulled up to the very edge of the salt circle, but the mystical barrier she'd laid down protected her. Jane had no such protection. Sally felt more than saw Jane's soul being ripped from her body and dragged into the tear where the Beast had once stood.

David's soul went next. Then the souls of every living being in the forest and the town beyond. The Gate had opened. It had opened between this world and the world beyond. The world from which it came. But the souls that passed through it did not automatically escape from the prison of Creation. They had to run a very deadly gauntlet first.

Sally witnessed the horde of Archons descend on the freshly harvested souls. She saw them devour, desecrate and despoil the most vital and divine part of David, Jane and every living soul that had lived in the town and the forest. Watched as they violated and annihilated that the part of them that had been God, but now was God no more.

Starved of sustenance for so long, the Archons were brutal and gluttonous in their feeding, and so were the *Bréostwylmas*. They swarmed round the Archons like a thick black cloud, with their famished mouths outstretched, drinking in the suffering and the agony of everything that had once inhabited the forest and the town of Dunballan.

Sally screamed at them, begged for them to show a little mercy, pressed up against the invisible barrier that protected her but left her impotent. Neither the souls, the Archons, nor the *Bréostwylmas* paid Sally's pleas the slightest attention. They were in a different realm of existence.

When it was over, the tear between worlds closed itself up and still, total silence fell once again on the clearing. When she'd finally cried herself out, Sally stood and kicked the salt over the embers of the fire.

She untied David, and walked the hollow shells that he and Jane had once inhabited back through the forest and into the town. The silence that dominated the clearing had now fallen everywhere.

EPILOGUE

The butcher's hand tightened, and whatever he had inside it must have cut into his palm. A thin trickle of blood spilled out from between his fingers.

Sally tried again to prise them apart, but the butcher was too strong. She wasn't used to being resisted in any way by the townsfolk, usually they were completely compliant. Sally realised that she wasn't going to able to get the butcher's hand open. She just didn't have the strength. That meant she couldn't tend to his cut and maybe she couldn't help him at all.

A wave of despondency broke over Sally and she couldn't hold back the hopelessness she'd been holding at bay. She felt all the energy drain from her and she sat down at a small, formica table and put her head in her hands.

She hadn't the strength for this job. She couldn't care for every person left in the town. She couldn't feed them all. She couldn't wash and clean them endlessly after they soiled themselves. Even after a couple of weeks, some of them were starting to waste away from neglect.

Soon, she would have to choose which of them she would keep alive and which she would allow to die. There simply wasn't the time, and she didn't have the physical energy, to care for them all. Her life was already one long round of drudgery, battling sixteen or more hours a day to keep them alive. Breaking into their homes, searching their larders for food and other stuff. She barely slept as it was.

Then there were the bodies she had to pull from the

aftermath of the traffic accidents, and the corpses of those that had fallen from ladders, or scaffolding. They had to be disposed of and there was never enough time to do that, not if she wanted to keep all the others alive.

Who else could she turn to for help? How would she explain what had happened to this remote, little community? Who would believe her, whatever she said? Sally was responsible for this. She carried the guilt. The burden of care for this town of soulless human shells fell on her shoulders alone.

Then, as if the mindless butcher had read Sally's mind, he opened his hand and its contents fell to the floor with a clatter. Sally glanced over at it, and laughed at the irony. A bitter laugh, but her first in over a week. An old, copper key lay on the linoleum, by the butcher's feet.

Then the tears came. She could never hold them at bay for long, nor the memories. Sally thought once more of the Beast, pressed up against the edge of the salt circle. It's watery, black eyes, alive with an unearthly mind, fixing her with their stare.

Sally also recalled the memories, and emotions, it had projected into her mind, burned there with a clarity and a precision that no memory or emotion of her own could ever hope to match.

She saw the Gate that McCavendish had seen, and she felt its deep sorrow. Saw how it was being used by the Archons as bait, to draw souls to it, so they could feed. Sally saw how much this pained the Gate, who was more conscious than McCavendish ever realised. The suffering of the Gate is what first drew the *Bréostwylmas*, who then flourished on the suffering of the Archons' victims. This only hurt the Gate more, and this, in turn, drew more *Bréostwylmas* to it.

The Gate found this situation unconscionable and intolerable. It was fashioned from the deepest vein of God's mercy. It was meant as an escape and a release. Not an instrument of torture, a lure to feed the most merciless and draconian elements of Creation.

So the Gate bided its time and waited. When McCavendish opened a portal into the Quiet Place, the Gate saw its chance to elude the Archons and the *Bréostwylmas*, and it slipped through into this world, taking the form of the Beast. Only a small number of the *Bréostwylmas* followed, and then it was their turn to bide their time, looking for slim pickings in the hedgerows and thickets, as Hettie.

Sally learned all this too late, and she still wasn't certain she'd have acted any differently if she'd known sooner. It was only David's last words to her, when she'd torn him from the Beast, that caused her to regret her actions. When she learned what McCavendish had meant in his final journal entry, and what he'd bequeathed to his successors.

"No Sally no!" David had shrieked. "I'm the key! It's me, I'm what's keeping it shut."

By then it was too late. The Gate had opened, and wherever it should have led, the Archons were waiting hungrily on the other side.

Sally had wanted to unlock David, practically from the moment she first met him. She was always afraid, of what the consequences of that might be though. Now she finally knew.

His living soul, the part of him that was God, had been torn out and devoured, along with everything that was Divine in every living being all around her.

Sally had always wanted to know how you could live in a world without God. If such a thing were even possible. She finally had her answer. It was where she found herself right now, and where she would probably die.

Jasper Bark
jasperbark.com

A.K. Benedict
akbenedict.com

Ray Cluley
probablymonsters.wordpress.com

James Everington
jameseverington.blogspot.com

Rich Hawkins
richwhawkins.blogspot.com

V.H. Leslie
vhleslie.wordpress.com

Laura Mauro
lauramauro.com

Adam Millard
adammillard.co.uk

David Moody
davidmoody.net

Simon Kurt Unsworth
simonkurtunsworth.wordpress.com

Barbie Wilde
barbiewilde.com

blackshuckbooks.co.uk

Lightning Source UK Ltd.
Milton Keynes UK
UKHW010616141022
410433UK00002B/592